Secret Places Revealed

To Arlena

God bless

Paul [illegible] Harper

9/22/2014

SECRET PLACES REVEALED

Paulette Harper

Thy Word Publishing
Antioch, CA

Cover Design and Images: AMB BRAND Management Design
Interior design by Tywebbin Creations LLC

Secret Places Revealed
Paulette Harper
info@pauletteharper.com
Author Website: www.pauletteharper.com
Amazon Author Profile and Full Book List:
http://tinyurl.com/mvzj65j

Library of Congress Cataloging-in-Publication Data

ISBN- 10:0-9899691-5-0 (p)
ISBN-13: 978-0-9899691-5-4 (p)
ISBN- 13:978-0-9899691-6-1 (e)

1. Inspirational Fiction. 2. Christian Fiction 3. African American Fiction 4. Women Fiction

Published and printed in the United States of America

Secret Places Revealed

Published by Thy Word Publishing
Antioch, CA 94531

Praise for Secret Places Revealed

"The characters of Aaron and Simone are both visions of beauty—internally and externally." – *D. Donovan, Senior Reviewer, Midwest Book Reviews*

"Paulette is a brilliant storyteller. With words, she paints such a vivid picture that it's almost like a movie going on in your head while reading. The beauty of Simone's character is that you can find a piece of you in her. This is definitely a story you can find yourself getting lost in." – *Cheryl Pullins, Iconic Legacy Brand Purveyor and Speaker*

"This book has a great combination of drama, suspense and comedy." – *Milton Kelly Author, Author of Walking In God's Path Toward Your Destinations*

"I could not turn the pages fast enough to see what would happen next." – *Deborah Dunson*

"This author brings it all out to the readers to see how God puts all the broken pieces together." – *Arlena Gordon Dean*

"A beautiful love story about second chances. Enjoyed it!" – *Myra Rutledge*

"A delightful story. Can hardly wait for more." – *Paulette Nunlee, Editor, Five Star Proofing*

"I thoroughly enjoyed this book and found it hard to put down." – *LaToya Murchison*

"I enjoyed this book with engaging characters and well-developed plot. It is a must read." – *Teresa Beasley, Authors & Readers Book Corner*

"Paulette Harper does an excellent job of unraveling the very complicated psyche of a young woman who deserves a second chance at love. In this lifechanging book, I gained hope again for my own personal journey." – *Sharon C. Jenkins, The Master Communicator*

"I am in LOVE with Simone and Aaron and felt myself rooting for them with every turn of the pages. I was pulled into their stories from page one and almost hated coming to the end. Such a beautiful love story and the perfect book to add to your holiday reading list." – *Cassiette Jefferson, Author*

"This book is a wonderful Christian romance; although love can be fearful, the truth will set you free." – *Bev S. Bush*

"Such honest and real writing! Paulette Harper brings you into a world where you feel like you've been before with relatable characters and situations that make you feel as if you are a part of the characters' lives. This is truly a gripping book that everyone should read." – *Jessica Starks, Social Media & Content Strategist*

"OMG this is my first time reading a book by this author and it will not be my last. I really enjoyed this story. If you are looking for a 5 star read this is the book for you." – *Ellowyn Young Bell*

"I absolutely loved reading this amazing, sensual, tantalizing story of love lost and then found. Suspenseful moments throughout the book kept me on the edge of my seat. I would recommend this book to all my friends." – *Yolando Cooksey*

Acknowledgements

My thoughts are filled with beautiful words for the king, and I will use my voice as a writer would use pen and ink. Psalm 45:1

I give thanks to God for once again allowing me the privilege to pen yet another book. Without Him none of this would be possible. He continues to amaze me. I praise Him because He gives me what to write and the stories to tell and for that I am eternally grateful. My desire is to bring Him glory with each book I write.

Secret Places Revealed is my first published inspirational fiction novel and it has been a tremendous joy writing, and I hope you'll love reading it as well.

I'm thankful for my family and friends who continue to support me by their prayers, contributions and encouragement.

Special thanks to readers and book clubs everywhere that have supported me. You have many books to choose from. Thank you for adding my books to your library.

Readers, are you ready? I introduce you to *Secret Places Revealed.*

Chapter 1

Simone Herron wanted to escape from the pain, and from life. At this time of the year, she always felt utterly lonely. It was like being in the middle of the ocean surrounded by only the waves. This was year number two without Joshua. Simone had family and friends, but it wasn't the same.

As if she weren't already miserable, the holiday season had arrived, with all of its cheery fanfare. She wished she could skip over November and December and head straight into January.

Pensive, Simone stared out her Fifth Avenue office window in the center of Manhattan, New York—the city that never slept. She could imagine that below her hordes of people bustled to and fro, arms laden with shopping bags, and tourists gawked at the beautiful and spectacular views from The Empire State Building to Times Square. Who wouldn't love it? But her heart was no longer enraptured by its beauty; the Big Apple wasn't the same anymore.

Simone turned away from the window. Even the busyness of the city and all it had to offer could no longer mask her restlessness. Something was missing. Could a move be the answer? A new locale would distract her and keep her mind off her personal life.

Sitting in the leather chair at her desk, she mindlessly shuffled the papers. When had her life fallen into this monotonous rut? For the past couple of years, she'd spent her Thanksgivings serving dinner at Shepherd's Gate, a women's shelter. Christmas was spent singing carols with her church at Faith Bible Center. She enjoyed those things, but she wanted more.

Maybe her boredom stemmed from the fact she'd buried her fiancé a few months before their marriage. But that was two years ago. She should have been enjoying life, but Joshua was gone and she was alive and still trying to remember how to put one foot in front of the other.

People told her time would heal her wounds and it would get easier day by day. And they were right—some days. People also told her never to question God, but those who knew her were aware that that was like asking an artist not to paint. There were days on which she felt she'd moved on, but others when the feelings in her heart and her dreams of him were as real as the love they'd once shared.

She couldn't understand why God had taken the only man she'd ever truly loved. Joshua had been her soulmate, her friend, the love of her life, her future children's father. The more she got to know him, the more she realized that meeting him had been something divine. He'd felt the same way.

There was an undeniable connection between them the first time their eyes met on their college campus in Manhattan. She wondered what their children might have looked like. Would they have had his dark eyes and curly black hair, or maybe brown eyes like hers?

The idea of not having a family hurt her to the core. Her parents were married for decades before her father suddenly died from a heart attack. They cherished one another and that's what she wanted for herself. For now, her dream of falling in love and having a family was tucked away somewhere in the back of her mind, preserved in the faint hope of a second chance.

Simone wasn't sure she believed there was such a thing as getting back to a normal life. She accepted what life had dealt her and was allowing her circumstances to bring her to a place of surrender. She learned to accept that when life brought pain, God would give her the strength to go through it.

Simone became teary-eyed as questions swirled

around in her head. Why, with all of her great accomplishments—she was a paralegal for a prestigious law firm, Armstrong and Armstrong; she worked with some of the most gifted and intelligent lawyers in the city—did she still feel like there was a void in her life? She needed a change. A fresh, new beginning. A move would make her feel differently and do her wonders.

She scanned her office. Her eyes drew to the plaques on the wall, awards she had received from her boss. Then she focused on the plaque on her desk, a gift from her pastor. Her favorite scripture was engraved in it, and the office light gleamed on the words. "*And we know that all things work together for good to them that love God, to them who are the called according to his purpose.*—Romans 8:28, KJV."

She knew God was in control, but sometimes, it was more difficult to accept when His plan superseded her own. She'd heard all the sermons. She was in all the prayer lines. She'd had plenty of oil poured on her head. But the pain remained unbearable. She was resilient, but felt weak, as though she hadn't slept in months. Externally, Simone had it all together, yet she felt detached. She was a fighter at the end of her fight.

A knock sounded on her office door. The door swung open and Terrance Armstrong strolled in. "Good afternoon, Simone. You not going to lunch?" Terrance, one of the firm's partners, was *the man*. He was a strong and capable real estate attorney, the best in the business, and sought out by all who could afford him.

Simone sat at her mahogany desk and cleared her throat. "I was busy working. Lost track of time."

Terrance was not only her boss; he was a good friend. If he could reverse the past for her, he would. She watched as he observed her. That was the thing... no one could change what had happened.

He claimed a seat in front of her desk. "Are you sure you want to do this? You think relocating is the answer?"

She grabbed the box of Kleenex from her desk, dabbed at her eyes, and nodded her head. "I do. Sometimes a change of atmosphere and surroundings is all that's needed. Besides, I don't have any real reason to stay. I love my job, you know that. But since Joshua's passing, being here's been much harder than I expected. Everything about New York reminds me of him."

"Are you sure you're not trying to run away from the memories? You can't outrun pain."

She leaned forward and took a deep breath. "No, not the memories. I'll treasure those forever. I believe this move will help me plant new roots. Besides, my family has been asking me to come home. My mom is getting up in age, and I want to spend as much time with her as I can. You know how beautiful Northern California is. Who wouldn't want to live in the Bay Area? Change is good, right? I think you told me that one day."

"Yeah, you're right. It's beautiful, and change is good. You got me there. You'll have to get used to the earthquakes, though." They both shared a hearty laugh.

"See, why did you have to go and bring up earthquakes?"

Terrance raised his hands in mock surrender, cocking an eyebrow as an easy smile formed on his lips. "Hey! I'm only being honest. Seriously, though, you know we'll always have a place here for you if you ever want to return, and we're only a flight away. I hate to see you leave. You've been like a little sister to me."

Simone's face softened. She gave him a slight nod and smiled.

Terrance continued, "I do have some connections in the Bay Area. Have you ever heard of the law firm Blackman and Blackman? They're one of the premier firms on the West Coast. I bet you would fit right in. Aaron and his brother Shaun are two of the best real estate attorneys in their field."

Simone listened attentively as he spoke. The more he talked, the more hopeful she felt and the more convinced she was that she was doing the right thing. "No, I don't believe I've heard of them. But I'm grateful for your connections. I wasn't sure where to begin. I know I can work anywhere, but it's better when firms come highly recommended and referred."

Terrance nodded in agreement. He continued, "I met Aaron at a conference last year. I'll give him a call first thing in the morning." Terrance paused for a moment and stared at her. "I'm being selfish. A change in location might be a good thing for you. I'll miss you, for sure, but I know that wherever you establish yourself, you'll do fine. Besides, any firm that hires you is getting a blessing, and I know, 'cause I taught you most everything you know."

They shared a rousing laugh. Simone rolled her eyes at his lack of humility. "Boy, whatever."

"Check with me in the morning, but first, lunch." He slid the chair back and stood, extending his hand. Simone accepted and squeezed his hand as they headed toward the door. At least someone was excited about her future.

Once she arrived home, Simone kicked off her shoes and burrowed into her favorite sofa, basking in the well-designed, unobtrusive beauty of her living room. After a short rest and dinner, she did some research on Blackman and Blackman. Terrance was correct. They were one of the premier law firms in Northern California and she was quite impressed with some of the accolades and awards they'd received, particularly for ethics. Aaron Blackman sat on the board of directors for the San Francisco Lawyers Association and had been featured on both national and local television programs. Furthermore, he'd authored several books and published articles in national magazines.

After reading about Blackman and Blackman, she was keyed up with anticipation at the prospect of working for this firm.

She got off the sofa and strolled into her bedroom, changed into her pajamas, and climbed into bed.

She tossed and turned all night. To make matters worse, her alarm was set to go off in a few hours. She lay there, looking at the ceiling, eyes wide open. She thought about reading, about working, about Blackman and Blackman.

What's wrong with me? It's only a phone call... a phone call that could change my life. Moving across states was a major task. She was excited and nervous at the same time. Would another law firm like her? Would they want to hire her? Would they keep her? She knew she was making herself restless for no reason.

As she pondered her fate, she tried to concentrate on the journey ahead. She was treading on unfamiliar territory. Would she be able to handle what the future held—good or bad—or would this move bring more heartache, like losing Joshua had?

Chapter 2

Simone looked out her living room window to inspect the weather conditions. Frost clung to the window. Light snow fell to the ground. She grabbed her black ColdGear parka to insulate herself, picked up her briefcase and purse, and headed to work.

An hour later, she was fighting with swarms of people to get into her favorite coffee shop. Meeting her best friend Kendra at the coffee house had been their ritual ever since they'd first met. Kendra, already seated at a window seat overlooking the congested sidewalk in downtown Manhattan, waved to Simone when she arrived.

Five feet six, Simone maintained her hourglass figure with a daily workout regimen. Her toasted caramel complexion complemented her long, thick, honey-brown hair, which she wore in twists.

She rushed over to her friend and slid into a chair. "Woo, it's cold out there. Sorry I'm late."

Kendra flashed Simone a smile. "Girl, don't I know it. I went ahead and ordered your caramel latte." She slid the cup toward Simone. "Can you believe I was able to snag this table with all these people in here?" Kendra looked around at the crowd.

Simone shook her head and swallowed some of her coffee. "You're the best, Kendra. What would I do without you?"

All of a sudden, she felt sentimental. The person sitting in front of her had been her best friend since college. If Simone and Joshua had gotten married, Kendra would have been her maid of honor. She remembered how Kendra had remained by her side when they first received the news of Joshua's accident. It was Kendra's beautiful, giving spirit and warm, bubbly personality that kept her going during that dark time. Had it not been for her prayers and constant encouragement, Simone would not have made it. They shared a special sister bond forged through the trials of life and lots of late-night conversations over ice cream.

Kendra's cough brought Simone back from her musing. "Girl, what's wrong with you?" She gave Simone a hard stare. "Don't even get started. We both are going to be weeping up in here."

Unbidden tears sparkled in Simone's eyes. She refused to allow them to fall. "I was thinking about all you've been to me. We've been through so much together. The thought of leaving you is so heartbreaking."

Kendra frowned. "You're really gonna leave? I know we've talked about it, but I can't believe it." She reached across the table for Simone's hands. "I'll miss you, sissy. Feels like we've been friends forever. I don't know what I'm going to do without my confidant, prayer partner... coffee partner. I don't even want to think about you not being here." Kendra squeezed her hand. "But... maybe a move is a good thing. In more ways than one."

Simone sat back and her hands flew to her chest. "Aw, sis. I'm going to miss you, too. The only thing that will separate us is a flight. Looks like we both will be racking up some frequent flier miles." She gave a slight laugh to lighten the mood.

"Well, maybe in Cali you'll meet someone special. Lord knows that wall you put up really needs to come down."

Simone didn't know if she could trust anyone else. What if they died, too? She had problems trusting herself. Could she really survive losing another love? There were only so many places to relocate to. Simone feigned indifference. "Oh my gosh! Girl, please. There you go, spoiling the moment. No walls here, girlfriend."

"You scared; that's what you are. Scared. Quit fooling yourself. I know you don't like to talk about it, but—"

"But you're going to bring it up anyways. Huh? And for your information, I'm not scared. Nope, I'm not scared of anything." Simone shook her head. "I haven't met anyone who piqued my interest." Simone folded her arms tightly across her chest.

"Ha!" Kendra blurted out. "Really? You must have forgotten who you're talking to. Remember, I called you the runner. Seriously though, you have got to take back your life. You only live once. Be happy. Let love find you again."

"Kendra, girl, I should be paying you instead of my counselor."

Kendra smiled. "Exactly."

"Whatever." They chortled.

"So tell me, how did Terrance take the news? When are you leaving? What are you going to do with your apartment?" Kendra fired off her questions without taking a breath.

Simone laughed again. Kendra's questions were putting her through the wringer. "Girl, I'll make sure you have all the 4-1-1. But right now, we don't have enough time to go over all the particulars. I will say this; after Terrance and I talked, he finally understood why I was moving." She wrapped her hands around her coffee cup, enjoying the warmth. "I'm actually looking forward to being near my family again."

Kendra paused long enough to savor a bit of her delicious steaming hot coffee, then crossed her arms and leaned back in her chair. "Really? I can see you saying that about your mother and your brother Devon, but what about Tori? Last time I remember, she was still jealous as ever. That girl is a piece of work. I know she's your sister, but she's a wild bull that's never been tamed."

Simone rolled her eyes. "Girl, I know. I'm hoping my time away would have changed our relationship. I can only hope for a miracle. I'm not the same person I was growing up, and I'm hoping she's matured. Some people you can't please, no matter what—"

Kendra raised her hand, stopping her midsentence. "Girl, please. You definitely going to need a miracle, some holy oil, and plenty of prayer."

"Well, getting back to Terrance...." Simone felt the need to change the subject. She clasped her hands together and placed them on the table. "He's actually going to connect me with a law firm in the San Francisco area."

"Uh, well, speaking of your fine boss, maybe I should try to come work for him. On second thought... hmm, maybe not. I wouldn't get any work done, 'cause he is definitely easy on the eyes."

Simone gave her a side eye. Her bestie was single and quite attractive. Her beautiful brown complexion and gorgeous smile reminded her of Salli Richardson-Whitfield. "Girl, what am I going to do with you? It's time to go to work."

Draining the last of their lattes, they stood from the table and headed in to the office.

"Good morning, Simone. I have a few messages for you." Patrice, her office intern, handed her several pink message slips.

Simone skimmed through them and took a deep breath. "Thank you. Is Terrance in his office?"

"Yes, but he's in a meeting. I'll let you know when he's done."

Simone nodded her head in acknowledgment. She and Patrice spent a few moments going over the week's calendar and duties. She had a tense week ahead.

"I'll be behind closed doors today. Please hold any calls for me and take messages the rest of the day."

Without saying a word, Patrice nodded.

Simone threw her briefcase on her desk and collapsed in her leather chair. She turned on the computer to check her emails. The inbox notification indicated that she had over a hundred waiting for her. She clicked on the Pandora music link in her favorites folder. The melodious sound of smooth jazz filled her office, calming the atmosphere.

She sat at her desk and stared at the stack of folders that needed her attention. She rubbed the back of her neck. "It's going to be a long day." Not able to concentrate fully, her eyes wandered to the picture of her family during happier times.

She loved her family, but the tension between her and her sister Tori had nearly torn the family apart.

Still, Simone loved her sister and was going to try her best to work on their relationship. She could only hope Tori would do the same. At the end of the day, they were family, and she would have to trust God to mend their relationship.

Hours later, Patrice buzzed her to tell her Terrance was available. Simone sashayed to his office, hoping he'd had an opportunity to contact Attorney Aaron Blackman on her behalf. She was anxious to hear what he had to say.

She knocked, then stepped inside his office. Simone sat in front of his desk. She placed her hands in her lap and took a deep breath.

Terrance leaned forward. His elbows rested on his desk, his hands clasped together. "So, I talked with Aaron and told him all about you returning to the Bay Area. I asked if he had any openings in his firm or knew of someone looking to hire a paralegal. Of course, I bragged about how fabulous you were and what a top rate, strong paralegal you were. As luck would have it, he's looking to add someone to his team and would be interested in speaking with you."

She shook her head vigorously. "Are you kidding? That's awesome. Wow, I never expected that. This is all happening so fast. I'm so excited. Thanks, Terrance. Seriously, thank you. This is incredible."

Terrance smiled and nodded, acknowledging her gratitude. They spent some time strategizing her next steps, deciding it was best for her to contact Aaron personally for a phone interview. Suddenly shocked by the possibilities of having a job solidified before she left New York, her emotions went into a tailspin. All at once, she was jubilant, scared, nervous, and happy. She got Aaron's contact information and told Terrance she would make the call.

God had used Terrance to open the door she needed. If things worked out, she could be returning to the Bay Area for the new year. Going into the new year with all new possibilities was music to her ears. She hoped it held the promise of a happier life.

Chapter 3

As real estate development attorneys, Aaron and his brother Shaun had partnered together and started Blackman and Blackman over six years ago. They'd done a remarkable job in bringing large businesses to the Oakland and San Francisco Bay Area. Their firm's mission was to create a gateway for African American businesses to access the area, providing support and legal services through stages: acquisition, planning, financing, construction, leasing, and selling.

Aaron sat on his bed and tied his tennis shoes. The Saturday morning air sent a chill through his body that forced him to grab his jacket from the closet. He picked up his gym bag, grabbed his car keys, and headed out the door.

Twenty minutes later, he made a sharp turn, maneuvering his silver 650i BMW into his brother

Shaun's driveway. He honked twice, letting Shaun know he had arrived. He popped a jazz album from Kim Waters into the CD player and allowed the melody to seep into his soul. Aaron had grown up loving jazz, and Kim Waters was one of his favorites. He drummed his fingers against the steering wheel. Shaun opened the car's back door and placed his gym bag on the floor, jolting Aaron from his musical bliss. The back door slammed shut. Shaun settled into the front seat on the passenger side, securing his seat belt. He greeted his brother with a fist bump. Aaron checked the rearview mirror, backed out of the driveway and headed to the gym.

"What's up, bro?"

"Hey," Shaun replied. A long silence filled the air. "A few of the fellas have been talking about taking a cruise. You want to join us?"

Aaron paused. "A cruise, huh? Man, I don't know. There's plenty to do, and somebody has to work in our office."

Shaun laughed. "I see you got jokes. Bro, when was the last time you went on a vacation? Have you even been on a cruise?"

Aaron shook his head. "Not you, too? I know you're not going to start. I've heard it from Mom and now you. Bro, please."

Shaun chuckled. "What did Mom say?"

Aaron gave him a quick glance and returned

his eyes to the road. "Don't pretend like you don't know."

Shaun quickly replied, "I don't. I haven't talked to Mom about you."

Aaron chuckled. "Yeah I bet. She told me exactly what you said." He took a deep breath. "She also suggested I find me someone to settle down with, get married, and have her some grandkids."

Shaun chuckled and replied, "For real?"

Aaron rolled his eyes. "Yeah, for real."

Clearing his throat, Shaun continued, "Don't you think you should get out and have some fun? It's been years. All you do is work."

Aaron clenched his jaw. He didn't have to be reminded of how long he had been out of the dating scene. He knew it all so well. He lived it. Falling in love was a sure guarantee that pain was soon to follow. So to avoid the pain, he chose not to love again. He kept telling himself that his career was the only thing that mattered with the exception of his immediate family. He was content. He couldn't understand why others couldn't accept what he wanted for his life. Maybe they were right. He did bury himself in everything other than a relationship.

Aaron countered. "Maybe right now that's all I want to do. We have plenty of work at the office to keep me busy for a long time. Anyways, man, women say they want a good man and when they have one, all they want is money and material stuff. And, let's not mention their lists, like 'my man gotta be this or that.'"

"Bro, you partially correct. But there are some good sistahs out there. You happened to pick someone who was crazy. I told you to leave that Macy chick alone." Shaun shook his head and said, "But you right about that list."

Aaron shot back, "Since you know so much about the good sistahs, how come you ain't hooked up with one?"

"Man, we ain't talking about *my* love life. We talking about *yours*, or your lack thereof. Plus, my love life is doing quite well." A smile tugged at his lips.

"Wait, I know you not trying to teach me a lesson on women, player-player!" The brothers shared a look and burst out laughing. Aaron's expression soured. "Man, don't remind me of Macy, and don't mention her name in my car. Believe me, she was the nightmare I'm glad I've awakened from. You talk about 'drama' with all capital letters." He shook his head in disgust.

They shared another laugh. "Naw, bro. I want you to enjoy life. It doesn't have to be serious. Some female company to take the edge off would do you some good. You know God created some gorgeous sistahs who are beautiful inside and out. Bro, you need to at least bring a date to the Christmas party."

"Shaun. Man, lay off. I'm thirty-six years old and I'm perfectly capable of handling that department all by myself. If I want to go solo for the holidays, I'm okay with that."

"You know what they say? All work and no play makes Aaron a dull boy."

"Bro, I should pull over and put you out of my car. I don't even know why I'm even listening to your butt." They laughed.

A moment of silence passed and Shaun said, "For real, bro, you want me to introduce you to someone? I know some nice-looking women at the gym."

Aaron gave Shaun a sidelong glance. "Naw, man. I don't need your matchmaking. Trust me. I got this. When the time is right, believe me, I know what to do."

Shaun threw up his hand in surrender. "Alright. Alright." He paused. "What you doing tomorrow?"

Aaron glanced over in Shaun's direction for a second. "I won't be around. I'm taking a drive down the coast. I'll be back tomorrow night." *Casino, here I come.*

"Oh. Okay."

Minutes later, Aaron pulled into the gym parking lot. They entered the gym and headed for their regular spot, joining all the other fellas in the weight lifting area.

A few minutes later, Aaron absentmindedly

stood over Shaun as he attempted to bench press. "Man, you going to spot me or what? Aaron? Aaron. What you daydreaming about?" Shaun looked up at Aaron.

Aaron's head jerked up. He wiped the sweat from his brow before assisting Shaun with his set. "Uh, nothing, man. Thinking about a phone call I received from Terrance Armstrong. You remember him?"

Shaun sat up on the bench and faced Aaron. "The attorney in New York?"

He nodded and tilted his water bottle to his lips. "Yeah, that's him."

Shaun placed his hands on his knees and leaned forward. "He called you? What did he want?"

"Wanted to know if we were looking to add additional staff. One of his paralegals is moving back to Northern California. He called to see if we could possibly use her in our firm or know of another where she might be placed."

Shaun tilted the bottle of water to his lips and took a long drink. "Hmm, what'd you say? I hope you told him yeah. Then we can get rid of Robin, because she ain't doing a good job. And don't get me started on your ex, Macy. She was the worst."

It didn't take Aaron long for his thoughts to find their way back to those two headaches: Robin and Macy. He would be the first to admit Shaun and he had not been successful in hiring paralegals.

The office couldn't function without someone, but the person had to be impeccable, intelligent, have integrity, and not be personally interested in either of them. Robin was not qualified. It was a wonder she'd lasted this long. Macy had appeared to be what they were looking for, but Aaron could kick himself for hiring her. Getting involved with her only added fuel to the fire.

The two Blackman men had agreed that neither one would mix work with pleasure. They both grabbed the forty-five pound hand weights from the floor and continued with their workout.

"I told Terrance I'd be interested in speaking with her. She's supposed to call and do a phone interview first, and then possibly fly out for a face-to-face interview."

Shaun wiped his brow. "So who is she? I guess if Terrance is speaking on her behalf, she must be quite good at her job. You get her résumé?"

Aaron gulped a sip of his water. "Her name is Simone. Terrance spoke highly of her and her work. She is supposed to be one of the best in his office. He went on and on about her. I forgot to ask him to shoot me a résumé. I'll do the phone interview first. If I think she could potentially be a good fit for us, I'll ask her to email it."

"Sounds good to me. Let's finish up and get out of here so we can get ready for tonight."

Aaron pulled into his three-car garage in Oakland Hills. Tired and exhausted, all he could think about doing was preparing a light meal, getting into his Jacuzzi, and taking a nap. But tonight was his turn to have the men over for a night of poker. No women, no crying kids, no interruptions; five men having fun. Perfection.

Oakland Hills subdivision overlooked both Oakland and Berkeley Hills. From his hilltop home, he enjoyed the spectacular views of the San Francisco Bay, and the East Bay Hills. Hidden behind evergreen trees, his two-story, four-bedroom home was perfect for any single man.

His mother had told him she wasn't getting any younger. She wanted him to settle down, get married and fill his house with kids. A day never failed to pass that she didn't say, "Make some babies, son. You got all those accolades, but no one to share the joy with. That goes for your brother Shaun, too. Life is too short. Fill your heart, not your bank account."

Aaron chuckled, thinking about his mom's advice. "Yes, Mom," was all Aaron could say. But his brother Shaun, on the other hand, didn't pay their mother any attention. What she said went in one ear and right out the other.

No matter how Aaron tried to explain to his mother that he was waiting on the right one, she didn't want to hear it. The truth of the matter was that Aaron immersed himself in his job, worked late hours, and spent more time at the gym rather than going home to an empty house. The idea of engaging another woman was not on his agenda. *There is no room on my plate for another relationship.* He wasn't going to make the time, either. He didn't have the energy to put the work into another relationship. His heart had been broken before, and he refused to allow it to be captured again.

Aaron entered the house and ambled into his den. His home was spacious. The interior decorator he worked with had created a warm, inviting space that was designed for entertaining. His kitchen featured all top-of-the-line Viking brand stainless steel appliances and granite countertops. The dark-stained oak cabinets completed an already elegant kitchen.

He made his way up the winding staircase and along the hallway to his master bedroom suite. Aaron tossed his keys and wallet atop the deep chocolate wooden desk. He kicked off his shoes next to the dark brown leather recliner that sat in one corner. He discarded his shirt, jacket, and tie across the foot of his king-size bed and clicked on the sixty-inch HD smart TV that was mounted on the wall.

He carried the gym bag into his bathroom area, tossed it on the floor, and removed his sweaty gym clothes, dropping them in the hamper. Aaron turned on his rainfall shower. The hot water felt good on his sore muscles.

His mind returned to his mother's words. "You need to get married." His mom was right. One day he would get married and have kids, but it was going to be years away. Right now, he was focused on his career, period.

Aaron hurried and dressed and went downstairs to ready the man cave for the guys.

Entering into his man cave, the room had dark hardwood floors and a custom card table surrounded by five brown leather chairs. A seventy-five-inch flat-screen HD TV was mounted on the wall in the bar area. The cherrywood bar had five tall, brown bar stools for easy viewing.

Aaron glided over to the bar area and filled a large bowl with chips and placed them on the bar with the dip. The refrigerator had a food tray filled with cold cuts, cheeses, fruits, and a bowl of potato salad made by their mother. He removed the tray and salad and set them next to one another on the bar.

He strolled over to the sound system, hit a few buttons, and the room livened up with soft sounds of jazz. As Aaron checked the time on his phone, the doorbell rang. The first three men to arrive were Shaun, Eric, and Jason.

"Hey, what's up?" Aaron said. Each man greeted Aaron with a fist bump and a few niceties. He opened the door wider to allow them entry, then turned and walked away. They trailed Aaron through the living room and ended up in the man cave, where they removed their coats and draped them over the back of their chairs.

"Y'all know the routine," Aaron said.

Each one of the men headed straight for the bar, grabbing drinks and food. After getting his drink and fixing his plate, Aaron heard the doorbell ring. He set his drink and plate down on the bar and strolled to the front door.

He opened the door for the last poker player. Benjamin entered, gave the customary greeting, and trailed Aaron back into the room.

Once inside, they were greeted by the other men, who were sipping on their drinks, munching on the food and talking trash about who was going to lose all their money.

Shaun leaned against the bar. "You'll get the opportunity to put your money where your mouth is," he said to Eric.

Eric tilted up his drink. "I hope you don't think I'm scared." Eric pulled out a wad of money from his pants pocket and showed Shaun who he was dealing with. Everyone laughed.

Benjamin shook his head. "Here y'all go talking all that smack. If I have anything to do with it, both of y'all might leave here broke."

Jason rolled his eyes. "Am I hearing that there's going to be a beat down up in here?"

"Sounds like it," Shaun replied.

Aaron interrupted, "Well, on that note... Let's

get this game going, and we'll see who leaves here with the clothes on his back."

Chapter 4

Aaron Blackman strode into the Grand Casino to try his luck once again. The sprawling casino had plenty of slot and video poker machines as well as a wide variety of table games. The gamblers were serious, focused on their machines, and focused on winning.

When he entered the casino, he heard the loud voices of those who were celebrating their new fortunes and saw the long faces of those who were not so lucky. Aaron rubbed his palms together. He stood tall in the middle of the casino, as if he owned the place. He had dropped plenty of money into the casinos, and this weekend he was determined to win some of it back. Losing wasn't fun, but it never deterred him from coming back.

In the past, coming to the Grand had been real good to Aaron. As of late, though, things were changing. His previous winning streak netted him over thirty thousand dollars, though that was quite some time ago.

Why quit now? He headed for the Party Pit with high expectations of coming out ahead. In his wallet, he had wads of money to play with, plus the "free" gambling money the casino placed on his gambling card.

With each step he took toward his favorite slot machine, The Triple Star, his heart raced with adrenaline. Nothing else came close to giving him that same high. Aaron positioned himself in a chair in front of the slot machine. He removed his cell from his side pocket and placed it on a chair next to him before inserting his gambling card.

Within moments, a small-framed woman greeted him with a smile. Her name tag read Barbara. "Good day, Mr. Blackman. Welcome to the Grand. I'm Barbara. I'll be serving you today. Can I bring you a drink?"

Their eyes met. Admiring her smile, he said, "Hi, Barbara. I'd love a Coke."

A few minutes later, Barbara returned with his drink. "I'll be back shortly to see if you want something else."

Aaron nodded his head in acknowledgment and glanced down at his Rolex. It was high noon. The day was still early, and he had time and money to enjoy till the wee hours of the morning. *Well, if I lose it all, or don't get ahead, I'll be heading back home... there is always next week.*

An hour later, Aaron was finally seeing a very small return on his investment. He took a sweep of his surroundings and noticed a lady headed in his direction. Sizing her up, he reached for his drink and took a sip. Five seven, shoulder-length brown hair and hazel eyes. *Attractive, if I was the least bit interested.*

"Hi. Looks like you're hitting it big. I'm Leah."

Aaron briefly looked away from the slot machine. With enough steel in his voice to let her know he wasn't interested, he responded, "Hi, Leah."

Barbara returned with another Coke. "Can I bring you a drink, Miss?"

She shook her head. "No, thank you." She watched Barbara walk off and turned her attention back to Aaron. "I didn't get your name."

"I didn't offer it." He took another sip of his drink and kept looking at the slot machine. *She's wasting her time and energy.*

When he was in his twenties, he would have jumped at the opportunity to talk to a gorgeous woman, but he was wiser, thanks to Macy, and he had no problem guarding his heart. Aaron was at the Grand to make his money back. And if that didn't happen today, he'd be back another day to try his luck again. But he wasn't interested in any side entertainment.

She searched his face. "I'm sorry. I didn't mean to interrupt you."

Aaron took his eyes off the slot machine. He noticed the deep frown on her face. "Hey, I'm sorry for being rude. I'm trying to stay focused in hopes of receiving a short win on this machine." He turned his attention back to the slot machine as if she was not there.

"Sure," she said, and quietly sauntered away.

Aaron continued putting his coins in the machine and drinking his Coke well into the evening without great success. He wasn't the kind to give up, but when the odds stacked up against him, he knew when to throw in the towel.

He leaned back in his chair and let his mind drift back to Leah. He had to admit he had been curt, which was not one of his distinguishing features. Had he allowed his guilty pleasure to transform his personality?

"What in the world is wrong with me?" he said out loud. He finished his drink, called it a night and headed home.

Chapter 5

Simone unlocked the front door, kicked off her Steve Madden boots and collapsed on her queen-size bed. She lay on her back and stared into space. Her mind was going in every direction. *How quickly things change.* A few years ago, she was planning a wedding, purchasing a new home, and thinking about kids. Now she was planning to relocate to another state, find a new job, and face family challenges that needed her attention.

Out of everything she needed to do, addressing her sister was the most difficult. In addition to Tori being a constant complainer, she was extremely selfish and self-centered. If something didn't benefit her, she wasn't going to do it. She had to be the center of attention.

Simone stole a cursory glance around the room. Her eyes focused on the clock located on the nightstand. She had enough time to change clothes and make a cup of green tea before calling Aaron Blackman.

She rolled out of bed and quickly undressed, dropping her clothes on the chaise. She sauntered into her kitchen and filled her tea kettle with water. While her water heated, she turned on her laptop and opened up the file folder that had her résumé in it. She looked it over and updated her skills to include added responsibilities from Armstrong and Armstrong.

Minutes later, the kettle whistled. She grabbed a cup from the cabinet, added a tea bag, and poured water in. Letting it steep and cool, she sipped the tea to calm her nerves. "Lord, if it is Your will, bless me with this position. Give me the right things to say, and may I not stumble as I speak."

Simone headed toward the living room. She sat on her sofa, placed her tea on the table, picked up the phone, and punched in the numbers. She frowned after the second ring, wondering if he was unavailable. When he finally answered after the third ring, Simone quickly silenced her runaway thoughts, worried that he had obviously gotten sidetracked or had possibly forgotten.

"Hello. May I speak with Mr. Aaron Blackman?"

Aaron stood in his kitchen, both hands filled with bags of groceries. Hurriedly, he placed the bags on the counter, reached in his pocket to retrieve his phone, and swiped the screen.

"This is Aaron," he said in his baritone voice. He took a step forward towards the kitchen table, pulled out one of the leather chairs, and sat down.

"Hi, Aaron. This is Simone Herron from Terrance Armstrong's office. Did I get the time wrong regarding our interview?"

He kicked off his shoes and loosened his tie. "Hi, Simone, nice to hear from you. No, you didn't get the time wrong. I apologize if I sound rushed. Something threw my schedule off a bit. Thank you for being prompt."

She grabbed the throw blanket off the sofa and wrapped it around herself. "Would you like to postpone the interview for another time?"

"No, not at all. I've been looking forward to speaking with you. Besides, you're going to be the one doing most of the talking anyways." They both chuckled. "But thank you for your thoughtfulness." There was a moment of silence before he continued. "Terrance spoke highly of you. And from our conversation, he tells me that you are moving to the Bay Area."

"Yes, that's correct. I have family there. And, it's time for a change. I'm excited to talk with you about the possibility of working for Blackman and Blackman."

Aaron activated the speaker and strolled upstairs to his bedroom to change into something more comfortable. He grabbed a pen and notepad from his briefcase and made his way to his desk.

"So, Simone, tell me about your work history and yourself."

Simone took the next few minutes to fill Aaron in on her job, skills, and experience working at Armstrong and Armstrong. The updated résumé jogged her memory about other duties Terrance had assigned her that allowed her to gain more knowledge in the field. She took a deep breath and mentioned her awards and recognitions. She told him of her love for Black art, writing, and her latest adventure, hiking.

They went back and forth conversing over her skills, abilities, and background. They discussed management styles, salary, and career development. He explained that if she was still interested in working for Blackman and Blackman, he would share his expectations and the job requirements.

Simone shifted on the couch and listened attentively. She could feel the passion in his strong voice as he talked about the job and his expectations. She was sure it would be an honor to work for such a prestigious firm.

Two hours later, Aaron said, "Well, Simone, I'm more than convinced that you could handle the job. Based upon Terrance's recommendation and our phone interview, I'd like to invite you for an on-site interview with my brother and me. This will allow us to go into more depth about the position, and it will give Shaun an opportunity to speak with you, as well. What do you think?"

"I think I'd be honored to fly there for a face-to-face interview. When would you like me to come?"

After agreeing that she would come the following week, the call ended. Simone, grateful for the open door, knelt and prayed. "Lord, thank You for ordering my steps and showing me that this is Your will for my life. I love You with all my heart."

She smiled at the thought of seeing her family, though the smile soon disappeared when she remembered Tori. "Help me, Lord," she said out loud.

Simone was in a zone. She had coffee from her favorite coffee house, soft music played on Pandora, and papers were scattered everywhere on her desk. She had been at work for two hours but hadn't seen Terrance. She couldn't wait to share the latest news regarding her travel plans with him.

Rapid taps on the door broke Simone's concentration. Terrance wandered in, holding his favorite New York Giants coffee mug. He folded himself into one of the chairs in front of her desk and crossed his legs at the ankle. "Good morning. I got your message. You wanted to speak with me."

"Good morning to you." Simone leaned back in her leather chair and stared into his eyes. "I wanted to tell you about my phone call with Aaron Blackman," she said with a smile.

Terrance tilted his coffee cup to his lips. "Obviously, it was a productive conversation. It's written all over your face."

"Oh, yes. You can say that. The interview went extremely well. He invited me to come and meet with him and Shaun. Looks like I'll be flying out next week to meet them."

"Awesome. This is what we were hoping for, right?" His lips curved in a smile. He reached over her desk and gave her a high-five.

She took a sip of her coffee. "Yes, and I owe it all to you. Thank you for making the connection. I couldn't have done it without you."

"You're more than welcome."

"Since you're here, I need to go over your calendar and discuss the action items that need your attention."

She handed him a printout of his court calendar and caseloads for the upcoming week. She'd already highlighted the dates and times his clients would be coming in for interviews. She provided him with the requested documentations and case files he needed to review before trial, and handed him several folders with contracts that needed his signature and court documents that needed to be filed. Simone assured him Patrice was more than able to handle any last minute changes, run errands, and do any and all research he might need while she was in California.

Terrance accepted his calendar and glanced over the entries, highlighting and making notes of priority items. He smiled. "You've been busy this morning."

"Yep. I want to make sure everything is covered before I leave. Patrice will have my number should you need me or can't find something. I have full confidence in her ability to handle anything until I come back."

"Okay. That sounds good. I better let you get back to work. By the looks of your desk, you still have a few items you're working on." Terrance gathered the folders and his coffee mug and treaded out of her office.

Chapter 6

Simone wasn't quite ready to leave the comfort of her bed. The cold air hovered in her apartment, and her bed was the warmest place to be. Hesitantly, she rolled out of bed, sauntered over to the window, and opened the blinds to let the heat from the sun warm her room. She'd make her way into the living room to click on the heater soon. For now, she was content in her bed under the warm electric blanket.

She reached over to her nightstand and picked up her cell phone. She had to call her mom about the finalized details of her trip home. Simone was excited to see her mom and the rest of the family. Some time had passed since she'd been home. After Joshua's death, her mother had asked her to move back. Simone wasn't ready then, but time had reversed her decision.

She hit one on the speed dial. The call connected after two rings. Early in the morning, her mother would be expecting to hear from her. "Good morning, Mom. How are you?"

"Morning, baby girl. I'm doing real well. I just finished my devotional time with the Lord. God is good."

"All the time, He is. I'm glad you're doing well, Ma. I was calling to tell you my trip is planned for next week. The only thing on my agenda is the interview I have. After that, I'll be able to spend some quality time with the family."

"That's good, baby girl. I can't wait to see you. It's been a while. Who's picking you up from the airport?"

Simone repositioned herself in bed and found a warmer spot. "Devon is picking me up. I've already texted him, so it's all been worked out."

"Okay. That's good. Tell me about this interview."

Simone talked her mother's ear off for an hour. She told her every detail she could remember and how Terrance had set the whole thing up.

"Daughter, I haven't heard you this excited in a long time. I'm glad you're finally coming around. I'm going to send up some prayers asking the Lord to bless you."

"Please do, and thank you for praying. I know you have His ear." Simone hesitated for a moment. "Ma, where is Tori?"

Her mother sighed deeply. “She getting ready for work.”

“Why the heavy sigh, Ma?”

“For somebody that works, she’s always broke. She never has money to pay bills, but I see she have money to shop.”

Simone waited. “Well, Ma, you have to put your foot down and give her another option. At this point in her life, she should have her own place.”

“Yeah, you’re right, Simone. But she keep telling me she can’t afford to move. Maybe when you come, you can talk to her.”

Here we go. This is not how I wanted to spend my vacation. “We’ll see, Ma. You know how Tori is when anyone says anything about her changing her ways.”

“Okay, baby girl. I know you need to get to work. I love you, can’t wait to see you.”

“Love you, too, Ma. See you soon.” Simone disconnected the call.

She crawled out of bed, took a shower, and got dressed. She padded into the kitchen and started making her morning coffee. The coffee percolator indicated it was time to have her first cup of caramel macchiato, but the ringing of her cell phone interrupted the moment.

She glanced at the name on the face of her phone and cringed. *Tori.*

“Hi, sis. What’s up?”

"Hi, Simone. Ma told me you were coming home."

"That's right. I'll be there next week. I have an interview."

"Um, sis, you know I hate to ask..."

Finally, the real reason for the call. "Ask me what?" Simone bit her lip. "What do you need?"

"Can you pay my car note?"

"Again, Tori?"

"I know, and I promise it will be the last time."

Simone rolled her eyes. She remembered the conversation she'd had with her mother about Tori's money problems and how much she loved to shop. Her mother said Tori's obsession with purses and clothes was out of hand, and she'd buy a purse before paying her cell phone bill, and pick up a new outfit for every occasion. Simone knew it was time to teach Tori a lesson.

"Sorry, Tori. Can't do it. My money is tied up with moving back, and I'm going to be spending some coin getting there." She said a silent prayer of forgiveness for lying. "Maybe you could ask for more hours at work."

"I can't get any more hours," she said in a startled tone.

"Well, sis, sorry I can't help you. I'm on my way out, so we'll have to talk when I arrive." Simone shook her head and disconnected the call. She hated lying to Tori about the money, but she was not going to continue helping her when she knew what Tori's problem was—shopping.

The truth of the matter, though, was that Simone was in superb financial health. Joshua had set her up quite well prior to his death. He'd already named her as the beneficiary on his insurance and investments. With the insurance payoff from his motorcycle accident and the investments that rolled into her account, she was set for life. She could still keep her apartment in New York for a vacation spot, and she'd also be able to buy a home in California once she got settled. She didn't need to work, but loved what she did. It kept her busy and her mind off her loneliness. Simone lacked for nothing, but she wasn't going to let Tori know it.

It never failed; each time Tori called or texted, she always wanted something. Usually, it was money. She never called to see how Simone was doing, or to see if she needed anything. It was always about her. *Selfish.*

Simone could never understand how she'd turned out the way she did. They were raised in the same household, were taught good morals and values, and even went to church. Both their parents worked hard to get what they had achieved in life. They owned not one, but several pieces of property in the San Francisco Bay Area. After their father's untimely death, they'd moved into a quiet neighborhood in the city. Maybe Tori thought the settlement their mother had received from their father's death was hers, too.

Returning to California had one challenge: her relationship with Tori.

Chapter 7

The next week raced by, and Simone was more than ready for her trip. She'd spent the last hour rechecking the contents of her luggage. Satisfied with what she'd packed, she deposited her luggage at the front door. While in the kitchen, preparing a little snack to take on her flight, her cell phone rang. She activated the speaker and set the phone on the kitchen table.

"Hey, girl, you ready?" Kendra asked when she answered.

"Yep. I've rechecked my bag twice to make sure I packed everything I need. I heard the weather was quite chilly in California, so I made sure to take a few more sweaters. I spoke with my mother, and she would like us to have a family meeting with Tori. That wasn't how I wanted to spend my time, but I'm going to do it. Maybe this time she'll get some help."

"Well, girl, you can lead a horse to water, but you can't make it drink. But, don't worry. Everything will be alright."

"Yeah, I know. We can always hope for the best."

"You call for Uber?"

Simone sighed. "Yes. They should be here in fifteen minutes, and I'll be ready."

They ended the call, and she finished preparing her snacks for her trip.

When Simone got to the airport, her flight to California had been delayed two hours due to bad weather. She wondered if that was a sign. Without giving it any consideration, she dismissed the thought. "This kind of stuff happens all the time," she said out loud.

Simone found a seat in the corner of the waiting area. She retrieved her laptop from her carry-on luggage, opened the cover, and powered it up. She pulled her cell phone out of her purse and called Devon.

"What's happening?" Devon said in his deep voice.

She sighed audibly. "Well, my flight has been delayed for two hours due to bad weather. I'll text you when we're about to board."

"Wow, really? Is it raining or something?"

"Thick fog. They're hoping it will lift soon, so we can be on our way."

"Alright. I'll be waiting on your text."

"Okay. See you later today."

They disconnected the call, and she placed the phone back into her purse.

Simone surveyed her surroundings. Her eyes collided with a handsome man seated several rows away. His full lips curved upwards, but only for a brief moment; he returned his attention to the paper he was reading.

For the next few hours, she checked California real estate websites for home listings. She was thrilled to be returning home, but even more thrilled that she'd be able to get her own place. She decided on purchasing a four-bedroom with two baths in Piedmont Hills in Oakland, so she could be close to her mom. It would also give her an extra bedroom for Kendra when she came to visit. Thankfully, it was a buyer's market. With no problem, she found several within her price range and sent her real estate agent the listings.

Two hours later, as the agent called for her flight to board, several waiting passengers clapped and cheered. *Hallelujah*, Simone thought. She sent a text to Devon, powered down her laptop, and waited for her section to be called. She could hardly believe she'd see her family in a few hours.

She boarded the flight along with the other first class passengers. Simone found her row. "Excuse me...." Her eyes collided once again with the handsome man from the waiting area. He was sitting in the aisle seat of the row she would occupy. Simone said, "I'm seated next to you."

The man was tall, well-built, with dimples. He reminded her of Rick Fox—definitely a piece of eye-candy. The gentleman stood to give Simone access to their row. He offered to help her place her carry-on in the overhead compartment.

Simone gladly accepted with a smile. "Thank you."

"My pleasure."

After she took her seat, she placed her laptop and purse in the available compartments for easy access.

He turned his head toward Simone. "How are you doing?"

"I'm doing well, thank you." She drew in a deep breath and exhaled. "I'm glad the fog lifted."

He chuckled. "I know that's right. That was a long delay. I'm looking forward to going home."

The flight attendant came by and offered juice before takeoff. Simone accepted orange juice and placed her drink on the table top.

After all the passengers were seated, the flight was cleared for take-off.

The handsome gentleman leaned forward. "By the way, I'm Lamont Willis."

"Uh... I'm Simone."

"Nice to meet you, Simone. So, what's taking you to California?"

"I'm actually headed to California for a job interview."

"That's great. What do you do?"

"I'm a paralegal."

"Small world. I'm an attorney. What firm are you interviewing with? I may know them."

"Blackman and Blackman. They're real estate development attorneys."

"I'm actually quite knowledgeable of the firm. We've done a few business transactions together in the past. Here, let me give you my business card."

Simone accepted the card and read it before placing it in her purse. "Oh wow. That's great. Thanks."

They spent the next hour talking about his visit to New York, the plays, politics, and living in California. As soon as the aircraft landed at San Francisco International Airport, the passengers were out of their seats, removing bags and waiting in the aisles.

Lamont eagerly retrieved her luggage from the overhead bin. "You have my card if things don't go as planned with Blackman and Blackman. We could always use help at our firm."

Simone nodded. "Okay, I'll keep that in mind. Thanks."

She grabbed her carry-on and headed to baggage claim, dodging swarms of people. By the time she arrived, the carrousel was filled with luggage. She waited patiently for hers to come through, but it never did. Most of the passengers, except Simone, had claimed their belongings. An uneasy feeling came over her. When the carrousel did its last turn and her luggage still was not accounted for, she knew her luggage was lost. It was the first time since traveling that the airlines had lost her luggage. *Well, there's a first time for everything.*

Too busy looking for her luggage, Simone hadn't noticed Lamont standing right beside her.

"Problem with your luggage?"

Simone blew out a breath. "Yeah, a small one. They lost it." She shook her head. "I can't believe this. First, the delay. Now, my luggage."

"Is there anything I can do to help?"

"No thanks. I'm going to file a claim and be on my way." She turned and stomped over to baggage claim. Simone appreciated his concern, but she didn't know him. She was not the type of woman to give strangers any ideas that would be misconstrued.

She gritted her teeth. She hadn't counted on losing her luggage. She couldn't believe it. Now she'd have to go shopping, especially for the interview. Something else not in her California plans.

Chapter 8

Simone was curbside when Devon arrived. He pulled up, gave her a hug, and quickly assisted her. Soon they were headed down Highway 80, bobbing their heads to the sultry sounds of Indie Arie's Christmas album.

She closed her eyes and let out a deep breath, allowing the music's melody to quiet her spirit. Her eyes opened when Devon interrupted, "How was your trip?"

She peered in his direction. "Well, besides the delay and my luggage getting lost, everything else was great." She paused. "I need to stop by the mall and pick up a few things. The flight was comfortable. I don't know why I hadn't traveled first class before."

They laughed, and she updated Devon on her plans for moving, her upcoming interview, and the house search. He, in turn, brought her up to date on all the family matters, his new house, his growing business, and the holiday festivities. Excitement filled the air when they started talking about the Golden State Warriors. Simone and her brother were both huge basketball fans.

He turned and grinned. "You know they have a home game while you're here?" He returned his attention to the road.

"Hmm." Her eyes lit up. "Let's see if we can get some tickets. I'd love to go. If you can find tickets, I'll buy them as an early Christmas gift to you. But promise not to say anything to Tori."

He pretended to zip a zipper across his lips. "I'm on it."

"What you going to do for a ride?"

"I need to get a rental."

"You can use my car. I have two, remember? After we eat and visit with Ma, you can drop me off at home. Keep this one until you leave."

Simone turned her head toward him. "Cool. Thank you. If I haven't said it yet, I need to tell you how much I appreciate you. I love you, bro."

A wistful grin lifted the corner of his mouth. "Love you, too, sis. We're family, and family sticks together. No matter what."

She turned her head and stared out the window. She hadn't realized how much she'd missed her brother. The daily phone calls, the board games on family nights. Growing up, Devon would beat up anyone who mistreated her. He was definitely a protector.

"Ugh. I see this traffic on 80 hasn't gotten any better."

Devon gave her a quick side glance. "It's probably gotten worse since you've last been here. But it can't be that bad after living in New York all these years."

"I mean, I'm quite used to the crowded roadway and the impatient drivers. Traffic in the city is bad, but I think 80 traffic is in a class by itself. It's all good, though. I'm happy to be home."

Devon reached over and squeezed her knee. "We're glad you're home, too, sis."

Despite the flight delay and the lost luggage, Simone was quite happy. She sent a text to Kendra. *Hey girl, finally landed safely in San Francisco. All is well. My flight was delayed and the airlines lost my luggage. Yep, that's how it started. How are you? TTYL. Love you.*

Moments later, she received a response. *Hey sissy, I was thinking about you. Bummer about your luggage. Glad you landed safely though. Talk soon. Miss you already. Love you, too.*

Simone read the text and turned her phone face down in her lap. She laid her head back on the headrest, closed her eyes and dozed off.

She woke up to Devon's voice. "Hey, sis. We're at the mall."

"Dang, I must have been tired. I didn't even realize I'd fallen asleep."

Devon looked at her. "Un huh, mouth open and all."

She gave him a look and playfully punched his arm. "Boy." They laughed.

"Come on, woman. Let's get this over with. You know Mom is waiting."

An hour or two later, they pulled into their mother's driveway. Exhausted, Simone slowly got out of the car, grabbed her purse, and ambled to the door of her mother's home.

Devon retrieved her carry-on luggage and the shopping bags that were on the back seat. She smiled. She was grateful for her brother and glad he always had her back. *He's going to be a great catch for someone one day: protective, handsome, and No Baby Mama Drama. Successful dentist, Dr. Devon Herron.*

The sound of her mother's voice drew her from her thoughts. "Simone! Look at you, baby girl." With outstretched arms, her mother greeted Simone at the door. They embraced one another with tight hugs and kisses on the cheek.

When her mother finally released her, Simone strolled over to the couch, plopped herself down, and removed her black stilettos. "How you doing, Ma?"

She grinned. "I'm doing well with the help of the Lord. I'm so glad you home. You hungry?"

The smell of her mother's fried chicken filled the air. Simone knew there would be a big spread of vegetables, cakes, and a tray of fruit to balance the meal. "I'm glad to be here, Ma. And, yes, I'm hungry. I haven't eaten since the flight."

Devon came in, smiled, and shook his head at the sight of his sister and mother all cozy on the couch. He deposited Simone's carry-on and shopping bags next to the couch. The smell of food lured him straight into the kitchen. Simone and their mother, Marie, pushed off the couch and joined Devon. The three fixed their plates. He poured two glasses of red Kool-Aid for himself and Simone and a glass of water for their mother. They pulled out their chairs and sat at the table.

"Simone, you only brought that small bag?" her mother asked.

"No, Ma. The airline lost my luggage. That's my carry-on. I kept waiting for it to come off the carousel, but it never did. I filed a claim. If they find it, they'll have someone from the airport drop it off here. That's why I have those shopping bags. Devon had to take me to the mall to buy some things for my interview and to get through the next few days. Hopefully, they'll find it soon."

"Lawd have mercy. I hope that didn't stress you

out." Her mother reached across the table and squeezed her hand.

"No, ma'am. Not too much anyway. It did slow me down from getting to you and this fried chicken." Devon and Simone laughed, and both leaned forward at the same time for a second helping.

Tori's key turned in the doorknob. She opened the front door and followed the sounds of laughter and the smell of food into the kitchen. "Hello, everyone."

Tori and Simone's eyes met. Tori headed for the kitchen sink to wash her hands. She dried her hands on a paper towel and pulled out a plate from the cabinet.

"Hey, Tori. How you doing?" Simone asked.

"Fine." She slammed the cabinet door.

Oh, here we go. "Hard day at work?"

Tori stomped over to the table and fixed her plate. "Nope."

Simone rolled her eyes. She wasn't in the mood to deal with Tori. She'd had a long day with the delay and her lost luggage. She didn't have the energy to address her sister. *Oh, well. She'll get over it.*

"I had to ride the bus. They repossessed my car." Tori yanked out a chair and sat across from Simone.

Devon and Marie kept eating.

Simone and Tori's eyes locked. "Well, appears

to me you need to be more disciplined with your money," Simone spoke candidly.

Tori swallowed a mouthful of potatoes. Rocking her neck as she spoke, she said, "Well, if you would have help me, I'd still be driving my car and we wouldn't be having this discussion."

Simone clenched her jaw and shot back, "Are you kidding? It's not my responsibility to pay your bills. I can't believe you."

Devon's nostrils flared, and he took a swallow of his drink. "Tori, you know we've all covered for you at one time or another. It comes a time in everyone's life when they need to take responsibility for their own actions."

Tori's eyes moved back and forth from Devon to Simone. "Are you two teaming up on me?"

"Y'all need some more to drink?" their mother asked, trying to break the tension. She stood, sashayed to the refrigerator, and filled the pitcher with more Kool-Aid from a large jug she always had in the fridge.

Simone shook her head as she chewed her food. She was annoyed. "We're not teaming up on you, Tori. We want you to be financially independent and not rely on others to meet your needs."

"Wait a minute, everybody. Everybody calm down," Marie interjected. "Lord Jesus, help us."

"That's right, Mama. Tell them," Tori said in frustration.

"I'm not telling them anything. I need to

address you, Tori." She stared at her sternly. "I've let you get away with a lot of stuff I shouldn't have, and for that, I apologize. I have allowed tension to come between my kids, and I want it to stop right now. I can't help what people did to you years ago, but we have done nothing but love you. You got to let the past go. That's the only way you 're going to have a better future."

Tori's mouth dropped open.

"Your brother and sister have helped you more than you know." Tori lowered her head as their mother continued her rebuke. "You need to be more responsible and take ownership of your behavior."

Devon swallowed hard, and Simone watched in shock. Their mom had finally stood up to Tori.

Tori's eye widened. "Okay, well, I'm trying. I needed a little help this month. Don't worry. I'm going to get myself together."

"God helps those who help themselves," Marie said.

They finished their dinner in icy silence.

Devon wiped his mouth on the napkin, stood, and took his plate to the sink. He turned back to the table. "Simone, when you get done, we can go so you can drop me off at home."

"I'm done." Simone got up and placed her plate in the sink.

"Wait a minute. Did I hear you correctly?

Simone is dropping you off at home? She's using your car?"

Devon eyes were cold. "Yes. She is."

Tori's eyebrow lifted as she cast a glance at Devon. "I wish I could have used one of your cars."

Devon and Simone cleared the table and cleaned the kitchen, while Tori sat there fuming.

She leaned back in her chair. "Wow, Simone could have rented a car and let me use your car. All the money she got from Joshua's settlement, she could buy two, three, four cars... yeah, I heard about the settlement."

"Tori. Didn't we have a talk? That's not a nice thing to say about Simone," their mother scolded her.

Simone gave Tori a stern look. "You know what, Tori? What I do with my money is my business. How can you be that insensitive and selfish? I can't believe you would be that heartless. Don't you ever say anything about Joshua, my money, or what I can buy. And don't ever ask me for help again. I love my family and I try to do the right thing as a Christian, but I'm tired of you thinking you can take advantage of people and then be all rude and nasty to them when you don't get your way."

Simone slammed the dishcloth onto the counter and left the kitchen abruptly. As she stomped into the living room, the tears fell from her eyes like a broken water dam. Simone would have traded all the money in the world to have Joshua still alive. *As if you can put a price tag on love.*

She remembered the last time she had heard his voice. They'd had a slight disagreement regarding his family, but to clear the air had confirmed their dinner date. How she wished that conversation had gone differently.

Chapter 9

After the drama with Tori, Simone was glad the day of her interview was finally here. She lay in bed listening to the falling drops of water coming down outside her window. It had rained the entire week, and the weatherman said it wasn't going to let up anytime soon. The one ray of sunshine in the week was the return of her luggage. Thankfully, none of the contents were missing or damaged.

As she thought about the interview process, Simone contemplated what she was going to wear. It had been years since she'd gone on an interview, and she was a bit nervous. She hoped Aaron was as cool in person as he sounded on the phone. If so, she'd be fine.

She remembered interviewing with Terrance. Fresh out of college, she was so nervous, she'd stumbled over her words more than once. She was glad Terrance had looked beyond her nervousness to see her potential.

It never dawned on her to schedule other interviews if this one wasn't successful. It wasn't like she was pressed for money; she had plenty. She had Lamont's card, but she wasn't going to call him. This interview was in the Lord's hands. If He wanted her to work at Blackman and Blackman, she would.

Thirty minutes later, she finally mustered enough energy to roll out of her comfortable queen-size bed. With both feet securely on the floor, she stood and made her way to the spacious walk-in closet to pick out her attire for the day. She'd decided on the navy pantsuit with her white blouse. This was definitely her power suit. She'd complete the outfit with navy three-inch stilettos and her white tote, which would be a stunning accessory. She hung the outfit over the closet door and made her way to the shower. Her cell phone rang. She stopped and glanced at the face of the name. It was Kendra.

Simone smiled as though Kendra could see her. "Hey, girl. What's up?" She put the call on speaker.

"Hey, girl. How you doing? Today's the big day. You ready?"

"I'm good; getting my thoughts together for the interview."

"You'll do fine. I heard the weather report. Be careful in all that rain."

Simone noted the concern in Kendra's voice. "I will. I'm going to leave in plenty of time. People don't know how to drive in this weather."

"How are things at home?"

"Well, girl, that's a longer story than I have time to discuss right now. I'll say this: Tori hasn't changed one bit. She is still the same self-absorbed person she's always been. When I get back, I'll tell you all about it."

"Okay, girl. I'm praying for you. Hit me up when you get back."

"For sho. We'll talk later." They disconnected the call, and Simone headed to the shower.

An hour later, she took a final look in her full-length mirror. Everything was to her satisfaction. Make-up flawless, twists perfect, and the suit screamed *Don't mess with me.*

She placed her phone and keys inside her tote and grabbed her outerwear, along with an umbrella. She snatched her updated résumé off the nightstand, placed it in her portfolio, and headed out the door.

Simone got into Devon's car, popped in a Lauryn Hill CD, and entered the address to the office building in the GPS. She backed out of the driveway and got on Highway 80 toward downtown Oakland.

The road was wet and slippery and the traffic appeared more congested due to the rain. She bounced to the music in her seat and tapped her fingers on the steering wheel, praying for a break in the traffic and no accidents. She'd left in plenty of time to pick up a coffee at Peet's and get to the interview with time to spare. Somewhere between talking to Kendra and the music, her nervousness dissipated.

She was excited to finally meet the Blackman brothers. The opportunity to work for them was promising. However, Simone knew better than anyone that nothing was guaranteed. She would go in and give it her best shot.

She was reminded of Proverbs 3:5-6, "*Trust in the Lord with all thine heart; and lean not unto thine own understanding. In all thy ways acknowledge him, and he shall direct thy paths.*"

Simone followed the directions from her GPS and turned into the parking garage. After circling the garage twice, she finally found an empty space. Taking a few minutes to do one last inspection of her face and hair, she applied a little more of her favorite lipstick, Rum Raisin. She put her phone on silent, grabbed her tote bag and suit jacket from the front passenger's seat, and stepped out of the car.

Aaron parked his car in his reserved parking stall at his place of business. He opened the back seat door, reached for his suit jacket, and put it on. He was dressed in a tailored dark blue Italian-made business suit—with a winter-white shirt and pin-stripe navy tie—that fit his broad shoulders with impeccable precision. On his feet, he wore blue wingtips. He grabbed his briefcase and activated the alarm in his car.

He'd arrived at his office a few hours earlier than usual. He needed to look over some files before his interview with Simone.

He threw his briefcase on his desk and hung his suit jacket on the rack. He opened his briefcase, pulled out his client folders, and collapsed into his leather chair. Simone's résumé was on top of the stack. Swiveling in his chair, he turned to face the full-length glass window in his corner office. In spite of the rain hitting the window, the view from his office was spectacular.

He looked over her résumé and highlighted a few conversation pieces to discuss. Aaron smiled as he remembered their previous conversation. They'd spent two hours conversing. She was easy to talk to. He knew it was their first conversation, but first impressions meant a lot and he was impressed. His mind lingered over her soft, gentle voice, so easy on his ears, and her consideration to postpone the interview.

He wasn't sure what it was, and why he was even thinking about her personal qualities because that really didn't matter. She was coming to interview for a job. Nothing more. He definitely wasn't hiring another Macy. Yet he couldn't help but smile when he remembered her laugh. *Aaron, get a hold of yourself. You're done with women for now. This is business, remember?*

He shook himself back to reality and turned to power up his laptop. He placed her résumé on his desk and checked his emails and appointment calendar. Certain emails required his immediate attention, and he focused on those first. The others would have to wait until later. His appointment calendar was clear for the rest of the day after his interview with Simone. He worked steadily for the next two hours, looking over new projects and building plans, and returning a few calls.

Two short knocks at the door interrupted his concentration. Shaun entered. "Hey, bro. What's happening?"

Aaron looked up and gazed at his brother. "I'm going over some of the city's proposed development projects before Simone's interview."

Shaun stood in front of Aaron's desk with his hands in his pants pockets. "Oh yeah, that's right."

Aaron leaned back in his chair. "She should be arriving shortly."

"Do you have the blueprints for the Oak Park housing project?"

Aaron eased out of the chair and stepped over to a table to retrieve the requested blueprints, but was unable to locate them. He cleared his throat. "I must have forgotten them in my car. I'll run down and see if they are in the trunk."

"Alright." Shaun left Aaron's office with determined strides.

Aaron retrieved his keys from his jacket pocket and moved steadily down the corridor toward the elevator. He pressed the down button and waited.

He was glancing at his watch when the elevator doors opened. A woman barely made it out the elevator door before she stumbled, lost her footing, and ran smack dab into him. Instinctively, Aaron reached out and grabbed her around the waist to steady her before she hit the floor.

For a moment, time stood still. Something hit him like a flash of lightning. Their eyes locked. "Whoa. Are you okay?"

The woman giggled. "Oh my. Yes, I'm quite alright. I am sooooooo sorry. My stupid heel got caught in the carpet."

He'd only held her for several seconds, but it felt like eternity. Aaron wondered where he had heard that soft voice before. Her beautiful laugh made his heart jump. *Who is this woman? She fits perfectly in my arms.* Aaron couldn't explain it. Holding on to this woman around her waist, it felt like something had awakened inside of him. Something he'd long buried, even before the fiasco with Macy. Something he hadn't felt in years.

The lady stuck out her hand. "I don't think

we've officially met. I'm Simone Herron. Please accept my apology for that mishap."

I knew it. It was her voice. I knew I'd heard it before. Wow. She's beautiful. A smile lit his face. He reached for her hand. "Well, hello, Simone. It's nice to meet you." Aaron's large hand engulfed her smaller one. "No apology necessary. I was too busy looking at my watch to pay attention." *Nope, Aaron, off limits. Remember your rule.*

She withdrew her hand, adjusted her clothes, and grabbed her tote off the floor. It appeared to have taken more of a beating.

Aaron could feel other people looking at them. He maneuvered her inside the foyer.

Simone joked, "Well, I'm glad it wasn't worse. If I'd fallen and broken my leg, I'd be suing you."

They laughed together. "Why don't I show you to my office? I was headed to my car, but it can wait until later."

She nodded.

He led her toward the receptionist's desk. Aaron gave her a quick introduction to their receptionist, Holly. Holly offered a half-smile and continued typing.

"My office is this way." He led her down the corridor to his spacious office.

"Come on in. Let me get that coat for you." Aaron hung her coat on the rack. "You're welcome to sit wherever you'd like. Would you like a drink? We have water, coffee, soda, and juice."

She sat in one of the empty seats in front of his desk and placed her tote bag next to her leg. She crossed her legs and adjusted herself in the chair. "I'll have some water. Thank you."

He sauntered over to his small office refrigerator, pulled out a water bottle, and brought it to her with a napkin.

As Aaron strolled back to his desk, he studied her profile. She was striking. Her tilted-up brown eyes were exotic and beautiful. Her smile held beautiful teeth, and was warmly inviting.

He placed a coaster on the desk in front of her. "Here you go." *Aaron, get your mind back on business,* he chided himself. Aaron took his seat behind his desk opposite her and put his keys in the desk drawer.

Finally breaking the awkward silence, Aaron said. "Well, welcome to Blackman and Blackman." He leaned back in his executive chair. "No problem finding the office?" Aaron tried his best to work his way through the first few minutes of the interview, but it was difficult. He was nervous. The embrace at the elevator sat between them, charged with electricity.

She smiled and tilted the water bottle to her lips. "No, not at all, but traffic was a beast. And the rain didn't help either. I left in plenty of time not to be rushed."

As their conversation continued, they talked about the inception of Blackman and Blackman, the projects the firm was currently working on, the position, and her role at the firm. Aaron shared a brief overview of the issues with Macy, though in carefully worded language.

He went over her résumé and asked a few questions he had highlighted. As she was talking, he drifted back to their phone conversation. She was unconsciously pulling him in now, more than she had on the phone.

"Aaron?"

"Huh, what? I'm sorry. What did you say?"

She chuckled. "I asked you if you had any more questions."

"Um, no. But I'm going to call Shaun. I want him to meet you." He dialed and Shaun answered on the first ring. "Hey, Shaun. Simone is here. Come on down and meet her."

"I'm on my way."

They ended the call. Within a few minutes, Shaun opened the door to Aaron's office. He wandered toward Simone and introduced himself as she stood to shake his hand. "Simone? Shaun Blackman. Great to make your acquaintance."

"Likewise, Mr. Blackman. It's a privilege to have this interview today."

"Please, call me Shaun." He smiled, unfastened his one-button jacket and sat opposite Aaron, gesturing for Simone to take her seat once again.

They spent the next thirty minutes getting acquainted. Simone shared her background and personal history, previous work experience, and her desire to be a part of their firm. Shaun seemed as impressed with her as Aaron. They finished the interview feeling confident in her skills, experience, and abilities.

Shaun appeared pleased with the way the interview had gone, and left Aaron's office for another meeting.

Aaron briefed her on the year-end calendar, the holiday events, and the upcoming attorney's conference that all their staff would attend. They ended the interview with the assurance that he'd contact her in a few days with their decision. Aaron stood and leaned across the desk to shake Simone's hand. The contact felt like an electric bolt. He could see in her eyes that she'd felt it, too.

Aaron quickly released her hand and looked away. He rubbed the palm of his hand against his pants leg. "Thanks for coming in, Simone. Let me walk you out."

Simone grabbed her tote from the floor and went to retrieve her coat from the coatrack. "Sure, Aaron. Thanks."

With distance between them, they sauntered out of his office in silence.

Chapter 10

Simone entered her bedroom, dropped down in the chair and kicked off her shoes. She closed her eyes and took a deep breath. Aaron Blackman. The picture on his website did him no justice. He was more distinguished and more handsome in person than she could have ever imagined: his full lips, framed by a manicured goatee; his hypnotizing cognac-brown eyes. Simone was sure she had gazed in them longer than was appropriate. But his long, black eyelashes framed his eyes and gave them the perfect shape. And the strong grip he'd had around her waist made her want to melt in his arms.

She sighed out loud and pressed her palm to her forehead. "Ugh! How stupid. Who almost falls and ends up in the hands of their potential boss? How embarrassing was that? Only you, Simone."

She shook her head. "And that receptionist, what was her deal? If looks could kill, someone would be planning my funeral. I wonder if they're dating. She sure looked like she had a claim."

Simone pushed off the chair and went to change into something more comfortable. She wished she could start her day all over. No, she needed to start the whole week over. From the flight delay, the lost luggage, Tori, and now the near-collision with Aaron. She pinched herself to see if she was really living through all of this. Maybe it was all a dream.

She couldn't imagine anything else going wrong. She pulled her Bible out of the desk drawer and opened it to Philippians 4:8. *"Finally, brethren, whatsoever things are true, whatsoever things are honest, whatsoever things are just, whatsoever things are pure, whatsoever things are lovely, whatsoever things are of good report; if there be any virtue, and if there be any praise, think on these things."* She smiled as she read it. God had everything under control.

She grabbed her jeans and a t-shirt out of the closet, changed her clothes, and collapsed on the bed. She stared into space, thinking about her misfortune.

She couldn't forget how uncomfortable she and Aaron were when she entered his office and took a seat. But why? It was nothing more than a slip. It was the first time she'd been in another man's arms since Joshua, and a long time since she'd felt safe. *Girl, please. Don't even go down that lane.*

Her cell phone rang. Startled, she jumped. She pulled her cell phone from the tote bag and glanced at the face of the phone. Kendra. Her timing was always perfect. Simone hit the speaker button.

"Hey, girl. I've been sitting up here waiting to hear all about the interview. How was it?"

"Well, the interview went great. But what happened before that..."

"Girl, what happened?"

Simone paused and took another deep breath before continuing. "I tripped and almost made a complete fool of myself coming out of the elevator."

"You have got to be kidding me! How did that happen?"

"My heel got caught in the carpet. Thankfully Aaron's strong arms broke my fall."

Kendra snickered. "Did you say you fell into Aaron's arms? Oh, no!"

Simone turned to lay on her stomach. "Oh, yes. That's exactly what happened. He was getting on the elevator and wasn't paying attention and before he knew what hit him, there I was. Talk about awkward."

"Girrrrrrl, give it up for the heel," Kendra chuckled. "Hmmm, that must have been nice. Wait... does he have muscles?"

"Kendra! Girl, you a hot mess!"

"Well, does he?"

"Girl, you too much. I'm glad you making light of my situation. And for the record, as if we both haven't already stared at his picture on the company's website, yes. The brother is fine. He's about five-eleven, chocolate skin like Hershey's cocoa powder mixed with a little milk, beautiful brown eyes, an inviting smile. His physique is well-toned, and yes, he's very muscular, with the most amazing broad shoulders and firm hands. Still, that was too close for comfort."

Silence filled the phone line for a moment. Kendra admitted, "Girl, you know pictures can be photoshopped, and I'm not laughing that you almost fell. At least you didn't fall straight on your face or your butt."

They both laughed. "True that," Simone replied. "Well, this is one picture that didn't do the real thing justice. He's more handsome in person." He was clearly one of Bay Area's most attractive bachelors. He was the perfect package—professionally successful, handsome, and financially secure. *But, of course, I wasn't paying attention.*

Simone had to catch herself. She'd already shared too many details. She knew her friend would make this into something bigger than what it was. Even she was surprised by how much she'd observed about Aaron in such a short amount of time. What she didn't want to share was just how flustered she felt being near him, and how he made her laugh. His powerful stride when he stepped, as if he owned the world.

"Yeah. Right. Did you forget who you talking to? So, did he offer you the job?"

Simone rolled her eyes at Kendra's reply. "He said he was going to let me know in a couple of days. I should have an answer before my return to New York." She let out a long, wistful sigh. "It would be great working there. I'm really excited about the new projects that are on the calendar and the major events coming up."

"Oh yeah. What events?"

Simone talked Kendra's ear off for almost an hour, sharing with her the list of upcoming events the firm would be attending and sponsoring. "There's a conference coming up, but he didn't have the location yet. It's one they attend every year, and there's a Christmas gala in Napa." She took another breath. "While I'm waiting to hear the final decision, I'm going house hunting."

"Make sure you find a house with an extra room for me."

"Already got you covered, sister-friend. There's no way I'm buying something that won't have space for you when you come to visit. I should let you get some rest, though. I know it's getting late there." Simone bid Kendra goodbye, checked her messages on her laptop, and went downstairs.

When he returned to his office, Aaron sat in his chair. He swiveled and turned to face the huge window. A storm had settled over the Bay Area. The rain beat steadily against the window. A chill hung in the air. But, Aaron could care less about the outside elements, he was too worried about what was brewing inside of him.

They'd wrapped up the interview thirty minutes ago. There were tons of other action items to occupy his mind, but still he found himself thinking about Simone. What was it about her that got him all twisted inside?

He could tell she was bright and intelligent, and would fit perfectly in the office. It was the exchange in the elevator that had him second-guessing himself. She had him feeling some kind of way. How could someone he'd so briefly known have that effect on him?

If he kept things on a professional level, all would be well. Crossing over into anything else would be out of the question.

He recalled Macy. When she came on board, he didn't realize how much of a self-centered woman she was. They'd gone out on a few dates, which was a big mistake. Aaron admitted his judgment was off, big time. By the time he ended what he'd considered a one-sided relationship, she'd already spread rumors about their affiliation. Once he got wind of her secretly sabotaging one of his development projects with a competitor, he fired her. *Never let a scorned woman work for you.*

Oh, no. He had to find a way not to hire Simone, he was way too attracted to her. But how? How could he convince Shaun of that without exposing himself? *Yeah, that's not going to happen.* He shook his head. What a quandary.

He turned and glanced at his law books on the bookshelf. Not one of them had the answer. He wrestled with his thoughts before accepting his reality. He had to hire Simone. If it was him making the decision, he'd make up some lame reason not to hire her. Now that Shaun had met her and was equally impressed, there was no way around it. Shaun would continue to pry until the truth was told. Aaron would rather deal with his feelings than hear Shaun's mouth. *Keep your feelings in check.*

Aaron sighed deeply. He retrieved a bottle of water from the refrigerator. Twisting off the cap, he took a sip. While treading back to his desk, two short knocks at the door interrupted his steps.

Before he could say a word, Shaun paced in and closed the door. "Hey, bro." Shaun collapsed into one of the chairs in front of his desk and crossed his leg. "That was a good interview. She seems to be perfect for the job. So we're hiring her, right?"

Aaron sat back down in his chair, looked at Shaun, and before he could catch himself, the words, "Oh, yeah. We're hiring her," came spilling out of his mouth.

Aaron knew his brother too well. There was no way to tell him about the elevator incident or the feelings that had been ignited in him. Shaun would not let him live it down. Aaron would allow the memory of Macy to keep him from detouring to the other side.

"Cool. The sooner, the better. When is she going to start?"

Aaron cleared his throat. "Well, she still needs to move here first. I'll give her a call tomorrow and offer her the job and get a start date. I'll let you know what we come up with."

Shaun gingerly pushed up from his seat. "Hmm. Okay. Did you have a chance to get the blueprints?"

Aaron shook his head. "Naw, man. Let me go now before I forget again." He pushed off the chair and strolled out the door with Shaun. When the elevator door swung open for a moment, he thought her scent was still present. *Fight it, man, fight.*

Chapter 11

The next morning, Simone and her realtor, Valerie, went to look at some properties. She had specifically instructed her realtor to focus on properties that were already unoccupied and would require no contingencies in the sale. She wanted to be able to fill the home with furniture and move in quickly.

The realtor angled in on homes located in Berkeley Hills. Simone looked at four houses before she finally settled on one she wanted in Claremont Hills.

"What do you think?" Valerie asked once she completed the tour.

"I love it."

The home was a European-inspired villa. It had a great view of both the bay and the bridge, complete with four bedrooms and three and a half baths. It was perfect, exactly what she had in mind. She gave Valerie the go-ahead to make an offer for the full price. She wanted it and had the money. There was no point in negotiating.

"I think you'll love the neighborhood. It's centrally located, and the home is a beauty. You've made an excellent choice."

Simone smiled. "I agree. Hopefully the owners will accept the offer and I can plan on moving in immediately."

"I know they're eager to sell and there are no other offers on it. Let's keep our fingers crossed."

Simone pointed her index finger toward the agent. "You cross your fingers. I'll pray."

They shared a laugh. "Okay, that sounds like a plan." They headed back to Valerie's office, where she wrote up the offer and submitted it.

Now came the waiting game, but Simone had time on her side. "Thanks for all of your help with this, Valerie. I appreciate it." She grabbed her purse, bounced out of Valerie's office, and headed to her mother's house.

Simone got behind the wheel. She sat quietly for a moment, reflecting on the past few days. She closed her eyes and said a prayer of thanksgiving. Tears of mixed emotions fell when she opened them.

Although she'd gotten a rough start to the week, she was overwhelmed with the possibility of purchasing this beautiful home. She was confident the owners would accept her offer. As she was ready to turn the key in the ignition, her cell phone started chiming.

She reached for her purse and removed her phone. Devon's face appeared on the screen. Her heart raced. He knew she was house hunting and would be unable to talk. He'd only call if it was important. "Devon, what's up? Is Mom okay?"

"Hey, Simone. Mom is fine."

Simone blew out a breath of relief.

"My bad to be calling you now, but Tori had an accident at work. We got a call from someone at her job saying they were taking her to Alta Bates. Apparently, she fell at work and is being treated."

"Is she okay?"

"Yeah. She's fine. They listed her as stable."

"Okay, good. I'm glad to hear that."

"We're on our way now. Mom wanted to see if you could swing by when you get done."

"Um, I'll be there shortly. I was leaving the realtor's office. What room is she in?"

"She's on the seventh floor. Room 712."

"Okay. See you in a few."

She put her phone in the console, started up the engine, and pulled off. The hospital was less than a twenty-minute commute.

The drive to the hospital took a little longer because of the rain and traffic. She trudged inside and headed for Tori's room. The elevator doors opened on the seventh floor. She strolled down the corridor to room 712. Devon, her mother and the doctor were inside.

Simone stepped into the room, halting the conversation that was going on among the three of them. "Hi, everyone." She went directly to her mother, who was sitting in a chair next to the bed, and embraced her.

Devon stood with his arms folded over his chest. The doctor, a middle-aged man, extended his hand for a handshake and introduced himself as Dr. Stevens.

Simone gave him a nice, firm handshake. "Hi. I'm Simone. Tori's sister. How's she doing?" Her eyes went from the doctor to Tori.

"She's fine. I was telling your family that she has a bad sprain and a little bump on her head that we are monitoring. I'm sure it's nothing, but we've run a few tests to make sure."

"How long is she going to stay?"

"At least overnight. Once we get the results back and everything looks good, she should be able to go home tomorrow."

"Oh, that's great." Simone smiled.

"She'll be in a little discomfort, but I have prescribed some medication that she can take. She might have a few headaches, but that's normal. No reason to be alarmed. I'll check on her a little later to see how she's doing."

"Thank you, Dr. Stevens," said Simone. The doctor nodded and headed out the door, back to work. Simone took a few steps closer to Tori. "How are you feeling?"

"I'm feeling fine." Other than the splint on her ankle and the little bump on her head, she did seem fine. But if she knew Tori, she was going to milk it for all it was worth.

"What happened?" Simone pulled up a chair and sat next to the bed.

"I missed my footing on the stepladder and landed on my ankle. And because I couldn't break the fall, I bumped my head."

"What were you doing on the ladder? Is that part of your job?" Devon asked.

Tori let out a breath in frustration. "No. It's not part of my job. I couldn't reach something, so I grabbed the ladder. It was an accident."

"Why didn't you ask somebody for help?"

Tori rolled her eyes at Simone, but didn't respond.

"Well, we're glad it wasn't anything worse." Their mom offered a smile.

"Dr. Stevens said he'd give me a week off work." Tori grinned. "Wish I could get at least two weeks."

Simone rolled her eyes. "Well, at least after one week, you'll be able to walk better, and that little bump on your head should be gone down by then. Besides, you don't get paid if you don't work, right?"

Tori ignored Simone. She went on and on about her accident and how her co-workers were trying to assist her before the ambulance arrived, and how she wished she could sue them. Then Tori prattled on about how short her paycheck was going to be and how she still didn't have a car.

Simone had had enough. She was thrilled when her phone chimed.

Tori raised her eyebrow. "You gon' take that call? I'm laying up here in all this pain, and you answering your phone. Really?"

Simone heaved a sigh. She checked the face on the screen. It was her realtor. "Yeeeeees, I am." She stood and walked down the corridor to the waiting room to take the call. She plopped into one of the empty seats at the table. "Hey, Valerie. I hope you have some good news."

"Hi, Simone. Well, yes and no. There was another offer that came in the same time we sent ours. The other offer is five thousand dollars more."

Simone closed her eyes for a second. "Okay, that's the bad news." She opened them. "What's the good news?"

"The owner is willing to see if you want to go higher."

"Hmm. You mean get into a bidding war?" *Welcome to California.*

"Yes, if you want the house. Remember, Simone, the house does have some equity and it is empty, so take that into consideration when deciding."

Simone mulled it over. "Tell the owners I'd be willing to pay ten thousand over, but that's my final offer."

"Okay. Let me present this counter-offer and I'll get back to you once I hear from them."

Simone shook her head. "They need to tell us ASAP, or I'm taking my offer elsewhere."

"Okay," Valerie said. "I will make sure I emphasize that." She ended the call.

Simone sat at the table, drained. She had been on the go since she arrived in California. A perfectly planned trip that was only expected to consist of going on one interview and looking at a few homes had turned into something completely exhausting. She cringed at the possibility of needing to stay a few more days to help her mother tend to Tori.

Yes, it was only a sprained ankle, but Tori knew how to make their mother feel guilty. Simone could only play it by ear and speak with her mother before she solidified her plans to return to New York. Simone wondered if her relationship with Tori would ever get better. *You would think that a bump on the head would have knocked some sense into her, but no. Well, at least, not today. Dear Lord, help us. What on earth would it take for someone to see that it's not all about them?*

In response, she felt the faintest impression upon her mind. *Patience, daughter. I'm working on you both.*

Simone leaned back in the chair. She was in no hurry to go sit through more of Tori's whining about being in pain. For the next few minutes, she checked her emails on her phone and placed a call to Kendra. She gave her the latest updates on the current events, including Tori's accident and her housing situation.

She hadn't yet heard from Aaron. She hoped to get the news real soon. She knew she needed to go back to Tori's room, but all she wanted to do was go to her mom's, take a nice long bath, and get some rest.

After thirty minutes of talking to Kendra, they ended the call and she placed the phone on the table. Simone folded her arms across her chest and looked at the ceiling. She was no longer alone in the waiting room. She could hear the chatter of family members discussing the sick and injured. She turned her head around to see a few people wiping away tears; no doubt they had received bad news.

Flashbacks of the last time she was at the hospital with Joshua pulled at her. She remembered the call, remembered driving hysterically and not caring if she broke any speeding laws. She remembered kissing him for the last time. The memories brought such deep pangs. Overwhelmed, she started to shake. She needed air. She wanted to get up and run, but couldn't. Her feet wouldn't move.

He that dwelleth in the secret place of the most High

shall abide under the shadow of the Almighty. I will say of the Lord, He is my refuge and my fortress: my God; in him will I trust.

A tear rolled down her cheek. Again, that soft whispered impression spoke to her. *You are safe with me.*

After a few seconds, she composed herself. Before she could make her way back to Tori's room to say goodbye, her phone danced and stopped her in her steps. Blackman and Blackman appeared on the screen. She swiped the answer icon and sat back down. Her stomach flipped. "Hello," her voice cracked.

"Hi, Simone. It's Aaron. How are you?"

You don't have enough time for me to tell you all that. She cleared her throat. "Hi, Aaron. I'm fine, and yourself?" She really wanted to tell him her stomach had been in knots waiting on his call.

"I'm good. Thanks for asking. Well, as promised, I said I would call today with a decision." There was a pause before he continued. "Shaun and I would like for you to come work for us. With that being said, we'd like to make you an offer. If you're still interested."

She smiled as she listened. "Still interested? As a matter of fact I am." Simone pressed her hand to her mouth to keep from squealing. "I'm so excited. Can't you tell?"

Silence traveled over the line. "You sure you're fine? I'm sorry. I don't mean to pry. It's that...." He paused and cleared his throat. "Well, okay. I guess this means you've accepted the position."

"You've guessed correctly."

"Great. We need to work out a start date. We're flexible. We know you're technically still living in New York."

"Ummm, yes I am. Can you give me a couple of weeks to get things in order? I want to give Terrance ample time to hire someone. I'm sure you understand that. If I know Terrance, he's probably covered himself already."

"That's fine. I'll have the offer letter emailed to you this evening." He sounded elated. "I believe you will be quite pleased with our proposal. When are you heading back to New York?"

"Well, my original plans were to leave in a few days. However, a family issue came up, so I might be here a few extra days." Simone's heart thumped.

"Oh really. Is everything alright?"

"Yes. My sister had an accident at work, but she's fine now."

"Oh, that's good to hear. Can you come in to fill out the paperwork before you leave? Let me know when so I can have everything ready for you when you arrive."

"No problem at all. I can swing by tomorrow around two o'clock. Will that work?"

Yes, that time looks good. So, we'll see you tomorrow. And, Simone, congratulations."

"See you tomorrow. Thanks, Aaron."

She disconnected the call. If only she didn't have to go say goodbye to her sister. She could sail right out of the waiting room into her brother's car.

Chapter 12

Aaron was determined to run today. Although the clouds hung low, the rain had finally stopped. There was a slight breeze from the wind but that wouldn't deter him. He dressed quickly, stuck his iPhone and headphones into his fanny pack, and made his way down the stairs to his kitchen. He grabbed a water bottle from the refrigerator and headed out for his run.

He pulled into an empty parking space at Lake Merritt. Aaron exited his car and did a series of stretches and side lunges to warm up his hamstrings and quads. He put on his headphones, zipped his jacket, and secured his black beanie on his head. At a touch of a button, the playlist on his music app started and Aaron set off on his run. At this hour of the morning, it was quiet and peaceful. Exactly what he needed.

Running cleared his head. The air felt good pushing against his lungs. He increased his pace. Everyone else around him became nonexistent; it was him and God.

It had been a while since he'd spoken to God. Somehow, with working and building a business, God had gotten pushed aside. Maybe that was where the breakdown had started. Aaron wasn't certain when it happened. He knew that somewhere along the journey, life had gotten complicated. On the outside, he had it all together: money, fame, cars, homes. He had achieved the American dream. But internally, something was missing.

What began as a fun, exciting, harmless pastime had turned out to be less pleasurable with each passing experience. Still, the adrenaline rush was like nothing he had experienced before. Nothing could match the euphoria of winning. The disappointment and letdowns of losing were equally brutal.

He couldn't stop chasing after the high of winning on the slots, though. It called to him. He was living for that rush. How did he let himself get to this point? Aaron wasn't quite ready to use the word addicted, but he did know how to recognize a problem when he saw one. *Recognizing a problem and doing something about it is totally different*, his conscience reminded him.

I can stop any time I want to.

Yeah, you've said that before, too.

No one knew his little secret, not even Shaun. He'd become a master at covering up his transgressions. Money was never a problem; he had plenty of it. He was paid well and his investments yielded great dividends. And, on quite a few occasions, he won big. Real big.

Keeping pace around the lake, he thought about the first time he'd started gambling. He was a college student in his twenties, betting on sporting games for fun. When he won, he'd use his winnings to place higher bets. He won some, he lost some. The fun continued. Over the years, the stakes got higher and higher.

Aaron never let his outside pleasures interfere with his professional business. Lately, his habit was consuming more of his time, more of his thoughts, and more of his money. He was ready to admit the time had come to reassess the situation.

You must not have any other God but me.

He hadn't heard God speak to him in a long time, but he didn't miss this rebuke. As if perfectly timed, the lyrics of a song leapt out at him. "The truth can hurt you or the truth can change you. What will truth do to you?"

Aaron continued his run. He silently poured out his heart to God. *God, I can't do this alone. I need You.* His feet pounded against the asphalt. *I need help. I don't want this thing to consume me.*

Aaron broke his stride. Bending at the waist,

he planted his hands on his thighs, lowered his head and stared at the grass. Aaron didn't dare lift his head. He feared the desperation he was feeling inside would be visible all over his face. The last thing he wanted was for someone who knew him to see him like this. Breathing heavily from the exertion of his pace, he uttered in anguish, "God, help me... please."

Aaron completed his four miles around the lake and made his way home. He stepped out of his sweaty running gear, showered, and dressed for work. He contrasted a striped, collared shirt with a double-breasted gray suit tailored to fit his frame, and complemented the outfit with a wool fedora. He looked in the full-length mirror. Satisfied with his appearance, he stuffed his cell phone into the interior breast pocket of his suit coat, jammed his keys and wallet into the pockets of his pants, and grabbed his briefcase. He jumped into his car and drove to work.

His workday started with an email from Simone. "Aaron, you and Shaun have been extremely generous in your offer. This is more than I expected. What a blessing! I'm honored to be working for Blackman and Blackman. See you around two o'clock. Best, Simone."

His lips curled up as he read the email. *Don't*

smile, man. She's your employee, he silently scolded himself. The hiring package was placed on the table in his office for her to sign. He had given instructions to Holly to get Simone's office prepared, stocked, and ready for her.

The office was in high spirits. Blackman and Blackman had successfully negotiated and signed off on three of the city's projects that would create sustainable employment for the city. Their firm was doing quite well with the acquisition of both commercial and industrial remodeling projects.

Aaron glanced at a few development contract agreements, making sure the language was correct and the scope of work and project milestones were clearly outlined. For the next two hours, his fingers danced across the keyboard, answering emails and drafting letters.

As he was about to exit his email program, he received an incoming message from the National Bar Association regarding the upcoming attorneys' conference.

Dear Mr. Aaron Blackman,

We are pleased to invite you to the Las Vegas Chapter of the National Bar Association's Annual Scholarship Gala in Las Vegas, Nevada. We would like to request your participation in this year's conference as the Keynote Speaker. In addition to having you serve as our Keynote Speaker, we want to honor your expertise in the area of real estate development by having you serve as a guest lecturer at our state bar continuing education program. We believe your contribution to the field of real estate development in the urban community is unparalleled, and a workshop on this topic will be an asset to our organization.

We look forward to a positive confirmation. It would indeed be an honor for us if you would accept our invitation. Kindly RSVP at your earliest convenience.

Aaron raised his eyebrows. "I don't believe it. Of all places to hold the conference this year. Las Vegas, the gambling capital of the world. God, this is hilarious. After I pour out my heart to you this morning, now this. I'm not going to accept the invitation. That's all there is to it." *That was easy*, he thought.

He exited out of his email program and wondered if Shaun was being invited to speak as well. If he was, that would blow any shot of him not accepting. Sometimes having a business with a family member was not good. Aaron sighed heavily and leaned back in his chair.

Shaun would be back in the office later today, and he'd confirm if both of them had received the invitation. Who was he fooling? He and Shaun were a team. They always taught at the same workshops. This one would be no different. Aaron's mind traveled back to earlier today at Lake Merritt. He shook his head. "The struggle is real. The struggle is real. Lord, help me.... Please."

A wise man will hear, and will increase learning; and a man of understanding shall attain unto wise counsels. Was this how God was going to help him? Was his situation so bad that he needed counseling? Who could he confide in? Who could he trust?

The only person he would even consider was his pastor. He cringed at the thought. "I can't. He's too busy. How could I even think about disturbing him?"

He forced the thoughts from his mind, searched his contacts in his phone, found the number, and placed the call.

Chapter 13

Simone pulled into the parking garage at 1:45 p.m. She secured a parking space close to the elevator, took one last look in the rearview mirror, refreshed her makeup, and applied a little more of her favorite lipstick. She'd fussed all morning about what she was going to wear, finally deciding on her white jeans, a black turtleneck sweater, and her black, four-inch, high-heeled boots. She grabbed her purse, turned off her cell phone, and headed upstairs to the office.

When the elevator doors opened, she walked toward Holly's desk and introduced herself again. "Hi, Holly. I'm Simone."

Holly looked at her and smiled slightly. Her disposition was more cordial today than when Simone had interviewed with Aaron. "Hi, Simone. I remember you." She paused before she continued. "Congratulations, by the way. Aaron is expecting you. I'll let him know you're here. If you'd like, you can have a seat in the sitting area."

Simone glanced over her shoulder. The sitting area provided a leather couch and two leather chairs for people to wait comfortably. She walked over to the sitting area, sat down in one of the chairs, and grabbed a magazine. Moments later, Holly came over and escorted her to Aaron's office.

After Holly closed the door, Aaron and Simone greeted each other warmly. Simone hadn't noticed his deep-set dimples before.

"May I take your coat?" Aaron asked.

"Oh, yeah. Thank you."

He grabbed her coat and hung it up on the coa-track. Simone felt the heat of Aaron's gaze as he studied her body.

He cleared his throat and pointed to one of the empty chairs in front of his desk. "Please, have a seat. How are you?" He returned to his desk and sat down across from her.

She sat and crossed her legs. "I'm well. A tad bit chilly today."

"You should be used to the cold weather. New York winters are harsh."

"You're right. No matter how long I've lived there, I still can't get used to the weather."

"Would you like something to drink? I can have Holly bring in some hot tea or coffee."

"No thanks. I'll warm up in a few."

He leaned back in his chair. "Okay, I have the package ready for you to review and sign. Once you get done, I'll show you your office." Aaron leaned across the desk, handing her the enormous folder. "You're welcome to sit at the table over there and complete these."

She grinned. "Thanks. By the way, I called Terrance and gave him the news."

He nodded his head. "I know. We spoke earlier. He's disappointed that you're leaving him, but extremely happy for you. Sounds like his loss is our gain."

Simone smiled. "Terrance is a great boss. I'm really going to miss him and the other people in our office. But I'll be able to visit."

"Wonderful. Well, I know you have a full schedule. I'll let you get started on the paperwork."

Simone stood and made her way to the table. She sat in one of the black leather chairs and proceeded to fill out every document.

An hour later, she was all done. She put her pen inside her purse, pushed away from the table and rose from the chair. She walked back to his desk and extended her arm to hand him the folder.

Sensing movement, Aaron swiveled in his chair and turned to face her. "You finished?"

"I am."

"Great. Let me show you where you'll be working."

He took the folder from her hand, placed it

atop his desk, and stood. Simone followed him out of his office to the office next door. Aaron leaned against the door frame and gestured for her to enter. "This is your office." She stepped in and scanned the room. His cologne tickled her nose as she glided by him. *Hmm, he smells so good.* She shook her head as if to clear the thought from her mind. *Simone, focus*, she chided herself internally.

Returning her attention to her office, she noted the cherry finish on the desk and the tilt and swivel leather desk chair with pneumatic lift. Her eyes widened. "Oh my. This is enormous. Now, I'm impressed." Her fingers walked atop her desk.

Aaron stuffed his hands into his pockets. "I'm guessing by your reaction that you like it. We wanted to make it as comfortable as possible since you're going to be spending plenty of time here."

He smiled. "I told Holly to stock it with everything you could possibly want."

She giggled. "Yes, I love it. This is nice. It's perfect." Simone looked at him and stilled.

His eyes were captivating. This couldn't be happening. Not with her new boss. She was still in love with Joshua. She wasn't ready for someone new. But something about Aaron had her feeling some kind of way. Simone willed herself to look away and walked toward the window.

"If you need anything, let Holly know. If we don't have it, she can order it for you."

"I sure will. Thank you, Aaron... for everything. The view is beautiful."

Looking down reminded her of New York: people everywhere, moving, coming and going. She would miss the city that never slept. Her thoughts drifted to Joshua. She reached for the engagement ring secured on her necklace and rubbed it.

Feeling melancholy, she turned around and walked back toward her desk. Her smile had disappeared.

"Simone, are you okay? Is the office not to your liking?"

"Oh, no. I'm good. The office is perfect. I was reflecting. You want to show me the rest of the offices?"

"Sure. Follow me."

Aaron took her on a tour of the office and introduced her to a few of her new co-workers. Then he walked her to the elevator and wished her safe travels. On the way to her car, Simone ran through her mental checklist of what she had left to do during her time in California. Things were slowly being checked off. She settled in Devon's car and powered on her cell phone.

There was a text message from Valerie. *Congratulations! The house is yours. Call me ASAP.*

Her smile returned. Job, check. House, check. Simone leaned her head against the headrest and gave God thanks. She put the key in the ignition and drove away, happy.

She couldn't wait until she got home to share her latest news. Her mom and Devon would be thrilled. She could care less how Tori would feel about it. She was overjoyed. Things were falling into place.

Simone parked in the driveway of her mother's home and rushed inside. She took off her black boots and placed them by the front door. She shed her outer garments, tossing her black trench coat and scarf on the accent chair next to the couch.

Tori was lying down on the living room couch, watching a reality show.

"Hey, Tori. How you feeling?"

Tori lifted her head. "Hey, Simone." She turned her attention back toward the TV without giving Simone any further regard.

The aroma of dinner permeated the air. Today's feast included red beans and rice, fried catfish, cornbread, and green beans. Simone also knew by the smell lingering in the air that a delicious pound cake awaited them for dessert. These were the kind of meals Simone missed being in New York. She could get similar food anywhere, but nobody could beat her mother's cooking.

Simone entered the kitchen. Her mom busied herself at the stove, while Devon sat at the table chatting with her about his growing dentistry practice.

"Hi, Mom. Hey, Devon." She walked over and gave her mom a hug and kissed her on the cheek. "Smells good up in here. I know I've gained a few pounds since I arrived." Simone patted her hips.

Marie tilted her head. "Another few pounds won't hurt you."

They laughed. "Yes, they will, Ma. That means more time on the treadmill," Simone said.

"Sis, you smiling again. More good news?" Devon asked.

Seconds later, the sound of movement came from the living room. Tori made her way into the kitchen, limping. Once the food finished cooking, Devon and Simone placed everything on the table. It was the tradition in their mom's house that everyone ate together. That was one thing that would never change.

After Devon said grace, they dove into the feast as though they hadn't eaten all week. Everyone except Simone piled their plates high. She was too busy watching her weight. Marie smiled and watched her three children interact, laugh, and converse.

Simone looked at her mom. She reached over and squeezed her hand.

"Mama, you cooked so much food," Tori said as she jabbed a fork into her fish.

"Yeah, I know. But, Lord willing, we'll see

tomorrow and y'all gon' be hungry. And you know your brother, he always takes a grocery bag full home with him."

Devon grinned at his mother. "Yep."

The dinner conversation ebbed and flowed from business to politics to the Bible and Devon's critique of the pastor's sermon.

"Tori, how is your ankle feeling?" Simone asked before she put a spoonful of rice and beans in her mouth.

Tori took a sip of her drink. "It's still a little sore. The doctor said it would get better as the week progressed."

Simone was glad to be moving back with her family. They needed each other. No matter how much they got on each other's nerves, they were family. These were the people God had put her with.

Conversation continued to flow. Food on the plates dwindled, and the pitcher of sweet tea was replenished. Simone filled them in on her plans for returning to New York, and Devon talked about the Warriors. Tori even engaged in the conversation by adding her two cents about the Splash Brothers.

Devon gazed at Simone. "Bummer we couldn't get tickets." He filled his mouth with food.

She looked up and met his eyes. "We need to get on the list so we can be season ticket holders."

Tori tilted her head and grinned. "Now would

that be season tickets for all of us?" She winked at Devon.

"Girl, you don't even like basketball." Devon winked back.

They chuckled.

"You all ready for dessert?" Marie asked, looking at her three children.

She walked over and placed the pound cake and a carton of vanilla ice cream on the table. Devon stood and went to the china cabinet. He retrieved four dessert bowls, the ice cream scoop and spoons.

When they were almost finished, Devon stared at Simone. "Sis, you were going to share your happy news with us."

Simone's eyes darted from Devon to Tori. Thinking of their conversation when she first arrived, she hesitated. She didn't mind sharing her good news with Devon and her mother. She knew they loved her and would be excited for her. But Tori was a cold piece of work. Simone's heart still held a little residue of pain from Tori's hurtful words earlier in the week.

She was torn. She wanted to share her good news, but she didn't want to listen to Tori whine about her self-inflicted life of poverty. Simone wasn't sure what she would do if things got out of hand.

Why did she always have to think about what Tori was going to say or what Tori was going to do before she did something? Their relationship was like a game of chess. She felt like she always had to be one or two steps ahead of her sister to outplay her. It was mentally and emotionally exhausting.

She looked up. Three pairs of eyes were glued to her, waiting.

"Yes, dear. Tell us what happened. What news did you get?" Her mother encouraged her.

"I got the house," she blurted out. "My realtor texted me while I was at the law office signing my papers. I'm so happy." She refused to look at Tori.

"I knew it!" Marie shouted. Her mother drew her in for a hug and kissed her on the forehead.

"This calls for another celebration," Devon said.

A chorus of cheers filled the air.

"Thank you. We've got plenty of time to celebrate. When I get the house all decorated, I'll have a housewarming party."

Devon raised his hand and offered her a high-five. "Dang, sis, feels like I've been giving you a lot of high-fives lately. Congratulations for real, though. You deserve every good thing that is happening to you."

"Thanks, big brother." She winked. "Everything is working out fine."

"God is good!" Marie exclaimed. "My family is all coming together. God has heard my cry."

Tori blurted out, "I owe you both an apology for the things I've said and done to you." Tears filled her eyes. She blinked rapidly to keep them from falling. "I know I have not been the best sister to live with, but I want to try to build a better relationship with you both...." She paused. "Congratulations, Simone." She took a sip of her drink, placed her cup on the table next to her plate, and looked at Simone and then Devon. "I do really mean that... I..." She cleared her throat.

Simone's eyes widened. Devon's mouth hung open in disbelief. Their mom's face held a slight grin. Simone couldn't remember the last time Tori apologized to anyone, except to their mother. Simone held Tori's gaze. She was assessing her to see if Tori was sincere or if she was trying to pull a fast one.

"For real," Tori said without breaking eye contact. "I'm really sorry. I know it might take some time to believe me, but I'm serious."

Simone fixed her face and swallowed hard. "Apology accepted."

Their mother shouted, "Hallelujah. She has seen the light." She stood up from her chair and offered a little praise dance to the Lord. "I knew you heard my prayers, Lord. Thank Ya."

Devon was speechless. He got up, cleared the table, and put the leftover food in the refrigerator. Simone put all the dirty dishes in the dishwasher and set it to start in an hour.

Tori and their mother were still chatting at the

table. Devon and Simone pulled out chairs and rejoined them.

The conversation turned toward Simone's new house. "I asked Valerie if I could bring you all to see the house and she said I could. I need to call her and make sure she is available to meet us there. Would y'all like to see it?"

A chorus of yeses filled the air.

Simone stood from the chair. She went into the living room where her purse was and removed her cell phone. She scrolled through her contacts, found the number, and placed the call. Valerie picked up the call and agreed to meet them at the house in an hour.

One hour later, Devon pulled into the driveway of her new home in Claremont Hills. He got out and opened the back door to assist Tori while Simone got out and assisted their mother.

They walked up the driveway to the front door. Valerie made her way through the living room and greeted them with a warm welcome. "Hello, everyone. How are you all doing?"

Simone greeted Valerie and introduced her family members. They all said hello.

"I'm sure you all are excited about seeing Simone's new house, so let's get started."

"I've already thought a lot about how I'd like to decorate and what my color scheme will be." Simone shared her ideas with the group as they moved slowly throughout the house, room-by-room. The house was rich with exotic finishes, a classic octagonal ceiling, a multi-room master suite, and gorgeous open common rooms with walls of glass, exquisite built-ins, and bonus areas. The European-inspired home, with its bay and bridge views, was breathtaking.

They oohed and aahed when Valerie brought them into the contemporary kitchen. The cabinets were a rich walnut finish with stainless steel appliances. A view from the kitchen window into the backyard showed a pool, Jacuzzi, and backyard kitchen.

Valerie opened the sliding glass door. They stepped outside to get a better view.

"I can see us having pool parties over here," Tori said out loud.

Marie surveyed the surroundings. "Beautiful, simply beautiful."

Devon raised his voice. "Wow. This backyard is an incredible sight. It's gorgeous, almost like a picture from a magazine."

Simone smiled and nodded her head in agreement. "I love the entire house, but this right here got me. When I saw this, I knew this was my house."

They finished touring the outside and made their way back inside. Valerie gave Simone an estimated closing date on the sale of the property.

"God is good, and everything is working out perfectly," Simone said.

Chapter 14

Aaron woke up with his stomach in knots. His mind had wrestled with itself all night, thinking about his first session with Pastor Williams. He got dressed, grabbed all his necessities, jumped into his car, and headed to the church office.

He walked into the church, where he was greeted warmly by the church secretary. "Good morning, sir. How may I help you?"

"Good morning. I'm Aaron Blackman. I'm here to see Pastor Williams."

"Yes. He is expecting you." She buzzed the pastor and informed him that his eight o'clock appointment had arrived. She escorted Aaron down the hallway to the pastor's office.

Inside Pastor Williams's office, he extended his hand for a handshake. "Aaron, it's so good to see you again. Come on in, and have a seat."

Aaron walked in, unbuttoned his jacket and sat. "Good to see you, too, Pastor Williams." Pastor Williams made his way to his black executive leather chair and offered Aaron something to drink. He declined.

Pastor Williams leaned back. "How have you been, son?"

Son? Some of the guilt Aaron had been feeling was erased when he heard his pastor refer to him that way. "I've been doing fine. Thank you for taking the time to see me. I know how busy you are."

Pastor Williams smiled. "My door is always open," he paused, "I want you to remember that."

Aaron nodded in agreement. "Yes, sir."

"Let us have a word of prayer before we continue." Pastor Williams prayed, and when he ended, the burden on Aaron's heart lifted slightly. "Son, what's on your heart?"

Aaron crossed his leg. "I've been dealing with something for quite some time, and I think it's time I got counseling."

"Son, I'm listening."

Aaron cleared his throat in hopes that the words would immediately flow out, but it was a lot harder for him to confess his transgressions once he was face-to-face with his pastor.

"Son, let me assure you that I won't judge you for what you have or have not done. I'm here to pray with you, counsel you and see that whatever brings you into my office is resolved. The Bible says, "for all have sinned and come short of the glory of God."

Aaron nodded. "Thanks, Pastor." He took a deep breath. "I have a gambling problem. Something that started out as fun is not so fun anymore." The moment he released those words, an overwhelming sense of relief came upon him.

A few seconds passed between them before his pastor responded. Pastor Williams leaned forward. "Son, that's how the devil works. At first, things appear like harmless play, and before you know it, you've gotten pulled deeper and deeper into the trap. Son, how long have you been having this problem?"

"Well, Pastor, to be totally honest with you, it started a long time ago. But, now I realize I need help in dealing with it—spiritual help."

"Well, son, you came to the right place. You've stepped over the first hurdle and that is admitting the problem. That's the first sign that you are on the path of recovery. I'm proud of you for doing that. Admitting our transgressions isn't easy, and repentance requires us to acknowledge our sins." Pastor Williams powered up his iPad and read from Psalm 32. "*I acknowledged my sin unto thee, and mine iniquity have I not hid. I said, I will confess my transgressions unto the Lord; and thou forgavest the iniquity of my sin.*"

"Pastor, I want to be totally free from the desire. Free from the guilt and shame."

"Counseling will help you cope with those issues. Counseling, plus scriptures, plus God are a sure ticket to recovery. But only if you apply it all to your life. That's where we mess up. We don't apply the principles that God has outlined for our lives and we find ourselves struggling in life."

"That is so true, Pastor. I know that in my head, but I need to reconcile that in my heart."

Pastor Williams grinned. "Yes, son. I couldn't have said it any better. God tells us in His Word what happens when we don't apply the scriptures to our lives. "*Thy word have I hid in mine heart, that I might not sin against thee.* Aaron, if you feel you need a support group, I can also recommend a few in the area. That's another option."

Aaron's jaw tightened. "No thanks, Pastor. I believe my counseling sessions with you are all I'll need."

Aaron looked intensely at his pastor as he gave Aaron several suggestions on where to begin the journey and scriptures to meditate on. "Before making the decision to gamble, stop and consider the consequences. You may not be hurting anyone else, but in the long run it could get worse for you and your loved ones. Son, you have to avoid environments that may tempt you to gamble."

Aaron nodded. "Yes, Pastor, you are absolutely correct, and that's my problem."

"Talk to me, son."

"I have a dilemma. This year's attorneys' conference is in Las Vegas, and they have asked me to be the keynote speaker."

"Umm," Pastor Williams said. "I see the dilemma. I guess you can't get out of going."

Aaron blew out a long breath. "Pastor, I wish it was that easy. Believe me, I thought about doing that, but it would raise too many questions from my brother Shaun. We attend this conference every year."

"Sin City, as some would call it. And I assume Shaun does not know about your problem."

"Exactly, Pastor."

It took a few minutes for Pastor Williams to respond. "Don't fret. We are going to work through this."

Aaron's eyebrows rose slightly. "I was hoping you could give me some advice on how I should handle this."

Finally, after a few seconds, his pastor made several suggestions. "Well, since you are going with your brother and I know there will be other people around, make sure you are not alone. While you're there, if time permits, schedule enjoyable recreational time for yourself that has nothing to do with gambling. And if you think you can't do that, tell the gambling establishment that you have a gambling problem and ask them to restrict you from entering."

Aaron's eyes widened and he shifted in his seat.

"I think those are great suggestions. I will definitely act on those."

"Give me a call, and tell me how things went when you return, and we can schedule another session then. How does that sound?"

"That sounds good."

"Before you leave, I want to pray for you. Heavenly Father, our awesome and powerful God, I pray strength for Aaron. He knows that You are with him, Father, and that You would not put more on him than he can bear. And we rejoice that Your Word would never return void. Bless Aaron with supernatural ability as he travels. So, now I ask, Lord, that Your power be manifested in his life and show Yourself strong on his behalf. We ask all this in Jesus' name. Amen and Amen."

After Aaron left his pastor's office, he felt stronger, encouraged and determined that he was going to win this battle. He had no doubt that God was going to answer his prayers.

Chapter 15

Aaron walked into Scott's Seafood Restaurant in Jack London Square, hoping that Shaun had arrived and was already seated. A young woman greeted him with a smile. "Welcome to Scott's."

"Thanks. I'm meeting someone here."

"Right this way, sir. The person you're looking for is already here," the hostess answered in a cheery tone. He followed her past the mirrored bar to the table, where Shaun sat looking over his menu.

"Hey, bro." They greeted each other with a fist bump.

The hostess handed Aaron a menu and told them what the chef's specials were, then left.

They scanned the menus. A server brought them water and placed the beverage on the table. Their waitress, an older woman with brown hair, brought a basket of hot bread and butter to the table and took their order.

"How are the projects you working on coming along?"

"Looking good." Shaun took a sip of his drink. "Everything is moving right along as planned. I've made connections with some developers and will be meeting with them later in the week."

"Cool," Aaron replied. "That's the way I like it. No surprises. Let me know if you need anything from me."

Shaun nodded. "So when is Simone's first day on the job?"

Aaron leaned back. The waiter returned and placed their meals on the table before them. They blessed their food. When they finished, they ate in silence for a few seconds. Aaron replied. "In a few weeks. She's headed back to New York to wrap up things there." He grabbed his napkin and dabbed his mouth.

"That's good to hear." Shaun put a spoonful of soup in his mouth.

"Hey, did you get the email regarding the conference in Las Vegas?" Aaron took a sip of his drink.

Shaun grinned. "Oh yeah, I did. They asked me to do a workshop. I know they asked you to do a workshop, right?"

Aaron nodded. "Yeah, they did. I haven't

replied. I was waiting to talk with you to see if we were doing that particular conference this year."

What's wrong with me? Aaron had never been afraid of anything. He had always faced and conquered challenges head on. So why was this thing eating him up? He had to admit that maybe this was much bigger than him. This was something that he couldn't fix by reading a textbook or writing a deposition. *God has not given you the spirit of fear.*

Shaun raised his eyebrows. "Man, you know we go to that same conference every year and every year we teach a workshop. The only thing different is that they having it in Las Vegas."

"True that. It should be alright." He kept repeating those words in his head. *I can handle this. It's going to work out.* But the words that came out of his mouth didn't match the words in his heart or the conversation that was playing in his head.

Shaun smiled. "We gon' have so much fun."

Aaron gave him a side eye before he swallowed a piece of his chicken.

Shaun cleared his throat. "I mean, after the conference."

Aaron paused for a second. "I'll have Holly make all the arrangements for us to attend."

Aaron had to concede; he couldn't think of any excuse not to attend. His back was against the wall. Any deviation from their normal routine when it came to the conference would raise a red flag with Shaun. *Remember Pastor Williams's suggestions.*

Shaun poked his steak with his fork. "You know this would be a good opportunity for Simone to join us."

Aaron titled his drink to his lips. He was already so caught up in the fact that he was going to be trying to quit gambling while in the very den of iniquity, that he didn't even think about the possible conflicts that might come up with Simone being there, too. "Yeah, man, you right. Might as well get her feet wet. I'll phone her tomorrow and talk with her about it." Aaron tilted his drink to his lips.

"Man, you get the suite for the Warriors game?"

"Yep. Secured that this morning. Everything is set. I think the staff will enjoy their early bonus."

"They better. If not, we know what not to do next year."

They laughed. "You hitting the gym tonight?"

Aaron cleared his throat. "Naw, not tonight. I'm going to Bible study."

Shaun's eyes widened as big as saucers. "Really? You going to Bible study?" He chuckled.

Aaron wiped his mouth. "Man, why you laugh? What's so funny?"

Shaun cocked his head to the side. "Naw, bro. It's cool. You haven't talked about going to Bible study in a long time." He placed his napkin on his empty plate and took a sip of his water.

Aaron leaned forward. "I know. I felt the need to attend."

"You going through some mid-life crisis I don't know about? You need to talk about something?"

Aaron laughed hysterically. "Mid-life crisis. Really? You serious?" He put his hand on his chin and met Shaun's eyes. "Naw, I'm not going through no mid-life crisis, and no I don't need to talk to you about anything. I'm good."

Shaun smiled at his brother. "Okay." He put his fist to his chest. "You know I'm here for you. I got you."

They laughed as Aaron signaled for the waitress to bring the check.

Aaron pulled into the parking lot at Grace Christian Center and parked his car. He unfastened his seat belt and took a deep breath. He whispered a prayer. "God, forgive me for all my sins. I know I have not been living right. Help me to overcome my struggles and live a life that is pleasing to you. In Jesus' name, amen."

He sat for a brief moment and watched the families going inside with Bibles or some electronic gadget in their hands. For the next hour or so, all attention would be on Pastor Darius Williams and the teachings from the Bible.

Aaron fought the urge to turn back around and go home, but quitting or giving up was not in him. Once he made up his mind about anything, he was determined to see it to the end.

He slipped on his jacket and stepped out of his car. With determined strides, he made his way into the church.

An usher greeted him with a warm handshake and handed him an offering envelope. Aaron received both with a smile. "Good evening. Thank you." He found a seat on the fifth pew. The praise and worship team was singing one of Jonathan McReynold's songs, "The Way That You Love Me."

God was all he needed. The words to the song began to minister to his heart. God had his full attention. He swayed to the melody of the sound and raised his hands in surrender to God.

Thirty minutes of worship passed. Pastor Williams emerged and took the podium. "Praise the Lord, saints. This is the day the Lord has made; let us rejoice and be glad," Pastor Williams's baritone voice reverberated throughout the sanctuary.

"Praise the Lord," echoed the congregation back to the pastor.

"Before we take our seats, let us greet our neighbors to the right and to the left of us." The congregation greeted one another and then took their seats.

"We are continuing our study on living a surrendered life," Pastor Williams said. "Turn with me to Galatians 5:1, which is our foundational scripture. I'll be reading from the Message translation. "Christ has set us free to live a free life. So take your stand! Never again let anyone put a harness of slavery on you."

Aaron couldn't believe what he was hearing. All he could do was shake his head. He hadn't stepped foot in church in quite some time, and the very night he decided to attend, God gave him exactly what he needed.

He listened attentively as the pastor taught the congregation the difference between living a life that is free when one surrenders to God and a life lived according to the passions of the flesh.

"We try to fill a void with superficial things that can only be filled by God. God is all you need. You've tried everything else... now try God," Pastor Williams exhorted.

"Preach, Pastor," someone from the congregation yelled.

Pastor Williams wiped the sweat from his brow with a handkerchief. "I know what I'm talking about. Been there and done it, too."

"Pastor, you all in my Kool-Aid," someone in the audience chimed in. Echoes of amens rang throughout the congregation.

"Sit down and let me teach, or I'm going to be here all night," Pastor Williams joked with his congregation.

Aaron looked around. He could see many were taking notes from the sermon and from the words written on the screen. Some in the congregation raised their hands as a sign of agreement. Praises and hallelujahs filled the sanctuary as one voice to God.

Aaron followed the pastor's word and took it all in like a sponge. His heart was happy. He knew this was where he belonged.

When Pastor Williams ended his message, he asked everyone to stand as he prayed over the entire congregation.

With his eyes closed, Aaron's mind traveled back in time, thinking of the goodness of God. When he opened his eyes, they were filled with tears. He blinked rapidly to stop the flow.

As the congregation dispersed, he stepped into the aisle and greeted other parishioners. Waiting to get a copy of the message, Aaron lingered inside the sanctuary where he noticed a few of his gym buddies chopping it up. Before he reached them, a couple of the sisters, single no doubt, stopped his forward motion.

"Hi, Aaron," they smiled, showing all their pearly whites. They were too obvious. That was one thing he didn't forget about some of the sistahs in the church. They let you know when they were interested. *What happened to, "When a man findeth a wife?"* he chuckled within.

"Hello, my sistahs." Aaron kept moving. He walked as fast as he could without it being apparent that he was running away from them. When he reached the other men, he greeted them with a fist bump. They talked for another ten minutes, and he excused himself to the copy center. He paid for a copy of that night's message and made his way to his car.

Once inside his car, he listened to Pastor Williams as he drove home. It felt like a burden had lifted off his shoulders. He knew that no matter what he was facing, God would see him through.

Chapter 16

Aaron had spent most of the morning outside the office, surveying a potential property. The land was a sixty-year-old former naval facility. If their firm secured the bid for the land, it would be developed to include restaurants, seniors' housing, and market-rate apartments. Because the purchase of land had become more competitive between developers, he knew if he wanted to move forward, he had to act immediately when a piece of property became available. Aaron was disappointed when he discovered LW Partners had already gained control of this particular piece of property.

By the time he arrived in the office, it was late afternoon. His jaw tightened. "Shoot."

"Good afternoon, Aaron. How are you?" Holly greeted him as he reached her desk.

"It's been a disappointing morning, Holly. Any messages?"

"Sorry to hear that, sir. You have several." She handed him several slips of paper.

"Thanks." Aaron took the messages from her and trudged to Shaun's office. He knocked on the door, opened it and walked in. He sat in one of the office chairs and looked at his brother.

"That Lamont Willis got the property."

"What? Wait. Which property?" Shaun put down his pen, leaned back in his seat and looked at his brother.

Aaron loosened his tie. "The naval facility."

"You've got to be kidding me."

"Man, I wish I was. I'm dead serious. How he got that prime piece of property before us is beyond me." Aaron shook his head.

"Bro, I don't know. You know how the business is. If you see something, you got to get on it really fast."

Aaron stared at him. "I thought I did. The listing came out a few days ago. He must have somebody working for him on the inside."

Shaun nodded. "Yeah, you know everybody in this business ain't honest. It can be cutthroat. You know he's a smooth talker, especially with the ladies. He could have gotten any one of those women down at the city planner's office to give him a heads-up before the listing was available to everybody else."

Aaron leaned forward. "I know. Well, what's done is done. But, I'm going to keep my eyes on that property and my ears open to the chatter between attorneys. We'll hear if his project is a go or not. You know how it is. Anything is possible, and everything could go wrong."

"True that. Securing financing, zoning permits, and getting government approvals can be a beast. We need to sit still and see what happens."

"Right. I'd like to know who'd hire him after those two last projects folded. That man is a thorn in my flesh. I still want to kick myself for investing in one of his failed projects."

"Man, that was years ago. Let it go. We've learned a whole lot from that experience," Shaun responded. "You know what Mama always says."

Aaron cut him a look. "Mama says a lot of stuff. Refresh my memory."

"What the Lord has for you—"

"Is for you," Aaron finished his brother's sentence. "Let me get out of here. I got contracts to sign, property evaluations to complete, letters to address, and a phone call to make to Simone." Aaron stood and walked out, closing the door behind him.

He strolled to his office, shut the door and took a seat at his desk. He powered up his computer and selected a few files to print. He thought about doing a little investigating to determine how Lamont had secured the property, but decided against it. Shaun was right. If that land was supposed to be acquired by Blackman and Blackman, it would become available again. Besides, they had other clients with larger projects that needed his attention.

Aaron's phone vibrated in his pocket. He removed his phone and saw he had a text from Kenny, his bookie. Kenny always checked in with him each month to see what Aaron was good for.

Hey Aaron, the boxing match is coming up. How much you good for, man?

Aaron closed his eyes and took a deep breath. *Lord, give me strength.*

Delete the text, son. Flee temptation.

He hoped his eyes were playing tricks on him. He opened his eyes and looked at his phone again. No such luck. *You can do this, Aaron. Say no.* Aaron placed both hands on his desk. He closed his eyes and prayed fervently, "Jesus, please help me. I cannot endure this without You. I'm trying to do the right thing. Please... help."

As if someone were whispering faintly, he heard the words of Second Peter 2:20. "*For if after they have escaped the pollutions of the world through the knowledge of the Lord and Saviour Jesus Christ, they are again entangled therein, and overcome, the latter end is worse than the beginning.*"

He leaned back in his chair and shook his head. He knew what he had to do. Aaron picked up his phone and texted, *Hey Kenny. Nah man. I'm going to pass.*

Kenny immediately replied. *WHAT! I don't believe it. You okay, man?*

Aaron felt like the devil was doing a tap dance in his head. *Go ahead. It's okay. One last time won't hurt you. You can always stop. Who will ever know?*

Aaron sent another text. *I'm good. But I'll contact you if I want to do business.*

Block his number from your phone, son. Submit to God. Resist the devil and he will flee from you.

Aaron placed his phone on his desk. He knew he was obviously hearing the Holy Spirit. There was no way he would be remembering all of these scriptures on his own.

You know how much money you could have made?

No, Aaron, resist it. Resist it. He was determined not to give in to the desire. A knock on the door interrupted the internal tug of war going on in his psyche. "Come in."

Holly poked her head in the door. "I'm heading out. Do you need anything before I go?"

"No, I'm good. See you tomorrow."

"Good night." Holly closed the door and left the office.

Aaron looked at his computer screen. A reminder email regarding the upcoming attorneys' conference awaited his response. He opened the email and typed out a response. After attending

Bible study and finally being true to himself, he felt confident about attending the conference.

I am with you. He was reminded of Matthew 28:20: "*Teaching them to observe all things whatsoever I have commanded you: and, lo, I am with you always, even unto the end of the world. Amen.*"

Two hours passed. It was six in the evening before Aaron even realized it. He didn't know if Simone was traveling or still in California. *Only one way to find out.*

His heart rate kicked up a notch. He shook his head. *Employee, Aaron. She's just another employee.* He picked up his phone, scrolled through his contacts, found her number, and placed the call. He couldn't explain why he was nervous about talking to Simone. He needed to keep reminding himself that she was off limits.

The phone rang twice before he heard her voice on the other end. "Hello, Aaron."

"Hi, Simone. Is this a good time to talk?"

"This is great, Aaron. How are you?"

I love how she says my name. Ugh. Off limits, Aaron. She's off limits. "I'm doing great."

"Is everything okay?"

"Everything is fine."

Simone sighed. "Great, that's good to hear."

He swiveled his chair and turned to face the window, crossing his legs at his ankles. "I wasn't sure if you were still in California or not."

"I'm still here. My flight leaves tomorrow afternoon."

"So you didn't have to stay and take care of your sister?"

"Oh, no. Tori is doing better. She'll be back to work next week."

"That's good." He cleared his throat. "Well, I wanted to give you the details about the attorneys' conference. I think I mentioned during our interview process that our office attends a conference every year."

"Yes, you did."

"Great. Well this year's conference will be held in Las Vegas. Since you're coming on board, we wanted to know if you'd be able to attend."

"Vegas, huh? When is the conference?"

Aaron covered all the details regarding the conference. He gave her an opportunity to check her calendar and was glad when she committed to attending. He was looking forward to having her on-board in a few weeks.

Simone lay in bed as long as she possibly could before her alarm went off. She reached for her phone, canceled the alarm, and placed it back on the nightstand. She let out a long breath and rolled out of bed. It was early morning, and her flight was scheduled for later that afternoon.

She could smell the aroma of fresh coffee and bacon coming through the vents. She showered quickly and headed downstairs with her belongings. Her phone beeped. She stopped on the steps and read the text message.

Flight on schedule. Those three words were music to her ears. The last thing she needed was a repeat delay. She opened the weather app on her phone. The weather in Berkeley was fifty degrees. A little chilly, no doubt. To a New Yorker, it would feel like thirty degrees.

She placed her purse and coat on the couch, deposited her luggage by the front door, and made her way to the aroma that was calling her name.

Simone kissed her mom and embraced her. "Good morning, Mom," Simone walked toward the cabinet and pulled out a coffee cup. She poured herself a cup of hazelnut coffee, her and her mother's favorite.

"Good morning. You all packed and ready to go?"

"Yes, ma'am. Devon should be here after he's done with his patient."

Her mom nodded. "Breakfast is ready. Go ahead and eat."

Simone grabbed a plate and a fork and sampled a little bit of everything she saw. "Where's Tori?"

"Still asleep."

They sat and chatted until they heard Devon coming through the front door. Devon entered the kitchen and rubbed his hands together with anticipation. "Perfect timing, if I must say so for myself."

"It's still hot. Grab a plate and eat. I want to make sure you eat plenty and get full."

"Ma, you don't have to worry about that." Devon scooped a few pieces of bacon onto his plate. He popped a piece in his mouth. "We got this."

Their mom playfully swatted Devon with the kitchen towel. "I know you do; please leave some for Tori."

The three of them enjoyed each other's company until it was time for Simone to leave. She put on her coat, while Devon put her luggage in the car.

"Leaving, huh?" Tori emerged into the kitchen.

Simone answered warily, "Yep. Guess I'll be seeing you in a few weeks. Bye, Ma. I'll call you when I land. I love you." Simone hugged her mother goodbye and stepped outside to join Devon in the car.

The cold air hit her like lightning. It felt like the wind went right through her body. She didn't think she had on enough layers to fight off the cold.

Devon turned the key in the ignition and the engine purred to life. Simone texted Kendra. They conversed back and forth until Devon pulled onto the freeway.

Devon angled his body in the seat to face her.

"It's going to be good having you back. Let me know how I can help with the move."

Simone put her phone down and focused on her brother, "Thank you. There is one thing you can do. I'll be shipping things to the house that are too heavy for Mom to lift, and I really don't want Tori in my stuff. If you can stop by and place them in the bedroom, I'd really appreciate that."

"No problem. I can handle that for you."

Twenty minutes later, he pulled curbside in front of San Francisco Terminal. He got out and assisted her with her luggage. They gave each other a quick hug and kiss before he pulled off.

Simone walked inside the terminal and checked the flight board. Her flight was still on time as the text had indicated. "Whew," she said out loud.

Her flight went off without a hitch. When she landed in New York, Kendra was there to pick her up. Simone loved her mom, but she was happy to be back in her own space. She dragged her luggage into her apartment, kicked off her shoes, dropped her purse and jacket on the chair, and went into the kitchen to make tea. She picked up the mail that Kendra had left on the table for her and went through each piece.

Simone was extremely busy over the next two

weeks. She kept a running list of things to do. At times, she felt overwhelmed, but realized more than ever moving home was the best decision. While she was in California, Kendra had gotten boxes for her and placed them in her apartment. Her next task was to pack and ship her belongings. Since she was going to keep her apartment, her packing was going to be selective—the Black art and her rare pieces would definitely be shipped to California.

She surveyed her apartment and walked over to her bookcase, where her pictures of Joshua were. She lifted the heart-shaped frame and traced her finger across the picture. No doubt she missed him. He would forever be sketched in her memory, but the woman she had become because of her pain, wasn't the woman she wanted to remain. She remembered the person she used to be—cheerful and enthusiastic. She was ready. Life was awaiting her return.

Simone closed her eyes and inhaled. She drew a sharp breath and shook her head to clear her thoughts. She had expected to see Joshua's face in her mind, picture herself in his arms. The way they used to be.

To her surprise, it wasn't Joshua's face at all that she saw when she closed her eyes. Aaron Blackman's milk chocolate skin, seductive brown eyes, and intoxicating cologne were indelibly etched upon her mind.

Chapter 17

By the time Simone returned to California, all of the boxes that had been shipped were waiting on her at her mom's house.

Simone walked out of the elevator into the offices of Blackman and Blackman like she was one of the partners. Despite the jitters she felt in her stomach, she strolled in in her knee-length black trench dress and her four-inch black stilettos with confidence and boldness. Lips painted a beautiful shade of red, she wore her long, thick twists pulled up in a pineapple, exposing her elegant neck.

She approached the receptionist's desk. Holly lifted her head from the computer and smiled at her. "Welcome, Ms. Herron. How are you today?"

She returned the smile. "Please, call me Simone. I'm doing good, Holly. And yourself?"

Holly nodded her head. "I'm well; thanks for

asking. I'll tell Aaron you are here." She buzzed Aaron. Within a few minutes, he was walking down the short hallway to greet her.

Simone turned toward Aaron, certain she'd heard him catch his breath. He was definitely checking her out. Was she imagining this chemistry between them? Before she had time to process it, Shaun came out of his office and came to stand with them at the receptionist's desk. "Good morning, Simone," they said in chorus.

She grinned. "Good morning to you both." She looked from one to the other.

Aaron addressed Holly, "Do I have any appointments today?"

"Yes, you have a three o'clock appointment with Mr. Hart regarding the Oakland Housing Facility project. Are you still available, or do I need to reschedule?"

"No, that's fine. Can you pull the file? And hold my calls from three to four."

"Will do, sir."

"Simone, I hope your day goes well, and depending on how much work Aaron has for you..." Shaun paused, "hopefully, we'll see you tomorrow if you are gone by the time I get back. But a warning to you—Aaron can be meticulous."

"Man, I'm standing right here. Really? Aren't you heading out?"

Simone chuckled as she watched the interaction between the two brothers. She loved it. It was obvious they had a close relationship.

"I'm heading to court and won't be back until later this afternoon." As Shaun walked toward the elevator, he looked over his shoulder and said, "Aaron, don't work her too hard on her first day."

"No worries, bro. I won't. At least, not today."

They laughed together as Aaron led her down the hallway. Simone took the opportunity to check out Aaron's body as he led her to his office. Without his jacket hiding his masculine physique, she noticed the way his black shirt clung to his shoulders, showing his toned upper back. *Tight. Nice. Down, girl.* Simone shook her head. Was she really ready for this? She lifted her eyes as he turned to face her.

"Go ahead and put your things in your office. Feel free to grab some coffee and then meet me in my office."

"Okay." She walked into her office, placed her coat on the rack, and secured her purse in her desk drawer. She grabbed a cup of coffee from the break room and strolled into Aaron's office with a quick knock on the doorjamb.

He looked up. "Come on in. We're going to work at the conference table."

Simone made her way to the table. She took a deep breath. There were mountains of folders, with yellow Post-It notes on each, spread all over the table.

Aaron joined her. She inhaled his cologne. It was intoxicating. She sipped her hot coffee to cool down. *Dear Lord, what in the world is wrong with me? Forgive me.*

Aaron smiled and spread his arms as if he was making a grand presentation. "Welcome to Blackman and Blackman." His tiny dimple danced at the corner of his full lips.

Their eyes met. "Looks like I'll have plenty of work to do. Enough to keep me busy for a while."

"It's not as bad as it appears. On each folder is a task that still needs to be done, either some type of property research or answering draft research memos or running reports for analyses."

He continued looking at her. *His eyes are captivating,* Simone thought.

Oblivious to her private thoughts, Aaron continued, "We'll start you on these so you can familiarize yourself with what is going on. Since you have experience, I'm sure it won't take you long to catch on."

Her attention went back to the folders. "No problem. I'm sure I can handle this. What about my computer?"

"Waiting for you to sign on. Take these few folders. You can work on these this morning. All logon instructions for your computer and for setting up your phone are on your desk. Let me know if you have any problems with anything."

"I will. I'll go get started." She took the folders from his hand and walked out of his office.

Relaxing in her black leather seat, she scanned her office. In less than two months, her life had changed drastically. She had moved across states, found a great job, and was waiting to close escrow on a home.

She signed on to the computer without any problems and maneuvered her way around. One of her first stops online was Pandora, where she set up her favorite channels of music. Being familiar with the software, it didn't take her any time to get into her rhythm.

Simone drank her coffee and settled in to tackle the tasks at hand.

Aaron stood. He walked over to his refrigerator and pulled out a bottle of apple juice. He wanted to check on Simone, but dismissed the urge.

He walked back to his desk, reclaimed his seat, and unscrewed the top of his juice so he could take a huge swig. He needed to get some work done before his client showed up for their appointment, but he could not get his mind off Simone. He smacked his hand against his forehead. *Ugh. Why do I keep thinking about my newest employee? Get it together, Aaron.*

He had plenty of work to do, but work was the

furthest thing from his mind. He wondered if her skin was as soft as it looked. Aaron wondered if she knew her brown eyes were beautiful or that her lips were enticingly kissable.

Who was he fooling? The only work he was accomplishing today was daydreaming about how much he enjoyed looking at Simone. *Stop it, now.* He scolded himself. *She is off limits, remember? Macy. Macy. Macy. Keep reminding yourself about the fiasco with Macy. No more dating employees.*

Keith Sweat's "Good Love" started playing from his phone. He snatched it off his desk and hit the forward control button. Tank's "Lost in You" began to play. He hit the pause button, shook his head, and laughed uncontrollably, but wondered if anyone else in the office heard him.

Surely he needed to pray more or find some scriptures to help him with this predicament. No, he needed to do *both.* He definitely needed help from on high for this one. He knew he didn't possess the willpower to fight this growing attraction on his own. *I'll add that to my prayer list.* Aaron groaned, "Lawd, help a brother out. Back to work, Aaron."

He went to the fax machine and pulled his clients' contracts, looking them over with a fine-toothed comb. For the next few hours, his time was completely consumed by contracts, proposals, plans, and blueprints, leaving him no time to think about Simone.

Hours later, he looked up from what he was doing. It was noon. *Time for lunch. I'm starving.* Simone had been as quiet as a church mouse. Aaron never even heard her leave her office. *Dedication. Now that's attractive.*

He stood and walked to her office. The door was ajar. Instead of walking in unannounced, he leaned against the doorframe. Hand in midair, he was about to knock when he noticed her standing in front of the window, looking out.

Without saying a word, he lowered his hand back to the doorframe and watched her for a brief second. He wanted to move, but his feet refused to obey his thoughts. He stood still as though his feet were cemented to the ground. *What are you doing, man?*

He tapped on the door. "Simone? I'm sorry. Did I disturb you?"

She turned around and met his eyes. "Oh no, not at all. Come on in. I was standing here trying to decide what I wanted to eat. I got so engrossed in my work I lost track of the time. I'm starved."

He moved toward her, "Well, that's why I'm here. I was going to see if you wanted to grab a bite to eat?"

Simone reached for her pendant. She held it between her thumb and forefinger, moving the ring back and forth. "I sure would."

There she goes, grabbing that necklace, Aaron

thought to himself. His smiled widened. "Okay. Great. Where should we go? Your pick."

"Do you like Le Cheval? It's close. The food is excellent and we'll get served fast."

"Yes. Le Cheval is perfect. And don't worry about the time. You're with the boss. Let me grab my jacket."

She pulled her purse out of her desk, put on her coat, and met Aaron as he was coming out of his office. They walked down the hallway toward the elevator. Before Aaron could hit the down button, the elevator doors swung open and Shaun walked out.

"Hey there. Y'all going to lunch?" Shaun looked at Aaron.

"Yep. You back from court?"

"Yeah. The judge rescheduled the litigation hearing." He smiled. "Perfect timing. Where y'all headed?"

"Simone has chosen Le Cheval."

Shaun met Simone's eyes. "Good choice."

"You want to join us, bro?" Given Aaron's thoughts earlier this morning, having a third wheel wasn't a bad idea. He was struggling to keep Simone in the 'employee' compartment of his mind.

"Yep. Don't mind if I do. Give me a second." Shaun strolled toward his office and returned without his attaché case.

They arrived at Le Cheval. To their amazement, it wasn't too crowded. The hostess seated them and handed them their menus. She introduced herself as Cecelia.

Simone settled herself in her seat. She looked around the restaurant and then at Aaron and Shaun. "This is one of my favorite places. I haven't been here in a long time, though."

Shaun replied. "Yeah, they're pretty high on my list, too. I was here a few weeks ago."

As they looked over their menus, the server approached them for their drink order. They all ordered water.

Aaron glanced around. "Looks like we beat the rush. It's really starting to fill up in here."

Shaun and Simone glanced up from their menu. They looked around, nodded in agreement, and returned to looking at their menus.

"I usually get the claypot rice. But today I'm going to step out of my box and try something new," Simone declared.

The brothers chuckled. The waiter placed a pitcher of water in the middle of the table. The hostess returned and took their orders.

They chatted about everything from music, to movies, to the upcoming plays in the Bay Area, to exercising and sports. Aaron wanted so badly to tell her about the Warriors tickets, but decided to wait until another time.

He studied her brown eyes. They sparkled when she talked about the Warriors. Her beautiful smile lit up the room. He loved how she wore her long natural tresses piled high on top of her head with a few tendrils hanging down, exposing her neck.

All he wanted to do was tattoo his lips on her neck. *Lord, forgive me.* As of late, Aaron had been asking for forgiveness a whole lot.

Simone didn't have much to add when they started talking about boxing. "I don't have a lot of interest in boxing. I don't like people getting beat up or all that blood. But, I do remember a Sugar somebody and a few others."

"You mean Sugar Ray Leonard?" Aaron helped her with the name.

Simone nodded, "Yeah, him."

They all laughed. "So, Simone, do you think you'll miss New York?" Shaun sipped his water.

She looked at him. "My best friend is there, so I'll certainly miss her... and a few others. But I'm keeping my apartment there so my family and I can have a vacation spot when we visit." The more they talked, the more impressed they were with her. Simone was proving to be quite the classy lady.

"Wow," Aaron said. "Didn't you tell me you were getting a house here, also?"

"I am." Excitement surfaced in her tone. "Escrow should be closing in a couple of weeks."

Well, she's not a gold digger. Any woman that can afford a place in New York and one here in California is obviously doing pretty well. Aaron smiled.

A chorus of congratulations filled the air. While the trio enjoyed their conversation, someone walked up to the table.

A baritone voice said, "Well, hello, Lady Simone." They all turned to see whose it was.

The man reached out and grabbed her hand. Before she could say or do anything, he kissed it. It happened so fast, Simone's breath caught. She was frozen in disbelief. Her forehead wrinkled with disgust. She quickly pulled her hand out of his grasp, trying to place the face and voice of the presumptuous man invading her space. Her eyes shuttered. She released a surprised gasp. "Ohh. Hi, Lamont. How are you?" Simone tried to sound cordial, though her voice came out a little strained.

Aaron cocked his head to the side and arched a brow. Shaun's mouth fell open.

Lamont held her gaze and winked before greeting both Aaron and Shaun with a half-smile. "Hey, how y'all doing?"

They acknowledged him with a fist bump as they exchanged pleasantries until the hostess brought their food. A few minutes later, Lamont stepped aside as the hostess placed their plates in front of each of them. "Here you are."

Lamont stared at Simone. "Lady Simone, it was good seeing you." He turned to walk away, then paused. Almost as an afterthought, he looked over his shoulder and grinned. "I take it you got the job."

She cleared her throat. "Yes, I did. Good seeing you as well, Lamont."

"Hope to see you again." Walking off he smiled and joined his party at the table in the far corner.

Simone inhaled. "Hope it tastes as good as it looks." After Lamont walked off, the table went silent. Lamont's appearance at their table also seemed to have upset the easy chemistry and conversation they had previously enjoyed. The frown on Aaron face convinced her that he was visibly upset.

"Why don't you bless our food, Lady Simone?" Aaron said sarcastically.

"Most definitely, Lady Simone. Do us the honors," Shaun teased.

She looked from one to the other. "Oh, I see. Y'all got jokes." They all laughed. "Lord, bless everybody's food at this table," she said out loud.

The brothers guffawed. Simone shook her head at their antics.

"So, Simone, how has your first day been? Aaron hasn't worked you too hard, has he?"

She shook her head. "Oh, no. He gave me instructions this morning and I've been taking my time getting acclimated with the process and familiarizing myself with the projects. It's been a great day so far." She took a bite of her food and wiped her mouth.

"You wouldn't have known she was there. She was so quiet," Aaron added. "Do you have any questions for us?"

She shook her head. "Nope, not yet. But, I will."

"Enough about work," Shaun interjected. "Aaron tells me you are a collector of Black art and you also like to hike." He inhaled a forkful of food.

The conversation continued until all the food was consumed. They chatted more after the hostess picked up their empty plates and dropped off the bill.

Chapter 18

Aaron made a sharp turn and pulled his car into his garage at six o'clock. The weather was still in the lower sixties with a slight breeze. Thankfully, he'd arrived home early enough to relax in the Jacuzzi.

Inside, he slipped into something more comfortable and headed to his kitchen. He grabbed some cold cuts, fruit, and a non-alcoholic beverage, then walked out to the Jacuzzi. He placed everything on the coffee table and went to retrieve a towel from the storage cabinet. He powered on the Jacuzzi.

All afternoon, Aaron had tried to put aside what had happened earlier at the restaurant, but his mind kept drifting back to the show Lamont put on at lunch. *Flaunting himself like he was some Casanova.*

Why was he surprised at seeing Lamont

respond to Simone like he did? After all, she was gorgeous, successful, and single. She could awaken any man in a heartbeat. She had brains and a beautiful body with curves in all the right places. Who wouldn't want Simone Herron on his arm? He couldn't get mad. Simone was free to be with whomever she wanted.

He snapped out of his momentary reverie when a call from Shaun came through. "Man, what was wrong with you earlier? You were a little quiet at work. I know we couldn't talk about what happened at lunch."

"Nothing was wrong with me. Was that a mess or what?" Aaron paused. "I didn't know they knew each other. I wonder how they met."

"I know, huh? Well, apparently they do. Pretty well, I might add," Shaun continued. "Small world. Lamont was smooth with the moves though. I gotta hand it to the brother."

"I'm not sure about that. From the look on Simone's face, she was as shocked at his behavior as we were."

"Speaking of facial expressions... and, you looked like you wanted to kill Lamont."

Aaron laughed. "Naw, man. He surprised the heck out of me when he kissed her hand."

"Uh hum. Bro... I saw how you were looking at her."

Aaron sat in one of the club chairs. "What you

mean?" He rubbed the back of his neck. He knew where the conversation was going.

Shaun hesitated. "Man, quit tripping. You were checking her out."

Aaron covered his face with one hand, glad his brother couldn't see him. "Man, you don't know what you talking about."

"Yeah, right. This is Shaun you talking to. Remember our agreement?"

"Man. I'm good. It's not like that."

"I'm watching you, bro." He laughed.

"Whatever, Shaun. I'm getting into the Jacuzzi. Later." He hung the phone.

Thoughts of her consumed him. He would tell no one, not even Simone. His vow to not repeat his previous experience would keep her at bay. No matter how hard it would be to resist her.

When Simone arrived at her mother's house, all she wanted to do was eat and soak in the whirlpool tub. She was quite pleased with how her first day at work had turned out, with the exception of the Lamont Willis escapade, which had totally caught her off guard. Truth be told, the only man that had ever kissed her hand was Joshua. The thought of another man extending the same gesture sent a slight chill to her core. Maybe it was the whole situation.

Inwardly, the more she thought about it, the more she chuckled. Aaron and Shaun's expressions were priceless.

Simone chatted with her mom while she finished her meal, then excused herself and headed upstairs to run a bath. She lit aromatic eucalyptus-scented candles around the tub and throughout the bathroom to create a spa feel.

She undressed and stepped into the whirlpool bath with the jets running full force. She moaned when her body hit the water, allowing the jets to do their magic. Simone leaned back against the bath pillow and closed her eyes. Before she realized it, she had fallen into a deep sleep.

The cooling water roused her. Not ready to withdraw, she turned the faucet on, added more hot water and continued to enjoy her soak. Satisfied with her relaxation, she finished bathing, pulled a towel off the heated towel rack, and dried herself off. Once she sprayed her perfume on, she slipped into her sleepwear.

Ten minutes later, she stretched across the bed and decided to call Kendra. Kendra answered on the first ring. "Hey yourself. How are you and how was your first day on the job?"

"I'm doing well. Girl, you know I always have a story to tell."

"Oh boy. What did Tori do now? I can't think of anyone else who would give you grief."

Simone chuckled. "Not Tori this time. Actually, she has gotten a whole lot better. Still needs some work, but we all do. She caught herself the other day about to say something negative. I gave her a hard stare before she even let the words out."

"Good. You don't need all that drama. Well, who is in your story today, Simone?"

"Do you remember me telling you about the Rick Fox lookalike on the plane?" She put the phone on speaker.

"Ohhhh, yes. I remember. How could I forget?"

"Well, I went to lunch with Aaron and Shaun today and he was there."

"What? No way." Kendra paused for a brief second. "What are the chances of that in such a big city?"

"No, that's it. It was totally by chance. But wait, there's more."

Silence traveled over the phone line, then Kendra said, "Okay, what happened? You're keeping me in suspense."

"Girl, Lamont came over to the table, greeted everyone and then kissed my hand."

"Simone... Nooooooooo. He didn't? I don't believe it!" she proclaimed. "What got into him? I'm waiting to hear what you did."

"Wait, girl. One question at a time. I don't know why he did that. He totally caught me off guard—"

"I'm sure," Kendra interrupted.

"As far as what got into him, you're asking the

wrong person. To answer your question how I responded. It happened so fast, I didn't have time to respond. I was shocked."

"Wait, he did that in front of your bosses? Wow. Bold man, I must say. How did they respond?"

"Well, I guess he felt since he knew them it was okay. And, yes, I agree with you. That was very bold. Girl, you should have been a crumb on the table. Aaron and Shaun looked at him sideways."

"Well, Simone, maybe once you get settled, you'll start dating."

Simone sucked in a deep breath and released it slowly. "Ummm, Kendra. Who said anything about dating? All I said was that the man kissed my hand, nothing more. Why you want to make something more out of it?"

"Simone, don't you think it's time? It's been two years, sissy."

Simone cleared her throat. "In time, Kendra. In time. I did not come to California to find a man. Hey, how are you doing?"

Kendra paused before continuing. "I'm doing well. Everything is everything over here. And don't try to change the subject."

Simone fluffed her pillow and changed her position. "Dating means bringing up the past, and I'm cool right where I am."

"You know you deserve someone to love you. It's been too long."

A few seconds of silence passed between the two. "Yeah, but falling in love hurts."

"Yes, Simone, I agree. But living without love hurts worse, and building walls don't help either."

Simone propped her pillow against the headboard and leaned against it. "Girlfriend, I know you mean well, but let's table this conversation. Okay?"

Simone knew Kendra all too well. She might table it for now, but as sure as it freezes in New York, Kendra was going to bring the subject up again. Let Kendra tell it, Simone should have been dating a long time ago. Thankfully, Kendra had decided to respect Simone's boundaries for the time being.

"Blackman and Blackman will be attending the attorneys' conference in Las Vegas. Is your firm attending this year?"

"Yes. We'll be in the house. We confirmed our invitation yesterday."

"Awesome. We'll have some downtime to relax, shop, and maybe even take in a show."

"That sounds good to me. I'm looking forward to it. Let me know when your flight arrangements are made and when you plan on arriving and I'll do the same. If we plan it right, we might be arriving around the same time."

"I know, huh? Too cool. I'll confirm everything with you in the next day or so."

Kendra yawned. "Time for me to hit the pillows."

"Me, too, sis. We'll talk tomorrow. Love you."

"Love you, too."

Simone crawled under the blankets and stared at the ceiling, pondering what her friend had said. Could it be time for her to date again? Was she willing to risk losing it all for love again? *Ugh*. The thought made her want to run away.

Chapter 19

"We have a delivery for a Lady Simone." The guy wore a City Bloom Florist polo shirt. "Am I in the right place?"

Holly looked up at the man. He held two dozen yellow roses in a decorative glass vase. She smiled. "Lady Simone, did you say?"

"Yes, that is correct. Lady Simone."

"You're in the right place. I'll make sure she gets them."

"Thank you." He placed the vase on top of the receptionist's desk and turned to leave.

Lady Simone, huh? Wonder who sent those? Think I'm going to take a peek. She surveyed her surroundings to see if anyone had come in without her knowledge. Holly rose from her seat and reached for the envelope to see if the flap was tucked in or sealed. "Shoot, it's sealed. Oh well. Maybe Lady

Simone will let us know who her Prince Charming is. I can't wait to see their faces when they enter the office."

She left her desk and walked into the break room, where she started the morning coffee and restocked the refrigerator with water and juice. Holly always arrived earlier than anyone else in the department to make sure the waiting area was neat, the conference room vacuumed, and the break room fully stocked with supplies. She glanced at the clock on the wall in the break room: 7:50 a.m. Holly finished tidying up and strolled back to her desk. The quiet office would soon perk up with staff, clients, contractors, vendors, and anyone else who wanted some of the Blackman brothers' time.

At 8:10, the elevator doors opened. Aaron arrived first.

"Good morning, Holly." As he approached her desk, his eyes darted from the vase to her, but he didn't say anything.

"Good morning. Here is your calendar for today's appointments."

He skimmed through his calendar and let out a deep sigh. "Full day for sure; hold all messages until this afternoon. Have you made the reservations for our trip to Las Vegas yet?"

"That's the first thing I'm doing this morning. I'll send emails out once I've booked everything, including the rooms."

"Okay. Thanks."

Seconds later, the elevator doors opened again. Shaun strolled in and stood next to Aaron at the desk.

"Good morning," Shaun said. His eyes went from the vase to Holly. She handed him his calendar and messages from last night's voicemails. "Wow, Holly. Did we miss your birthday?"

She stared at Shaun. "No you didn't miss my birthday," she said in a tight tone.

Shaun winced. "My apologies."

Aaron interjected, "Well, what did Travis do this time? Those roses say 'I'm sorry, please forgive me.'" Shaun and Aaron looked at each other and shared a laugh.

She rolled her eyes. "Y'all laughing at me? That ain't right. Travis ain't done..." She stopped and thought about her response. "Whatever, those are not my roses."

Their laughter stopped abruptly. "If those are not your roses, then who are they for?"

Silence filled the air for a moment, then Holly said. "Oh, those roses belong to... Laaaady Siiimoooonne."

Aaron and Shaun's eyes held for a brief second. "Lady Simone. Really?" Aaron said.

She nodded. "Yep, Simone. She obviously has somebody's attention."

Seconds later, the elevator doors opened. Simone sauntered in. "Good morning, everyone."

"Good morning, Simone," Holly greeted her

with a big welcoming smile as she walked into the office.

"Good morning, Simone," Aaron and Shaun said in harmony.

Simone looked at Holly. "Those roses are gorgeous."

"I agree," Holly said. "They are simply beautiful." She smiled at the men and quickly turned her attention back to Simone. "Someone has an admirer."

Simone replied with an agreeable nod to Holly. "Yes. It appears like it. Are those yours, Holly?"

"Nope. Unfortunately, my man don't get down like that. But, when I talk to him in a few minutes, that is going to change," Holly said in a heated voice.

"Oh," Simone replied.

Holly leaned back in her seat. "Lady Simone, this beautiful bouquet of roses is for you."

"Lady Simone? Who...?" Simone stammered. Everyone was looking at her. She blinked in confusion, paused for a moment, then responded, "Did you say those are my roses? Surely there's a mistake." She tucked her hair behind her ear.

"Yes. That's what I said." Holly replied.

"Oh. Okay." Simone placed her tote bag on the desk and slowly searched for the card. She was about to open it to see who the flowers were from. Feeling six eyes intensely locked on her movement, she hesitated. She slung her tote on her shoulder, took a deep breath and grabbed the roses. She strolled down the corridor. Aaron, Shaun and Holly stood with their mouths agape.

"Oh, she left us hanging," Holly said.

Simone smiled all the way down the hallway. Once inside her office, she shut the door, placed the vase on her desk, and pulled out the card. The note read: *Congratulations. Wishing you all the best. Lamont.* As she expected, they were from him. A perfectly innocent note. But what man sends flowers without wanting something in return? Now she had to call him and say thanks. Not that calling him was a bad thing, but she remembered how he had looked at her with a gleam in his eye. And how could she forget the kiss on her hand?

She didn't know what to do about Lamont. He was definitely eye-candy, but a person's exterior could change; it was just a matter of time. True quality shone from within. Besides, there was no spark with Lamont, not like the spark she had felt when she'd landed in Aaron's arms or even the spark she got when she'd first met Joshua. Now Simone had two problems—Lamont Willis and Aaron Blackman.

It was obvious from Lamont's gestures that he wanted more. She would find out how much more when she spoke with him. And the other problem was she knew any spark she was feeling toward Aaron Blackman was going to have to be suppressed. After all, he was her boss. Liking him was wrong on so many levels. She was definitely in a different place, and quite frankly, she didn't like it at all.

She snapped out of her musing. "I need to make that call." She pulled Lamont's business card from her tote, picked up her cell phone off the desk, and keyed in his number. Her fingers danced atop her desk while she waited for him to answer.

"Hi, Lamont. This is Simone." She paused. "I hope I'm not interrupting...." She waited for his response.

"Well, hello, Lady Simone. No interruption at all. You caught me as I was going into the office."

She hesitated. "Oh, okay. I wanted to call and say I love the roses. Thank you so much. They are beautiful."

Silence filled the air. She didn't know what else to say. She figured the conversation would come to an end, but he continued it, "I'm glad you like your gift. A little somethin' somethin'. I hope I'm not being too forward by sending the roses."

Did he say he hoped he wasn't being too forward? Hmmm, a kiss on the hand and now roses.... Naw, dude. You not forward at all. "No problem at all. But I better let you get to work. I'm sure you're a busy man."

"Would it be okay if I locked your phone number in my contact list? I promise not to blow your phone up too much."

What kind of question was that? *Do I have the option of saying no?* She didn't know how to respond, so she said, "Okay."

Simone, really? Okay. Is that all you got? Maybe Kendra was right; she obviously had been out of the dating scene longer than she realized. At thirty-five, she should have a bag full of comebacks, but she didn't have one.

They chatted a few more minutes. Simone finally persuaded him to hang up, but not before she thanked him again for the roses.

"Okay, Lady Simone, it was good hearing your voice. Have a great day."

They ended the conversation without him asking to take her to lunch or dinner. Maybe that was a good sign that he didn't want anything more out of the relationship. Maybe he was being polite and kind to her without any strings attached. She'd keep her fingers crossed, and for added measures, she'd cross her toes, too.

I don't believe it. She left us standing there. Aaron sat at his desk and replayed the conversation with Simone. When he thought he was going to get confirmation that Lamont had sent the roses, Simone had dodged the bullet. His lips curled into a smile when he thought about how she'd managed to elude them all. *The mystery continues.*

Distracting thoughts about her had him day-dreaming when his mind should be on purchasing land, financing more real estate deals, and working on their next major building project. He shook his head and returned to sorting through his messages. He glanced at the clock. His new client was scheduled to be in his office shortly. He had two hours to prepare for the presentation.

He pulled their folders from his briefcase and placed them across his desk. Out of all the projects they were working on, this was one of the biggest. The proposed Nevali Project was a 250-foot high-rise tower with office space, 150 residential units, retail, and a boutique hotel with penthouses on the top floors. The 150,000 square feet of creative office space would include larger floor plans, higher ceilings, and more glass. It would also include terraced outdoor decks with panoramic views of the city.

He studied the blueprints, but his mind wandered back to the marigold dress she'd worn. It was simple but elegant, and it fit perfectly on her thick body.

Aaron's thoughts shifted back to work, although he didn't want them to. He sorted through the piles of paperwork on his desk and double-checked the finances for the hundredth time. He'd done the research. He knew what his client wanted and the PowerPoint slides were ready. He had no doubt he was going to knock this one out the park. Aaron was ready with his A-game.

His cell phone beeped. Aaron leaned back in his chair. He had a text message from Kenny. *Hey, Aaron. Checking in with you.*

Aaron blew out a heavy sigh. *Didn't I tell him I would contact him if I wanted to place any bets? Nobody but the devil, always prowling. Get thee behind me.* Aaron hit the delete button. He noted it had been weeks since he'd placed a bet or even had a desire to gamble, but he wasn't going to let his guard down. *Neither give place to the devil. Let him that stole steal no more.*

He picked up his phone and blocked Kenny's number. With the Lord's help, he was overcoming this battle with gambling. He no longer needed to keep the devil on speed dial.

Ten minutes later, Simone knocked on his door. She waited until she heard Aaron's muffled voice tell her to come in. She gave him a smile as she crossed his threshold holding folders in her arms.

"Have a seat."

She settled in one of the chairs in front of his desk and handed him the pile of folders. Simone crossed her legs and watched him glance through each one.

After a few minutes, she interrupted, "How does it look to you? As you can see, I've completed the to-do list and run reports where needed. I took it upon myself to run the analysis for several projects. I hope that was okay."

He lifted his head. Their eyes met. "Yes. That would have been the next step, so you are ahead of the game. I'll take a better look at each folder later today after my meeting. We have a new client coming within the hour for a presentation."

She tilted her head to the side. "Oh. Okay. I'm sorry. I should let you prepare for your meeting."

"Oh, no. You're fine." *Yes, you are.* "I'm all ready to go. In fact, I think it might be good for you to sit in on it. It's one of our biggest projects, and you'll be able to see how we put the entire project together from conception to finish; at least, on paper, that is."

She pushed her twists behind one ear and smiled. "Okay. I'd like that."

For the next few minutes, they discussed a few details of the project and potential problems that could arise from such an enormous undertaking. While they were conversing, an email came through from Holly confirming all flights, hotel rooms, and conference registration for the entire staff. Everything was all set. They'd be on their way to Las Vegas in a few days.

Chapter 20

Simone loved that she could still rock her fitted blue jeans. She decided on the magenta blouse and a pair of black slip-on shoes. She ambled over to her full-length floor mirror and took one last look from head to toe. Fully satisfied with her appearance, she grabbed her small weekend bag and waited on the limo to pick her up. As promised, the limo pulled up to her mother's house at seven o'clock to take her and the rest of the staff to the Oakland Airport.

Inside the luxury vehicle, Simone got a better look at Aaron. She'd always seen him wearing one of his tailored suits, but today he was casually dressed in a blue short-sleeved polo shirt which showed off his broad shoulders and toned arms. He finished the look with fitted black jeans and black Doc Martens boots. He could dress down and still look good. The fresh scent of his cologne exuded confidence and strength, but created chaos with her senses. She took note of the two diamond studs he wore in his ears, something he must only wear outside the office, because she'd never seen those before, either.

When they disembarked from the plane, a shuttle was waiting to take them to the Mirage Hotel, the host hotel for the conference. The hotel's lobby was full and noisy with people checking in. Attorneys from all over were present along with other professionals.

"This is nice, Aaron." Simone pushed her twists behind one ear and surveyed the fixtures in the lobby and the well-appointed stately décor.

Their eyes held as they moved closer to the check-in desk. "I think we are going to enjoy our stay. At least, I hope we do." He replied.

"No doubt about it. I plan on it. I needed this mini-getaway." Simone said.

Once they all checked into the hotel and were given their room keys, the concierge placed their luggage on the cart and guided them to the elevator and up to their respective rooms. They chatted in the elevator about the itinerary and lunch. They all agreed to meet back in the lobby for lunch in an hour once they settled in.

Simone's cell phone beeped. She had a text from Kendra. *En route. Should be at the hotel shortly.*

Simone texted back, *Okay.*

She slid her key into the door and ambled into a mini-suite. "Wow." Her eyes roamed the room. She had a spectacular view overlooking parts of Vegas and all the amenities that would make staying there the next few days extremely pleasurable.

"Enjoy your stay, Miss. If there is anything we can do for you, please let us know." The concierge deposited her luggage inside the room.

"Thank you so much." She gave him a tip and closed the door.

The room was perfect for her and Kendra. Besides the conference, they were looking forward to some sister time. Tonight, they would walk the strip, have dinner, or hang out at the hotel. While she unpacked, she could hear voices coming from the hallway. In a few seconds, the door lock clicked.

"Hey, sis," Kendra said.

"Hey yourself. Glad you made it."

The concierge deposited her luggage on the floor. Kendra gave him a tip and sent him on his way. The ladies hugged as though they hadn't seen each other in years. Kendra walked around the room and gave it a thumbs-up.

"Did you have any plans for lunch with your group?"

Kendra stretched across the bed she would occupy for the next few days. "Nope, not for lunch. I told them I would probably be hanging with you."

Simone smiled. "Cool. We're meeting down in

the lobby in about forty-five minutes for lunch. You have time to freshen up. You're finally going to meet the Blackman brothers."

Kendra eyes glowed like a candle had been lit inside her. "I'm looking forward to it. Who all from the firm is here?"

"Girl, everybody is here. They believe in bringing the staff. All four of us road the limo together and flew on the same flight."

"That's great. I love it when a company invests in their people."

They laughed and chatted while they compared itineraries for the next few days. After taking a moment to freshen up, they headed out the door for lunch.

When the elevator doors opened, they had to maneuver through the crowd of people waiting to get on. As they walked toward the lobby, a voice called out Simone's name and caught her attention.

Simone and Kendra's eyes locked. "Girl, who's calling for you?" Kendra asked.

"Hmm, that voice does sound familiar." Simone turned around.

Lamont Willis headed in her direction. "Well, hello, Lady Simone. You're looking lovely as ever. I had no idea you would be here."

"Hey, Lamont, and thank you. We got in a couple hours ago." They moved over to the side to allow other guests to pass. "Lamont, let me introduce you to one of my friends. This is Kendra."

"Hello, Lady Kendra. Nice to meet you."

"Hello, Lamont." They exchanged pleasantries.

His attention went back to Simone. "Where are you two ladies headed?"

"We're headed to lunch with my coworkers."

"Oh. I did see the two brothers in the lobby. They are patiently waiting on you, so I'll let you go. Perhaps we'll run into each other again."

"Perhaps we will," Simone replied.

"Lady Kendra, it was a pleasure meeting you."

"Same here."

Lamont turned and walked toward the elevator. Simone and Kendra proceeded to the lobby to meet everyone else.

"Lawd hammercy. He does look like Rick Fox. He's gorgeous!" Kendra quipped.

Aaron and Shaun sat in the hotel lobby, reading the newspaper and checking messages on their phones. Aaron observed the crowded hotel filled with people. He reflected on his journey and was quite pleased with his progress. *Thank you, Lord. I can do all things with Christ, who strengthens me.* Other than the fluttering in his stomach when they'd first landed, he didn't have any desire to gamble. Some people wouldn't believe him if he told them his struggles, but he learned when you give something to God and you commit to change—all things are possible if you believe.

He rummaged through the paper and then tossed it on the center table. He looked up and noticed Lamont having a conversation with Simone. Aaron's eyes flitted between Lamont and Simone. His jaw tightened and he narrowed his eyes. "What in the world is the great Casanova saying now?"

Shaun raised his head and met Aaron's eyes. "Man, who you talking about?"

Aaron lifted his chin in Simone's direction and replied in a dry tone, "Lamont Willis over there is talking to Simone."

Shaun immediately turned his eyes in their direction, made contact and brought his attention back to his brother. "Oh. Looks to me like he's talking to Simone and what's her friend's name?"

Aaron crossed his leg and stared. "I believe it's Kendra."

The corner of Shaun's lip curved into a smile. "She's cute."

"I think I'm going to say something to Simone about Lamont. I don't want her to get hurt."

"C'mon, man. You can't do that." Shaun let out a heavy sigh. "You don't even know what, if anything, is going on between the two. Don't make any assumptions. Let me remind you, Simone isn't our sister. She's an employee. She can see and talk to whomever she pleases."

Aaron shrugged his brother off, and then relented. "Yeah, maybe you're right." He wasn't sure what made his jaw clench more–what Shaun had said or the cheerful smile Lamont had on his face when their eyes met.

"Man, I thought you told me it wasn't like that. I didn't think you were into her," Shaun quickly reminded him of their previous conversation. "Hmmm, seems to me that maybe you're a little jealous, and I'm going to leave that right there."

Oh, yes, he was jealous. Jealous, frustrated, and annoyed. And, couldn't do a thing about it unless he crossed the line of no return. He rolled his eyes at Shaun.

Before he could respond, Simone and Kendra walked toward them. They rose from their seats as the ladies approached.

Simone smiled. "Hello there." Her eyes darted between the two. "Aaron and Shaun, this is my friend Kendra, from New York. She'll be joining us for lunch, remember?"

They smiled and extended their hands. They shared pleasantries for a few minutes. Simone took an aerial view of her surroundings while the three became acquainted and noticed that Holly and her other co-workers were missing. "Where is Holly and the rest of the team? Are they not joining us?"

Aaron replied, "Holly decided to have room

service and rest. Everyone else begged off as well. It looks like it's the four of us."

"Mmm. Okay. Did we decide where we are having lunch?" Simone asked.

Shaun answered. "While we were waiting, we took a look around and spotted a few good restaurants. If you ladies want something light like salad, there is Paradise Café or the Roasted Bean."

"A salad is fine with me," Kendra replied, keeping her eyes on Shaun.

Simone nodded. "Salad it is."

They navigated the masses of people in the lobby and inside the restaurant, dodging several women whose eyes were fixated on the two brothers. Paradise Café was crowded, as expected, but they managed to get seated in twenty minutes. They requested outside seating so they could enjoy the weather and the serene sounds of the waterfall. The waitress handed them their menus and told them the specials. A few seconds later, the waiter placed water on the table.

After looking over the menu, Kendra blurted out, "Everything looks good."

"I know, right?" Simone agreed. "I'm having something light. I might splurge at dinner."

The men closed their menus. Aaron asked, "How's your room?" His eyes darted between Simone and Kendra.

Simone replied, "Awww. It's so nice and the view is gorgeous."

Kendra nodded in agreement. "I'm looking forward to some downtime to hit the pool."

Shaun said, "That's good. I'm glad you like your room." He looked at Kendra. "Yeah, we checked out the pool, too. Hopefully, we can do the same."

The waitress returned and took their orders. The men ordered sandwiches while the women decided on salads. As they waited for their meals, they chatted about the conference, the weather, recent movies they'd seen, and their latest projects. They laughed and joked about everything from the presidential candidates to Kevin Hart's latest movie. The conversation flowed easily. They were enjoying one another's company until a voice from the past crept into the present.

"Aaron, you always did like Kevin Hart," the soft voice said. Aaron would have recognized that voice anywhere: Macy Lewis, his ex-girlfriend and disgruntled ex-employee.

"Don't look so surprised to see me here. You know this is the circle I roll with," Macy said.

The muscles in Aaron's face tightened. Simone and Kendra looked at the woman causing his discomfort.

Shaun lifted his glass of water before speaking. "Hey, Macy."

"Hello, Shaun. You're looking as handsome as ever. How are you, Aaron?" she said in a monotonous tone.

"I'm doing quite well."

"Aaron, where are your manners? Aren't you going to introduce me to your guests?" Her eyes went from Aaron to Simone and Kendra.

He paused for a second before he decided to introduce them. "Macy, this is Simone and her friend, Kendra."

"Well. Hello, ladies. I do believe I've heard a little about Simone. Nice to meet you both."

Simone's eyes widened in surprise as she returned the greeting.

Kendra leaned her elbows on the table. "Hello, Macy."

The server placed their lunch orders in front of them and told them the owner would come by shortly to check on them.

"Well, I guess that's my cue to leave."

Aaron wiped the sweat from his forehead with his handkerchief. *Good.*

"Bye," Shaun said under his breath.

"But before I leave," she looked at Simone, "here's a word of caution for you. Don't even think you and Aaron are going to be a couple. After what happened between us, I bet he won't cross that line again."

Simone jerked her head around and glared at her.

Aaron frowned. "Excuse me. Bye, Macy. Don't you have somewhere else to go? If you don't, pretend you do and leave." His cold glass of water never looked so good. *This witch. Why she trying to jump stupid here in Vegas?*

He shook his head and stared at her as she pivoted and sashayed off. Aaron turned. His eyes connected with Simone. "I'm so sorry about that. I must apologize to both you and Kendra for her outburst."

"She's a piece of work," Shaun said in a harsh voice. He swallowed hard. "Nothing like a scorned ex."

Simone blinked in confusion. "Wow. A piece of work is an understatement. She has some major issues. Who does stuff like that?"

Kendra shook her head in amazement.

"Would you mind if I blessed the food?" Simone asked. They all bowed their heads. When she finished, they ate in silence for a few minutes.

Aaron's heart raced. He couldn't believe Macy would pull a stunt like that. He cocked his head to the side and looked at Simone, breaking the awkward silence. "Macy worked at the office as a paralegal. I made the mistake of getting involved with her, and when I broke it off... well, you see the results of that."

Shaun took a bite of his sandwich. "Yep. That pretty much sums it up. She was bad for our business."

Simone raised her eyebrows. "Okay. But, that was so foul." She tilted the water to her lips and took a sip. "Believe me, that won't happen to me again."

Kendra frowned. "Wow, is that how these California women are? They come out of nowhere and make a scene like that?"

Aaron took a breath in an attempt to suppress his frustration before he continued. "Please accept my apologies for what happened. Simone, I'm not sure how she even knew you. But news travels fast in this industry." He paused for a moment. "I ended up firing her because she started sabotaging our work, and we couldn't have that."

"Really?" Kendra said. "Wow. I can see why."

Aaron's intense eyes stared at Simone for a second, but he quickly looked down at his food. "Because of that experience, I promised I would never get involved with anyone at the office ever again." He felt a kick in the pit of his stomach. "It makes things too complicated. And when things don't work... stuff like this happens."

She blinked several times and released his gaze. "That's completely understandable," she said.

He glanced around. What was not being said between the two of them felt palpable. Aaron wanted to see if anyone else could feel it, too.

Shaun chimed in, "We don't do well in hiring paralegals."

Simone gave him a hard stare. Kendra looked at him sideways.

"Oops. Wrong answer, brother. You on your

own." Aaron lowered his head and took a bite of his chicken sandwich. He lifted his eyes and looked at the sweat beads forming on Shaun's brow.

A well-dressed man approached their table. "Hello, my special guests. How's everything here at your table? Is the food to your liking?"

Shaun let out a deep breath. "Perfect timing," he mumbled.

All four heads turned and looked at the man who held their attention. "Everything is great," they all said in unison.

"That's good to hear. Please let us know if there is anything we can do to make your experience more pleasurable here."

They nodded their heads in acknowledgement as the owner turned to leave.

Shaun cleared his throat and stared at Simone and Kendra. "That didn't come out right. What I meant to say is that the people we've previously hired had ulterior motives for wanting to work for us."

Aaron grinned. "He's right. We've hired people who couldn't do the job and who weren't a good fit for our firm."

Simone swallowed hard. "And what makes you think I'm not like any of your ex-employees?" she asked them both, but her attention was on Aaron.

Aaron and Shaun's eyes met, then darted back to her. Shaun answered first. "Well, you come highly recommended by one of the best attorneys in New York. Any misrepresentation on your part is a reflection on him, and I don't think that's the kind of person you are... nor is he from what I know of him."

She cocked her head to the side and looked at Aaron. "Well, Aaron... earth to Aaron."

Her voice captured his attention. It took him a few seconds to answer. "Well, in addition to what Shaun has said, I remember your first day at work. My table was filled with folders with all those Post-Its. Do you remember that?"

She chuckled and answered. "Do I? Oh, yeah. I remember."

"You didn't flinch at all. It didn't move you one bit. That told me right there that you were a committed and determined employee. You have this confident poise about you that's undeniable. You're focused and quite organized. I can tell you are teachable, driven with a passion to learn, yet you're also intelligent enough to work independently and get the job done." He took a breath. "You want me to continue?"

She smiled and held up her hand to motion him to stop. "Naw. That's good. Okay, I wanted to make sure y'all didn't think I was anything like... what's her name?"

The brothers looked at one another, but Aaron said, "Macy." They all broke out in laughter.

"Well, my sister, you've made a great impression on these two. I didn't doubt it at all," Kendra added.

"Oh, no, Simone, you're nothing like our previous employees," Aaron said.

Shaun immediately nodded in agreement. "Yes. Thank God."

In spite of the interruption, they finished their meals with pleasure. The conversation shifted to the upcoming Christmas party the Blackmans would be hosting at their vineyards in Napa.

At the conclusion of the conference, he and Simone would return home and diligently work side-by-side on the Nevali project. Aaron had drawn the line and made himself quite clear regarding his personal life. He only hoped he could keep his own promise.

A table had been reserved for Blackman and Blackman near the front of the room. They walked through the crowd, spotted the reserved sign on one of the tables and took their seats. Aaron slid into the seat next to Simone. On several occasions, his leg brushed hers. He smiled. "Excuse me. I didn't mean to bump your leg."

She forced a platonic smile to her face, enough so the sides of her mouth curved upward instead of down into a frown. *What's wrong with him? Bumping my leg like he didn't mean to.*

She tried not to look in his direction, but her eyes shifted Aaron's way several times. Each time, she caught him staring.

"Good evening, everyone!" The president of the association called the meeting to order, then gave the history of the organization, the organization's accomplishments, and the purpose of the gala. Simone focused her attention on his speech.

"Today's speaker is a graduate of the University of San Francisco School of Law. He passed the bar in the top ten percent of his class. He has received many awards locally, as well as internationally. He and his brother Shaun have done an outstanding job in bridging the gap between real estate developers and cities in the San Francisco Bay Area. Together, they own Blackman and Blackman, one of the leading real estate development law firms in their part of the world. He has authored many articles that have appeared in *California Law Magazine* and *Real Estate Developers' Journal*. He is active in many different organizations within the San Francisco Bay Area, and has donated his time, energy, and money to help many. The company has been a major contributor to this organization and is this year's recipient of the Firm of the Year Award. It is my distinct pleasure to introduce to you, Mr. Aaron Blackman."

The room filled with applause. Simone looked at Aaron and smiled. Joining the crowd, she proudly stood as a member of the firm.

Aaron rose and made his way to the stage. He had swagger about him that oozed power and confidence. He wore a grey suit—with a striped blue shirt, and a blue and pink checkered tie—with a blue silk handkerchief in the pocket. He looked so good that he turned heads with every step.

Simone surveyed the room and chuckled inside when she noticed women fanning themselves, while others sat mesmerized. He did have that effect on women, but he'd never find out she was one of them. She turned her attention back to Aaron and caught his gorgeous smile.

He addressed the audience with thanks before he delivered his speech. Simone was captivated. She had no idea he was such a good speaker. He spoke about the organization's goal to raise funds for scholarships for law students who were committed to serving minority, low-income, and other underserved communities.

She could feel the passion in his message; it roused the audience as they clapped throughout the duration of his speech. He had a way with words that drew them in, like a sweet dessert. He held everyone's attention, including hers.

Throughout his speech, her eyes kept colliding with Aaron's. The man stirred up so many emotions in her—emotions that hadn't surfaced in years that needed to be checked. Emotions that she would suppress if she was going to continue working for them.

He confused her. Obviously the vibes she was getting from Aaron did not match what he had said at lunch the other day. But it didn't matter what she felt or what she thought he felt. The only thing that mattered now was that he had set the rules, and she was going to go by his playbook.

Relieved, she sighed inwardly. She wouldn't have to put on her running shoes once she found a flaw in him, because he'd already set the boundaries and determined who would cross his finish line. She was good. All good. He'd made it perfectly clear she was not in the running.

She listened intently as he finished his speech and presented the awards. Who would want to run from a man like Aaron Blackman?

Chapter 21

Aaron enjoyed Las Vegas and his time away from the office. He'd managed to come back without giving in to the temptation to gamble. He had to admit Simone Herron was likely the reason why. Thoughts of her consumed him most of the time. There wasn't much time left to even think about gambling.

He placed a call to Pastor Williams and told him, although the thoughts to gamble were present, he didn't give in. They chatted for a few minutes before his pastor had to end the call, but not before Aaron made another appointment for his counseling session.

Aaron returned his thoughts to Vegas. His only regret about the trip was sharing his no-fraternization rule with Simone and Kendra at lunch. As soon as he'd said it, he'd wanted to take the words back. But it was too late. He'd put it out there, everything except his true feelings for Simone. His vow to not repeat his previous experience would keep her away, no matter how hard it would be to resist her.

His mind drifted back to the gala. He hadn't been able to keep his eyes off her. He loved the off-white suit she wore. Her skirt had clung to her shapely figure quite well. The head wrap she covered her hair with was a little different, but he liked it. No, he loved it. It brought more attention to her already beautiful skin tone. The woman was too gorgeous for her own good.

Stop right now. Aaron shifted his mind back to work. The presentation with Mr. Kane prior to their departure for Las Vegas had been a great success. He was pleased with Aaron's idea and gave the approval to begin the project. The Nevali project was his number one priority. It was full speed ahead. He couldn't spend the day dreaming about Simone; he needed to step things up. They were in the beginning stages, where anything could happen to delay or even abort the project. Millions of dollars hung in the balance. Aaron knew it meant less sleep and longer hours, but in the end, it would be worth every sacrifice.

Aaron called a meeting with the staff to share the latest news and updates. Everyone would be given specific duties and responsibilities and provided with a schedule listing all deadlines. He took his laptop and walked into the conference room to set up the presentation.

The staff entered the room. Simone walked in with a writing tablet and a pen. She surveyed her options for available seating. The only seat open was across from Aaron. Simone plopped herself in the seat, reached for the water pitcher and poured herself a cup of water. Their eyes met. He looked straight at her as if no one else was in the room. She quickly lowered her eyes, tucked her hair behind her ear, and took a big sip of water.

Something magnetic drew him in every time she came around. He had to get a grip on himself. He couldn't afford to break his cardinal rule.

Holly cleared her throat to get Aaron's attention. "Aaron, are you ready to begin?"

Aaron blinked his eyes rapidly. "Yes. Go ahead and pass out the agenda and the Nevali package."

Simone peered at the agenda. She released a heavy sigh and twisted in her seat.

Aaron stood, adjusted his jacket, and paced the length of the room discussing the project, environmental matters, and the pros and cons of such an investment. He pushed the button for the first slide. He went through the four bullet points, which highlighted the benefits of the project, the market analysis, the business model, and the marketing plans. He continued for the next thirty minutes, covering the agenda, and then opened the floor for questions and answers.

"Aaron, I see overtime and some weekends might be required," one of the clerks inquired.

"Yes. If we are to keep the deadline and schedule, we're going to have to put in more time. If that becomes a problem, you know we're flexible. Family always comes first."

Simone toyed with her necklace when she heard him discussing overtime. He assured them they would be rewarded handsomely for their efforts.

They went back and forth with questions and answers from both brothers. After the presentation, Aaron and Shaun had two more items to discuss. "Well, as you know, the holidays are coming up. We will once again host the Christmas party in beautiful Napa County. Keeping with the annual tradition, our Christmas party will be at the Blackman Estates and Winery. You are welcome to bring one guest."

Clapping and cheering echoed throughout the room. Everyone was giddy with excitement.

Simone put her elbow on the table and rested her chin in her hand. She looked around at all the happy faces and smiled. Aaron had Holly bring over a large box that was sitting in his chair. He opened the box and pulled out what appeared to be apparel boxes. He and Shaun handed each staff member a box. As the boxes were passed out, Aaron said crisply, "Do not open the boxes until everybody has received one."

"They know how to take care of their employees," one of the employees whispered to Simone.

"I've heard about how generous they are. Wonder what's inside," she whispered back to her coworker as she shook her box.

"Does everyone have a box?"

"Yes."

"Okay. Go ahead and open them."

Someone jumped up and screamed, "Oh my goodness, I got a Warriors ticket and a Steph Curry royal blue jersey." Seconds later, other staff members added their shouts and rejoices. The room exploded like firecrackers on the Fourth of July.

One lady did a little praise dance and gave God the glory for hers.

Simone couldn't open her box fast enough. Once opened, she took out the jersey and inspected the front and back. "Oh my goodness," she said.

Grinning, she put the jersey down long enough to clap her hands. Excited, she followed suit with shouts of thanks.

A few seconds later, another employee shouted, "We have tickets in one of the suites."

"Whaaaattt?" another employee blurted out.

Simone looked at her ticket. The Blackman brothers had rented out one of the suites in Oracle Arena. She uttered, "Wow. Amazing. Fabulous. Hallelujah. Thank you, Jesus."

The entire staff was on cloud nine. The early

Christmas gifts seemed to have washed over the fact they would be working overtime and possibly some Saturdays. At that point, nobody seemed to care.

She turned to find Aaron staring at her. One corner of his mouth lifted to a half smile. She mouthed, "Thank you," and immediately turned her head and joined the rest of the employees giving everybody high-fives.

After all the excitement finally settled down and everyone reclaimed their seats, Shaun took over the meeting. "Okay, everyone. Inside the box is an arena map where we will be meeting at. Get there by five. That night, the first ten thousand fans get a splash towel. We want to make sure y'all enjoy the entire experience."

More oohs and aahs echoed throughout the room. "This is getting better and better," one employee shouted out loud.

"It sure is," Simone added, "Wow. I started at the right time. I'm blessed."

Thirty minutes later, Simone was back in her office. She sat at her desk, reflecting on the last hour. She chuckled to herself. *What a clever, well-thought-out plan to get your employees on board with overtime. Very calculated. Very strategic. I have to give*

it to Aaron and Shaun; they knew exactly what they needed to do to win their staff over.

She was blown away at their generosity and couldn't wait until the game to wear her jersey. *Too bad Devon couldn't get Warriors tickets; at least we're on the waiting list for season tickets.* Once she came down from the euphoria, she began closing several transactions regarding land and office buildings. After that was completed, she made a few minor changes on some annual reports.

Her cell phone rang. It was the title company telling her to come to the office and sign the paperwork. "We are ready to close," the title officer acknowledged.

"Awesome. I'm so excited." She had been waiting patiently for weeks to hear those words. Finally, the keys to her new home would be in her possession and she could move into her own place.

She immediately called Kendra to tell her the good news. Simone leaned back in her chair and put the call on speaker.

"Girl, I'm going to get the keys to my new house shortly."

"Simone, that is so awesome. Congratulations. I'm so happy for you. We will definitely have to celebrate when I come to California."

"Yes. I can't wait until you see it. You'll love it like I do."

"I'm sure. Look, chica. I don't mean to switch subjects, but we never did get a chance to discuss what happened at lunch when we were in Vegas. What in the world was that all about?"

Simone hadn't given much thought to the Macy incident since she returned. She felt sorry for women like her, beautiful on the outside with no substance inside. Simone thought maybe Macy was insecure, but that was not Simone's problem. She had her own concerns to deal with, and Macy was not one of them.

"That's a good question, girl. You tell me. That was beyond ridiculous."

"And that speech Aaron gave. Who was he trying to convince? You know—his speech about not getting involved with anyone from work. It was obvious he already broke that promise."

Simone raised her eyebrows in surprise. "Kendra, what are you talking about?"

"Girl, he couldn't keep his eyes off you at lunch." Kendra chuckled and mumbled, "Looks like you have two admirers."

"Girl, please! One is enough. I'm doing all I can to avoid Lamont Willis."

"Bestie, you've been out of the scene way too long. Anybody can see Aaron Blackman is into you."

"Nope. Not true. The only thing he's into is his business. And you need to get that out of your mind, because it is surely not in mine. Didn't you hear what he confessed at lunch?"

"Yeah, I heard him. And believe me, he would

not get any awards for that awful performance. Girl, he couldn't even fool himself with that whole spiel."

"Umm. sissy, you so wrong. That's my boss, remember?"

"Oh. I know he's your boss. But, he's also a man. A fiiine man."

Simone fiddled with the stapler on her desk. "Girl, you crazy. Please. Get serious. Ain't nothing going to happen over here. I came to this firm to work and do my job and that's what I'm going to do."

"Yeah. Whatever. Speaking of brothers, how is that other piece of fine chocolate doing? Shaun. He's a cutie pie."

"Kendra, I'm about to go. I've heard enough. We'll talk later."

"Wait. One more thing." Kendra hesitated before speaking. "You know Joshua would want you to move on, sissy. Keeping it one hundred. Love you."

"Love you, too. I'll call you tomorrow." She pressed *end* on her phone.

Simone tried to refocus her attention back on work, but her mind traveled back to her phone call from the title company. In less than two hours, she had been blessed with the most exciting news—the closing of her home and a ticket to the Warriors game. Life was good.

She spun in her chair and yelled, "Thank you,

Jesus." She texted Devon and shared her good news, then called her mother.

She composed herself and focused on the picture on her wall. Devon had given her a poster with the scripture Jeremiah 29:11, "*For I know the plans I have for you," declares the LORD, "plans to prosper you and not to harm you, plans to give you hope and a future.*"

Those words imprinted on that poster became more real to her than ever before. Things really were working out wonderfully. She toyed with the ring on her necklace. Simone knew how easily that could all change.

Chapter 22

Drops of sweat ran down Aaron's head as he thought about the stunt Macy had pulled in Las Vegas. He wiped the sweat from his brow with a handkerchief.

He'd been caught totally off guard by her sudden intrusion that sent the entire lunch in a different direction. The more he thought about it, the angrier he became. Macy was a thorn in his flesh. Aaron slammed his fist down on his desk so hard his coffee cup jumped. *The nerve of her!* He twisted, leaned back in his chair, and stared at the ceiling as though there was an answer in the sky.

How could I have fallen for her? She was the most selfish and uncaring person he had known. He could deal with her bad-mouthing him and dragging his name in the ground; he really didn't care about that. He cared about Simone and what Macy had said to her. That was what bothered him. The woman knew how to push the wrong button and get the wrong response out of him.

"Lord, I need help dealing with her." He shook his head and remembered a scripture his pastor had recently preached from the Message translation of Ephesians 4:26-27, "*Go ahead and be angry. You do well to be angry—but don't use your anger as fuel for revenge. And don't stay angry. Don't go to bed angry. Don't give the Devil that kind of foothold in your life.*"

There was a light tap on his door. "Aaron, may I speak with you for a moment?"

He spun around in his chair. Holly stood in the doorway. "Come on in." From the dazed look on her face, he could tell it was something important. Slowly, she approached his desk. She folded her arms across her chest and paused for a second before she continued, "Macy is here to see you."

To keep from allowing Holly to see the emotions on his face, Aaron lowered his head, closed his eyes, and said a prayer. He allowed a few seconds to pass before he lifted his head. "Macy? Did you say Macy is here to see me? What in the world does she want?"

Holly's eyebrows rose. She switched her body weight from one leg to the other. "Yes, sir. She is asking to see you. She's in the sitting area."

He leaned back in his chair and looked her straight in the eyes. "Is that right?" The irritation in his voice stood out. He quickly remembered his little conversation with God. Now his test was waiting to come into his office. Yes, it was a test, one he was determined to pass.

Holly stood and waited patiently until he spoke. "Give me a few minutes. Then send her in."

Simone's personal life was moving in the right direction. She would be in her new home in a few short weeks, so decorating and shopping for new furniture were high on her agenda. With a list of great things on the horizon and feeling good within, she rose from her desk and strolled down the hallway. She halted abruptly when she saw Macy coming in her direction.

Macy smiled. "Hi, Simone."

Simone looked at her with a stern expression and gave her a sideways look. "Hi."

A few days ago, Macy had been nasty and rude to her. Now the woman was all smiles. Simone would never show her true emotions, but the comment Macy had made to her in Vegas was quite disturbing. To see her again only reinforced Simone's position to keep her feelings in check.

"I'm glad I ran into you. I wanted to apologize for my outburst the other day. I don't *know* what got into me."

Did she mock me? Simone's eyes narrowed

before she exhaled. "Macy, we don't know each other, and I'm not really sure why you felt you had to embarrass me. But, don't ever try that mess again," Simone put her hand on her hip and lowered her voice, "or I'll slap you into tomorrow."

That got a reaction out of Macy. Her eyebrows lifted, causing her eyes to widen. "Well, you don't have to resort to violence," her voice cracked.

"I'm just saying."

Macy had no idea who she was facing. Simone had grace and dignity, but when she had to get a fool straight—she did. And no doubt, a fool was standing in front of her.

After leaving his seat, Aaron found himself standing at his door. With the door slightly ajar, he heard voices speaking. He waited before interrupting, but when he heard Simone say, "I'll slap you into tomorrow," he almost choked laughing.

Aaron whispered the words to himself. "I'll slap you into tomorrow." He couldn't help but laugh. "Well, looking at her, she doesn't appear to have an ounce of cruelty in her. But I guess I was wrong. It's obvious Simone can handle her own." He shook his head in amazement.

His lips curved upwards when he saw how sassy she looked with her hand on her hip.

Aaron swung his office door open. He leaned a shoulder along the doorjamb, folded his arms across his chest, crossed his ankles and gave Macy a hard stare.

He turned his head. His eyes met Simone's. "Simone, is everything okay?"

"Yeah, Aaron." She pushed her honey brown twists behind one ear and let out a heavy sigh. "Everything is fine."

Aaron returned his attention to Macy. "My meeting with you will be real short, like ten minutes or less," he responded in a harsh tone.

Macy's face dropped.

His eyes shot back to Simone. "Come by in ten minutes so we can go over the Nevali reports."

Simone gave him an exasperated look. She didn't know if he really wanted to meet with her or if that was his way of getting rid of Macy. If it was the latter, she didn't want to be a part of his game. The last thing she needed was to be in the middle of a love/hate war between those two.

Clearly, Macy wasn't about to wave her white flag in surrender. That was evident from her tight dress and the cleavage that protruded from her low-cut neckline.

Simone hesitated. "Sure, Aaron. I'll have everything ready." She trudged past Macy and gagged and coughed as she inhaled her cheap perfume.

With ten minutes to spare, Simone headed to the receptionist's desk and handed folders off to Holly for filing. Stopping by the restroom, she checked her makeup, her hair and clothes. While alone, she prayed. *Lord, forgive me. I know You were not glorified with that confrontation. I have to do better. I will do better with Your help. In Jesus' name, amen.*

Simone tried to shake off the thoughts that roamed through her head, but the visions of seeing Aaron come to her rescue, like a knight in shining armor, sent shivers through her body. He dominated her thoughts. She shook her head to rid her thoughts of all visions of him—but no such luck.

Aaron walked into his office without shutting the door. He turned and faced Macy.

"Hi, Aaron," Macy said in a sexy tone.

Aaron frowned, but didn't respond.

He stood in the center of his office and refused to move. "You have five minutes. Why are you here?"

"I thought you were giving me ten? Aren't you going to offer me a seat?"

He stuffed his hands in his pants pockets. "Now, you have four."

Her mouth dropped. "Okay, Aaron. I came by to apologize for my behavior in Las Vegas." She moved toward him.

He took a step back. "Okay, but you could have done that over the phone. Besides, you really need to apologize to Simone, not me."

"I did. You can ask her."

"I will."

"Seeing you the other day brought back all those sweet memories of what we had before. I know we can make it this time if we try. Please forgive me for the wrong I've done." She looked like she was trying to muster some tears, but couldn't.

He looked at the clock. "Well, since you only have two minutes left, I will use those instead." He pierced her with a pointed expression. "Let me make myself perfectly clear. We are done. There is no more us. Read my lips. We will not be getting back together."

Macy stood motionless. Her mouth hung open in disbelief.

"Now, if you don't mind, I have work to do."

She rolled her head and put her hands on her hips. "Well, you'll miss me, and you'll come begging for me to come back. You wait and see."

"I doubt that."

She pivoted and stormed out the office, muttering about how much she hated him. She almost bumped into Simone.

The tension in the room was palpable. Aaron shut the door and strode back to his desk.

"Macy won't be coming around here anymore. Let me take care of something before we get started." He contacted security.

Simone toyed with her necklace as she listened to Aaron on the phone.

"If Macy Lewis shows her face in our building again, escort her out immediately. No questions asked. She's not to be allowed inside again." He hung up the receiver.

Their eyes met for what seemed like forever. His stare was intense, disturbing. Simone blinked to break his gaze and jumped right into the meeting. "I have the Nevali folder with all the reports, figures and some references for contractors."

He smiled. "Are you okay?"

She appreciated the compassion and concern in his voice, but she was determined not to read anything into it. He was her boss. His only concern was for her safety. "Thanks, Aaron. I'm good—all good. I believe Macy and I have a good understanding."

"Okay, but first, let's clear the air." He leaned forward, looking directly at her. "Did she apologize to you?"

"Yeah, she did. But people like her usually don't mean it."

"I don't want you to think I bring my personal business into my office. I was surprised to see her. I thought I had seen the last of her in Las Vegas."

"No problem at all." She paused. "Aaron, you don't owe me any explanation. I came here to do my job, and that's what I'm going to do."

Aaron took the Nevali files from Simone's

hand. He flipped through the pages, meticulously rechecking the data, making notations. His lip curved into a smile.

Simone cocked her head to the side as she watched him. "What are you smiling about? My work?"

"Simone... you told that girl you would slap her into tomorrow." Aaron burst out laughing.

"Ugh. I am so embarrassed." Simone hid her face in her hands. "I can't believe you heard that."

Aaron gently touched her hand. "It's okay, Simone. I'm sorry it happened. I want you to know that nothing like that will ever happen again."

She looked up at him. "Thanks, Aaron. I believe you."

Simone wanted to forget the whole ordeal and move on. The Nevali project would require zero acceptance for errors. She couldn't afford to give any of her time, thoughts, or energy to Macy's foolery. Her energy would be used towards making sure she did a good job. Simone wanted to reassure the firm they had hired the right person.

While Aaron continued to peruse the documents, she stood and observed his collection of books on his bookshelf and his awards on the wall. She looked over her shoulder. "I checked the reports three times to make sure everything was accurate."

"Everything looks in order."

Their eyes held. She forced herself to look away

when she felt the spark. "Impressive... collection of books and awards."

"Thank you."

Her fingers ran across each book reading the titles. With a smile, she blurted out, "By the way, I got the keys to my house."

His head jerked up. His eyelids blinked rapidly. "You got the keys to your house?"

She gave him a slight head nod as she bit her lip, toying with the ring on her necklace.

"That's awesome, Simone. Congratulations." He paused. "So, when's the moving date? Where exactly is your house? Do you need any help moving? We have great connections with some moving companies."

Simone chuckled at Aaron's interrogation. She smiled, debriefed him, then returned to admiring his book collection and all of his awards. Walking toward his desk, she stood behind the chair she had been sitting in. "Aaron, I was wondering if I could possibly bring two people to the Christmas party? I know you said one, but I would love to bring Kendra."

"Most definitely," he said with excitement. "You'll love the party, too."

She smiled. "I'm sure I will."

"You ready for the game?"

Simone smiled from ear-to-ear. "Oh my, am I ready! That literally blew me away. Thank you again. And seating in the suites is the icing on the cake."

His own grin matched hers. "Well, the reports I'm running now will be part of the package to Mr. Kane. If you can grab them and put the package together, then send it to Mr. Kane with the corresponding letter I'm emailing to you now, we'll be good to go."

"Okay. Wonderful. I'll send them out in the morning."

Simone walked over to the printer and grabbed the documents, then ambled back to her office.

Simone checked her phone. There was a missed call from Lamont. She retrieved her voice message. *Hello, Lady Simone. This is Lamont. How are you? If you don't have any plans for lunch today, I'd be honored if you would join me. Give me a call at your earliest convenience.*

Leaning back in her chair, she hit the *delete* button. She hesitated, unsure of whether or not she should accept.

Her mind traveled back to their few meetings. Other than the encounter at the restaurant where he kissed her hand, he had been a gentleman and had not made any advances toward her. Maybe if she accepted, he would quit beating around the bush and come out about his feelings. She decided she would accept his invitation and find out.

She returned the call and told Lamont she would meet him for lunch. They agreed to meet at noon for Mexican at Obelisco Restaurant.

She disconnected the call and looked at the clock. Simone had about an hour before she needed to leave. She used the time to double-check the reports, Aaron's letter and all the other supporting documents, then finished preparing the package for Mr. Kane.

Two short knocks at the door interrupted her concentration. Holly peeked her head through the crack. "Simone, you have a visitor. Mr. Lamont Willis is in the lobby."

Her head snapped up. *Did she say Lamont was in the lobby?* "Okay, I'll be out in a minute."

Simone tossed her pen down on the desk and retraced their phone conversation. She'd told him she would meet him at the restaurant. What part of that conversation did he not understand? She couldn't believe he'd disrespected her request. That was her number one pet peeve. Why would he do that? She didn't know what kind of game Lamont was playing, but she was not going to be one of his chess pieces. If she didn't know what his intentions were before, she did now.

She pushed herself from the desk, grabbed Mr. Kane's envelope, and headed down the corridor. Her steps stopped before she reached the lobby.

She heard Aaron's and Lamont's voices. Her mouth dropped. She couldn't believe it. Maybe she should have stayed in New York. Why was all this mess happening since she arrived at the firm? *First, Macy. Now, Lamont.*

Aaron asked suspiciously, "Hey Lamont. What's up?"

"Hey, Aaron," Lamont said, smiling. "Picking up Simone for lunch."

Aaron stared at him for a few seconds. "Oh. Okay."

Simone cringed at Lamont's response. Undeniably, Lamont enjoyed annoying Aaron. She wasn't sure why, but she didn't want any part in it. She sprinted quickly toward the lobby before their conversation went any further—or got out of hand.

"Hey, Lamont." Irritated, she held up her hand. "Did we have a misunderstanding or something?"

"Hi, Lady Simone. Forgive me for the intrusion, but my mother taught me better manners. When I invite anyone out, the proper thing to do is pick them up."

"Well, did your mother also tell you to honor other people's requests?" Simone retorted.

Holly's eyes were glued to them as if she was watching an episode of *Atlanta Housewives*. By the expression on Aaron's face, Simone could see he was a little disturbed, though she wasn't sure why. They were not in a relationship. He'd made himself perfectly clear. He was not getting involved with anyone at work.

Aaron marched back into his office.

As far as Simone was concerned, she was going to dump them both before anything got started. Aaron—for his double standard, and Lamont—for his blatant disrespect of her wishes.

Simone focused her attention back to Holly and gave her instructions on mailing out Mr. Kane's package. Once Simone finished speaking with Holly, she turned to Lamont and invited him back to her office.

"Come in, Lamont." Simone scowled.

Lamont stood and faced her from a distance. "Simone, before you get started. Please accept my apology. I can tell by the disappointment in your eyes that me coming here was not a good idea." He paused and caught his breath. "Believe me, it won't happen again. Forgive me?"

She folded her arms and pursed her lips. "You're correct. I am disappointed. I never want to feel like I don't have a voice in anything that pertains to me. Your plans superseded my request, and I can't have that."

"I understand, Lady Simone. It won't happen again."

"I've lost my appetite. So, why don't I give you a call and let you know when we can do lunch."

With a sly grin, he responded, "Hmmm. Oh,

okay, Lady Simone. You going to let me know when you want to do lunch?"

She nodded, took a deep breath, and opened her office door.

Lamont tucked his hands in his pockets and stepped into the corridor. He swung around. "I hope I won't be waiting too long to hear from you."

She smiled politely and responded, "Have a great day, Lamont," then firmly shut her office door.

Chapter 23

When Aaron and Shaun arrived at Oracle Arena, the crowds were beginning to pile in. Rain and a slight wind were expected in Oakland, but that didn't deter faithful fans. Aaron and Shaun knew their employees well, and didn't flinch at the cost for the event. Aaron and Shaun made it a point to show them how much they were valued.

Aaron parked his car in VIP parking, turned off the ignition, and waited for everyone else to arrive. Minutes later, the rest of the group rolled up. Aaron and Shaun grabbed their Warriors jackets from the back seat and got out of the car. Aaron hit the lock on his key. The employees congregated around Aaron's car with high-fives, fist bumps, and hugs.

Simone rolled up and parked her car in one of the available parking stalls. She grabbed her coat out of the car and put it on. After securing her car, she surveyed the area and caught sight of the others in the group. Excited, she scurried along to join the group. Before she could reach her destination, a young man in his early twenties stopped her in her tracks.

"Hey, beautiful."

Even with his jacket on, she could tell he wore baggy pants that showed his underwear. Had it not been for his belt, he definitely would have lost his pants. In disbelief that this young man was trying to flirt with her, she looked over her shoulder to see if he was talking to someone else. Seeing no one else close enough for him to be addressing, she shrugged her shoulders.

He laughed. "Yeah, you." He fixed his eyes on Simone, "You think I can holla at ya?"

She gave him a hard stare. "Young man, you talking to me? And no, you can't holla at me. I could be your sister."

"Awww. Wow." He laughed again. "It's like that?" He rubbed his chin trying to look older than he was. "You need someone to escort you?"

Simone held a straight face. "Is it like that? Ummm. Yeah. I'm flattered and thank you for the compliment, but it ain't happening here. And no, I don't need you to escort me. I'm good."

"Alright, beautiful." She watched the young man dart across the parking lot.

Simone resumed her stroll and joined the group, shaking her head all the way.

Meanwhile, Aaron scanned the parking lot for the last missing person—Simone.

Shaun caught his attention. "Let me guess. You looking for Simone, right?"

Aaron rolled his eyes. "Man, don't even start with that mess."

Shaun stuffed his hands in his jacket pockets. "I ain't saying nothing else. I asked a simple question."

"Good."

"But here she comes," Shaun said, smiling.

"Man, thought you wasn't saying another word."

"Well, I lied. My bad."

"Let's enjoy the game. This is going to be a good one," Aaron responded. They solidified the statement with a fist bump, calling a truce.

Aaron turned and watched Simone approach. His brown eyes glowed as he beheld her. She was a vision of beauty—even in a Warriors jersey, jeans, and tennis shoes.

When Simone joined the group, she gave her salutations to everyone and beamed a genuine smile. Aaron noticed she wore her Warriors cap with a ponytail pulled through the back. Without her heels, she stood a few inches below his shoulders.

Anticipation and excitement for the game was evident. They could hear the fans chanting, "Go Warriors!"

With everyone accounted for, they all headed to the north side of the arena. A line had already formed. The young man who had accosted Simone before headed in her direction.

The young man looked at Simone and tried once more. "Hey, beautiful. You know age is only a number."

Aaron's eyes widened.

A frown settled on Simone's face. "Are you serious?"

Aaron looked at her, then at the guy. "Simone, is this guy bothering you?"

Simone took a deep breath. "Well, seems like the young man can't take no for an answer. I already told him I wasn't interested."

Aaron honed in on the young man. "Young man, she already told you she wasn't interested. I think you better get on before you get a spanking."

The employees laughed in chorus. Aaron and Shaun encircled the young man. The young man sized them up, then retreated. He marched off, holding a tight grip on his falling pants.

Aaron glanced at Simone. She still wore a frown on her face. "Are you okay?"

"Oh, yeah. I'm fine. Thank you."

Once the doors opened, the greeter handed them a splash towel. The mob of fans stampeded toward the food, drinks, and souvenir lines. The party was about to begin, and they were ready to watch their team kick some booty.

They made their way up the stairs to the premium suites. The host asked Aaron for the suite number so she could open the doors and let them in. When they marched into the suite, a feast awaited them. There were trays of food—hot dogs, chili cheese fries, ribs, chicken, links, and fruit and vegetable trays. To wash the food down, there were all kinds of drinks—nonalcoholic and alcoholic.

The employees secured their seats and assembled in line to get their delectable refreshments. "Girl, look at all this food. I think I've gained three pounds trying to decide what I'm going to eat," a coworker said to Simone as they waited in line.

"I know, right? I'm not even going to think about all these extra calories. I'll worry about shedding them tomorrow. Tonight, I'm determined to enjoy every moment. Who knows when I'll get to another game?" Simone smiled.

"That's what I'm saying. Is this your first game?"

"It is, and I'm loving it. The view overlooking the court is amazing. I keep wanting to pinch myself to make sure I'm not dreaming."

Her co-worker balanced her plate and smiled.

"It's all so surreal. Girl, let me find a seat. I can't believe I wore these heels to the game."

"Enjoy the game," Simone said as her colleague walked away. She moved over to the side and examined her surroundings.

Aaron's mind traveled back to the previous encounter with the young man. He smiled slightly. *She really does need protecting. She got Lamont on one side and the juveniles on the other.*

He couldn't get too mad at the young man. As young as he was, he did have good taste in women. Coming that close to a woman like Simone would mess with a brother's mind.

He shook his head. *I ain't having it.* Every time he was around her, his thoughts were all mixed up. One moment, he played with the idea of being in a committed relationship. The next, he talked himself back into reason.

Aaron appraised her from a distance before he approached. She looked like a kid in Disneyland. His heart warmed. Seeing Simone happy pleased him. He wasn't sure why. She did something to him he couldn't quite explain.

David, one of the employees, bumped him, breaking his concentration. "A penny for your thoughts, boss."

Aaron looked away. "Oh, hey, David. I was wondering if this spread is enough. Let me go check on a few things. Enjoy yourself."

Aaron walked away. He decided to invade

Simone's space. "Amazing, huh? First time in a suite? Or first time at a professional game?"

Simone angled her body. "Is it that obvious?" She snickered. "Actually, first time for both."

He laughed and tilted his head to the side. "Really? That explains it, then. The experience is awesome. But wait until you see the fire show at the beginning. You'll love that, too."

"Yeah, I'm looking forward to seeing it. I heard it was really great." She nodded and briefly glanced away.

The jubilance in her voice made him smile.

Simone grinned at him. "I better find somewhere to sit with this plate." She'd decided on chicken, salad, and fruit. "Those BBQ ribs sure looked enticing, but the last thing I need is to have meat stuck between my teeth or barbecue sauce running down my brand-new jersey." She laughed. "Don't let me hold you up. Thank you again for all of this."

Before he could respond, she pivoted her body and headed toward one of the club chairs in the suite. Aaron put his hands in his pockets and watched her walk away.

"Hey, Simone," Holly said as she sat next to Simone. "How you doing?"

The two exchanged small talk, then Holly leaned in closer and whispered, "That Macy is something else, isn't she? She my friend and all, but sometimes... she does too much."

Simone cocked her head to the side and arched a brow. "Well, it's like this...."

Holly leaned forward expectantly.

Simone continued, "My pastor once gave me the best advice, and I use it daily. Pray. Yup. Prayer works every time. You should think about doing that for her."

Holly reeled back as if she'd been slapped. She let out an audible gasp.

With that, Simone grabbed her things and marched her way to a different seat with a better view of the court.

The entire arena went pitch black. Lights shone on the court floor. The voice of the emcee reverberated through the speakers. "Whoop, whoop, whoop, Warriors' fans, it's go time. Let's get hyped and make some noise." The crowd went crazy. On the screen, were the words GET UP ON YOUR FEET AND GREET YOUR NBA CHAMPIONS....

At the command of the announcer, everyone stood and obeyed his instructions. The noise and excitement brought goose bumps to Simone's arms. The place was electrifying. Everyone chanted, "Warriors! Warriors!" The music had heads bobbing, bodies shaking. When Simone thought it couldn't get any louder, it did. The lights shone on the starting lineup as they were introduced. Inside the suite, everyone joined in on the Warriors' dance. When she turned around, she met Aaron's eyes. She gave him a thumbs-up and a wide, gorgeous smile. He responded with an electrifying grin and a head nod.

For the next two and a half hours, the suite was filled with oohs and aahs, plenty of high-fives, and jaw-dropping moments as Steph and Klay hit three-point shots. As predicted, the Warriors kicked some Los Angeles Clippers booty.

On the drive home, Aaron thought about Simone. He would pay for another suite to watch her face light up again the way it had tonight. *If I broke my rule for her, would that make her face light up?*

He'd sworn off women, at least for a while. In the past, all he had to do was think about Macy Lewis and his whole body would rebel at the idea of being in a relationship. Then Simone Herron had bumped into him coming off the elevator and managed to get past all of his defenses without even trying. Was she worth the risk? His heart said *yes*.

Chapter 24

The delivery truck arrived promptly at seven o'clock in the morning with a truckload full of furniture to fill every room in Simone's house. Her shipment of African art had arrived a few days before, along with the rare pieces of art she had collected. Simone and her family had arrived at the house around six to bless her new home and to assist in whatever way was needed.

Three hours later, after the furniture was placed in each room, her family assembled in the kitchen for a light brunch. They pulled out their chairs and sat across from one another, helping themselves to the delicious spread Simone had provided. Plates filled, the table fell silent. They bowed their heads while Marie asked God's blessing over the food.

"Simone, your new home is so beautiful," Marie said. "God has really blessed you."

"Yes, ma'am, He has. I'm thankful and appreciative of His many blessings."

"Sis, you gon' fit one of those rooms for me?" Tori smiled.

Simone filled her mouth with food and lowered her head, pretending not to hear. Tori was always looking for somebody to take care of her.

"I know you hear me. But, it's okay. I ain't gon' trip."

"Oh, hallelujah," their mother blurted out.

They all shared a laugh.

"Tori, you're welcome to visit, but I know you'll be better off when you get your own place, with nobody telling you what to do or when to come home." Simone winked at her and took a sip of her drink.

"I know. I know," Tori responded. "I'm going to get my own place. Y'all will see."

Devon reached for his sister's hand. "Let me know if you need help with anything else." He flexed his bicep muscle. "All hands will be on deck."

Simone smiled at her brother and rested her elbow on the table. Chin in hand, she soaked in her surroundings. "I'm sitting here amazed at God. When Joshua died, I didn't know how I would live. I couldn't imagine putting one foot in front of the other and living another day." She sat up and reached for her necklace, holding on to the ring. Tears filled her eyes, but she kept them at bay.

Her mom reached for her hand. Simone squeezed it lightly, acknowledging her mother's comfort. She continued, "You know the last two years have been hard, real hard. But there's also been some good in the midst of my pain." She looked at her family. "Especially now. I'm back home with all of you. I'm happy with my new job. And now this." Simone looked around at her new home.

The changes in her life were beginning to pay off. As far as she was concerned, she welcomed the new chapters. In a few days, Kendra would be flying in for the holiday party. Simone was delighted. She couldn't have been in a better place.

Life wasn't perfect, but it was as close as it could get.

Chapter 25

Simone and Kendra had gone on their annual pampering day, which included shopping, facials, and mani-pedis. Later, they would get their hair and makeup done. It had been a long time since Simone had splurged on herself. She'd actually forgotten how good it felt. They finished up their last-minute shopping and headed back to Simone's house.

Simone showed Kendra the Blackman Estate and Winery on the website. From the pictures, they were in for a night of elegance. The winery was highly sought-after for parties and weekend getaways. Devon had arranged for a limo to pick them all up and drive them to Napa. Instead of driving back to the Bay Area after the party, they'd booked two rooms at one of the bed and breakfasts nearby.

Simone chose to wear a Jennifer Lopez *Maid in*

Manhattan replica design. She'd had a seamstress design the long peach chiffon strapless dress after falling in love with the movie. Simone wanted the same spellbound look and completely speechless response from the crowds that Jennifer Lopez had gotten when she walked into the benefit party where she was meeting Ralph Fiennes.

She carefully placed the dress over her head, adjusting it as it fell down over her hips to the floor. Everything was in place. Her makeup was flawless and the dress flowed perfectly. She looked good and she felt good. Her beautician had curled her hair, so she decided to wear it piled high on her head, with a few curls falling to her face. Simone was feeling herself.

"Girl, you killin' it," Kendra said.

Kendra had decided on a blue paneled silk evening gown with cap sleeves, a black waist belt, and plunging scoop back with a flared hem. Her toned body filled her dress quite nicely. She wore her natural hair in a short coil hairdo like Wanda Sykes.

Simone looked at Kendra. "And you *slaying*."

One final look in Simone's full-length mirror warranted a few simple last-minute adjustments. Outside, the limousine and Devon waited.

The party was in full swing when they arrived. Simone and Devon stood at the entrance, her arm looped in his. Kendra followed close behind. As

Simone hoped, heads turned in their direction. She could feel all eyes on them.

Kendra moved next to Simone. "Girl, we got everyone looking over here. I love it. I'm going to have a great time."

They smiled and laughed in chorus.

Heads continued to turn as they made their way down the stairs.

Simone glanced around. Her eyes rested on Aaron. He tilted his head and smiled. She willed herself to turn her head, but seeing him in that black double-breasted tuxedo arrested her attention. His eyes held her captive for a few seconds. She had seen him all dressed up before, but tonight, there was something different about him. His hair cut low and his goatee spaced perfectly around his lips sent shivers all through her body. What kept her attention was his beautiful dark eyes, his chiseled jaw, and his well-formed bone structure. All of it made him strikingly handsome. The diamond studs in his ears made him more attractive.

A bump from Kendra got her attention.

The room was filled with hundreds of people, all mingling, drinking, and enjoying the soft, smooth sound of jazz. Simone remembered some of the faces from their trip to Las Vegas and a few other networking events she had attended. This event definitely brought out the who's who in the industry. As they moved throughout the room, they were greeted by waitresses and waiters dressed in all-white offering trays of appetizers and champagne.

The décor was absolutely breathtaking. Looking around the spacious room, Simone could tell a pretty penny had been spent on decorations. A tall, fully-decorated Christmas tree about eighteen feet tall stood in one corner of the room. Each table was covered with a white linen tablecloth and adorned with a glass vase filled with all white flowers—roses, orchids and carnations accented by green holly leaves and small white baby's breath clusters. As they walked further into the center of the room, an ice sculpture of an angel grabbed their attention. The craftsmanship was mesmerizing.

"Wow, this is gorgeous," Kendra said, looking at the twelve-light heritage crystal chandelier hanging from the ceiling.

"I agree," Simone replied. "And that tree is simply beautiful. This is so much more than I expected. They've outdone themselves."

"Pretty cool," Devon said as he walked around the sculpture, admiring all the intricate details. He stuffed his hands in his pockets. "The person that carved this has mad skills."

When Aaron laid eyes on her, she took his breath

away. She was... striking, breathtaking, gorgeous, and stunning. Yet those words were not enough to describe her beauty. He smiled as he appraised her from head to toe.

His smile fell when he saw she was not alone. A tall, distinguished man in an Armani suit escorted her. Aaron's eyes went back and forth from Simone to her escort. Well, at least it isn't Lamont. Aaron suddenly felt jealous, wishing she could have been on his arms. He made his way to his guests.

From across the room, Aaron watched Simone introducing her well-groomed escort and her friend Kendra to those she knew. A few people seemed familiar with her escort based on their responses with the brotherhood fist bump.

"Man, you got it bad. The doleful expression on your face says it all," Shaun said. "You have no cause to be jealous, right?"

Aaron snapped. "Naw, I'm good. And no. I'm not jealous." He paused. "Brother, don't you have some mingling to do?"

"I'm so done with you both pretending like y'all not interested in each other. I know you are. Who penned the phrase 'to thine own self be true'?"

Aaron couldn't dispute the obvious anymore. He'd spent the last few weeks debating what his next step would be. Tonight should have been the night to confess his feelings to her, disregard his promise to himself, and forget about trying to keep some rule that denied him love. His plan for the evening had included a romantic setting in the wine cellar, a small replica of the decorations they had throughout the event, dancing, and a toast to new beginnings. But here she was, with another man, and looking happy....

Aaron tilted his drink to his lips and took a sip. "Yep, you're right once again, my brother. But, it appears Simone has found someone already." He paused. "And she looks beautifully happy."

Shaun stepped closer and patted him on the shoulder. "Um, yeah. And you look like you ready to kill the brother." Shaun paused. "Shoot man, she is looking really good, too. Her and that Kendra got everybody's head turning in their direction."

Aaron gave him an icy stare. "Really, Shaun?"

"Brace yourself. They're headed over here. We're about to find out who the blessed man is that seems to have taken your place, Aaron." Shaun winked at his brother.

Aaron shrugged. "Whatever. I should have gotten me something to drink."

"Man, you don't drink. On the other hand, maybe a drink will loosen you up."

"Well, I might make an exception tonight." He tried to rush off to the bar, but it was too late. Simone, Kendra and Devon approached them as Aaron made a move to leave.

"Hello, gentlemen. Lovely party. We're having

a great time." Simone looked back and forth between Aaron and Shaun.

Kendra was delighted to agree. "Yes. This is more than I could have imagined. Thank you for the invite." She addressed them both, but her eyes were stuck on Shaun.

Simone interjected, "You both remember Kendra?"

Shaun locked eyes with Kendra. He reached out his hand, and she accepted. "Hello, Kendra. Good to see you again."

She smiled. "Thank you. Same here."

"I must say, you both are looking beautiful tonight," Shaun complimented them.

The ladies blushed. "Thank you," they responded in unison.

"I'd like you both to meet someone else who's special to me." Simone's head turned toward Devon. "He's been my rock and my confidante. I don't think I could have gotten through those rough times in my life without him." She gave her brother a thousand-watt smile, then looked directly at Aaron.

A pained look crossed Aaron's face. Shaun's eyes darted back and forth between Simone and Aaron. He hurt for his brother.

Simone tightened her grip on Devon's arm. "Aaron and Shaun, this is Devon."

Devon removed his arm from her grasp to give them both a fist bump. "Aaron, nice to meet you," he paused for a second and continued, "Shaun, nice to meet you as well. I'm Simone's... brother."

Aaron released a jagged breath.

Shaun laughed. "Simone's brother, huh?"

"Yup, brother. Dr. Devon Herron."

"Cool." Aaron nodded his head, smiling from ear to ear. "Real cool."

The ladies excused themselves and went to the rest room to freshen up. On their way, they felt the presence of eyes staring at them. Several attractive men looked in their direction. No one bothered to turn away; instead, they kept their gaze boldly on them. Several men saluted them with their drinks and smiled.

The men conversed a little bit longer with Simone's brother, realizing they shared several things in common. Shaun was a golf enthusiast like Devon. Aaron and Devon realized they shared similar interests in the same sports teams, namely the Warriors, Giants, and the 49ers. Devon also told them about his practice. He gave them both a business card and invited them to his office should they need any dental work.

When the DJ kicked the music up a notch, Simone and Kendra bobbed their heads as they returned to the three men still huddled in a circle. It was apparent the ladies were ready to join the others on the dance floor. Devon swooped Kendra to the floor, and Shaun grabbed Simone, leaving Aaron as the observer once more. They danced, sweated, and danced some more. Simone hadn't moved like that in years. She'd probably regret it tomorrow.

Kendra leaned in close to her ear, "Looks like Stella is getting her groove back."

Simone leaned over and responded with a smile, "Well, I don't know if I'm getting my groove back, but I'm definitely getting a callus. Girl, I'm cute alright, but my dogs are barking."

The DJ played a few more upbeat songs, then changed the tempo of the music.

Simone was about to walk off the floor, but Shaun stepped back and waited for permission to continue dancing with her. He quickly slid his arm around her waist and pulled her closer to him, but left enough space between them so she didn't feel uncomfortable.

Their eyes held. "Please forgive me for not waiting until you said okay, but I'm working on a plan, and I already know my brother is going to kill me."

She frowned, "I'm sorry. What plan is that, Shaun? And what in the world are you talking about, Aaron is going to kill you?"

"Simone, you know Aaron is attracted to you, right?"

She gasped. "Shaun, are you serious? Hmm, no, I didn't know that. But I do know about your brother's rule. Besides, I'm not interested."

He turned his head to the side. "You not interested? Really. You two need to stop. Clearly, your eyes are telling on the both of you."

Her mouth fell open. She had no comeback at all. Shaun had called it like it was. She mumbled under her breath, "Oh, gosh. New York seems so appealing right about now."

"Can I ask you to trust me?" Before she could utter a word, Shaun gave her a twist and the twist turned into a dip. It happened so fast he didn't give her time to think or even catch her breath. The next thing she heard, Shaun was counting backwards. Everything else was a complete blank.

She was boiling. "Shaun, what has gotten into you?" She glanced around the room to see who else had witnessed their episode of *Dancing with the Stars* and caught Aaron's eye.

Shaun kept counting, "Five, four, three, two, one."

Aaron blinked rapidly, hoping what he'd seen wasn't real. Did he watch his brother dip Simone? He had had enough of Shaun. That was the breaking point. He stood there contemplating his next move. He placed his glass on the table and moved with determination and poise through the crowd. *Told him I didn't need help with women.*

He approached them, tapped Shaun on the shoulder, and whispered in his ear, "I'm going to deal with you later. You best count on it." Shaun released his grip on Simone and offered Aaron a fist bump as a truce. Aaron left him hanging. Shaun left smiling.

Aaron looked deep into Simone's eyes and slid his arms around her waist. He pulled her close to his body. If she was going to object, now was the time.

Her previous thoughts and plans about dumping Aaron Blackman fell to the ground. She wrapped her arms around his neck. Her knees weakened as they swayed to the music. He smelled so good. The only man that had ever been that close to her was Joshua. Was she ready to allow someone else to fill that space?

He whispered in her ear. "You remember that rule I had about not getting involved with anyone at work?"

She looked at him. "Yes. I do."

He smiled. "I'm breaking it. I'm breaking it for you." He brushed his lips against hers. Her heart jackhammered louder than the music.

His flashback of their first encounter by the elevator doors stayed with him. She fit perfectly in his arms. The only difference now was that he was ready to be open and honest about his feelings. *Can't fight love when it's real.*

The DJ played another slow song.

Aaron pulled away from the embrace and looked into her eyes. "Will you come with me? We need to talk." He waited patiently for her response.

She looked puzzled at his request. "Okay."

A smile crossed his face. He grabbed her hand and led her down the stairwell to the wine cellar. Simone looked back over her shoulder. Her eyes connected with Kendra who gave her a nod of approval. Devon's eyes narrowed in confusion and Shaun grinned. Everybody else was too busy on the dance floor, dancing or drinking and having a good time, to notice they were leaving. Everyone except Holly, who stood with her mouth wide open, taking in everything that had transpired between Shaun, Simone, and Aaron.

A small table with two wine glasses and a bottle of chilled cider stood in the center of the wine cellar. The lights were turned down low. A small lit candle on the table added to the ambience.

She walked over to the table. "Well, counselor, looks like you had something planned."

"Yes. I did. I was waiting for the right moment."

She turned and made eye contact with him. "What if I'd said no?"

"I was hoping you'd say yes."

They smiled at each other. Standing a little distance away, Aaron could tell she was a little nervous. He took a step and asked, "Why are you nervous?"

"I haven't allowed any man to get this close to me in a long time."

As he walked closer, he could see that her body trembled slightly. He pulled her in. "Well, all of that is about change." The only space between them was the fresh breath they shared with each other.

Her breath caught. "You wanted to talk."

"Yes. But after."

"After what?"

He lowered his head and touched his mouth to hers; once, twice, three times. She wrapped her arms around his neck, grabbed the back of his head, and kept it in place as they enjoyed the moment. The more she responded, the longer the kiss lasted and the tighter his grip was on her.

After releasing her from the embrace, he cleared his throat. "After that. Hmm... like I envisioned, but so much better."

She gasped for air.

"Come, have a seat. Let me pour us something to drink."

Simone could have used something a little stronger to calm her nerves, but she'd have to settle on the cider. He poured her glass first. She downed it before he poured himself one.

He chuckled. It was the perfect cold drink to put out the flame that burned inside her. They looked at each other and broke out laughing. "You want some more?"

"Yes, please. Thank you."

He poured her a second serving, then poured himself a glass and sat next to her at the table.

She waited until he was settled in his seat

before she interrogated him. "What happened to your cardinal rule?"

His dimples showed when he smiled. "Well, some rules are meant to be broken, especially when it deals with matters of the heart."

She took a sip of her cider. "So, how are we supposed to work together?"

"Don't worry. We'll figure it out. Let's promise that our relationship won't interfere with our jobs and we won't bring what happens in our personal lives to work. Last thing we need is people snooping in our business." He took a sip of his drink.

She nodded. "I agree."

They talked back and forth, asking questions and getting to know one another better. "Simone, I have a question for you. You don't have to answer if you don't want to."

She nodded. "Go ahead."

"What's the story behind the necklace I see you wearing at times?" He leaned in, extending his hand to her. She gladly accepted.

"My necklace. Do we have that much time to discuss it?"

"Tell you what; why don't you give me the short version and if I have more questions, we can pick it up from there. How does that sound?"

She shut her eyes for a moment and took a deep breath. When she opened her eyes, she looked straight at him. "Okay, that sounds good. I was engaged two years ago to a really good man who was killed in a motorcycle accident." She paused. "His name was Joshua."

She preceded to give him the short version of their relationship, how they met, the-wedding-that-wasn't, and her ultimate move to California. He uttered not a word, sitting silently in shock.

Aaron had no idea she carried all that pain. To go through such heartache and still be willing to try love again.... Was she truly ready? She had loved Joshua. No doubt about it. And she was the woman Aaron needed, but would he have to compete with memories from the grave?

The recollection of her past was more than Aaron had expected. Tears welled up in her eyes as she talked more about her past. He reached out and wiped away the tears on her cheeks with his thumb.

His heart filled with compassion.

He saw the pain in her eyes, he could tell it was still hard for her to discuss. Maybe this wasn't the best time to open a can of worms. Now that he knew, he could help her get through it.

"The necklace holds my engagement ring." Her fingers trembled.

He pushed back his chair, stood and reached for her hand. She folded her hands into his and stood with him. Aaron wrapped his muscular arms around her waist and drew her to him. He spread butterfly kisses across her forehead. "I'm sorry.

Maybe now wasn't the best time. We don't have to discuss it anymore."

She looked at him and gave a half-smile. "Okay."

"Are you okay?"

She nodded and placed her head on his chest, relaxing in the warmth of the embrace. "Hold me." Obeying her request, he held her tighter.

Simone felt safe in Aaron's arms. She didn't want the moment to end. For the first time in years, she was in a place where she didn't need to put up any walls or barriers. Nothing mattered at that moment, all her cares and concerns were far away. Being with him felt… *right*.

Anxiously, she lifted her head and glanced up. Aaron was staring down at her. "This feels perfect. I don't want this to end," he said.

Their lips touched again. She sighed. "Why do I feel like a 'but' is coming?"

He laughed. "Because we better get back to the party before somebody sends the police looking for us."

Her smile widened. "I know, huh? And you're right. Kendra might start thinking you kidnapped me."

His eyes enlarged. "Don't give me any ideas. I have the perfect place. A little island in Bermuda."

She chuckled in disbelief. "Are you serious?"

"Yes. I'm serious. Have you been to Bermuda?"

"No, I haven't been there. But I've seen pictures. It's beautiful."

"I'd love to take you there one day."

She smiled. "I'd like that." Her inviting smile yielded another kiss on her lips.

He teased, "Now, let me show you how to really dance like the stars."

"Oh, Lawd. My feet are not going to like me in the morning."

"Don't worry. I give a mean foot massage."

"Oohee. I like that, too."

Chapter 26

"Man, you going to spot me or what?" Shaun said to Aaron while lying on the bench trying to bench press two hundred pounds.

"I ought to leave you hanging for that foolishness you pulled with Simone."

Shaun's head jerked around. He lifted up from the bench and eyeballed Aaron. "It worked, didn't it?"

Aaron's face tightened. "No. It didn't work. And, I told you to back off. I didn't need any help."

Shaun remained silent. He had a smart comeback, but thought better of it.

"From now on, I don't want you messing in my business, especially when it comes to me and Simone." Aaron lifted his water bottle and took a sip. The cold, hard stare Aaron gave Shaun was a clear indication he meant what he said.

Shaun wiped the sweat from his brow with his tee shirt. "Alright, man, my bad. I'm sorry. I overstepped my bounds. It won't happen again."

"Good."

Shaun held up his hand. "Point taken. I was wrong."

Aaron eyed his brother and smiled. "Yes, you were wrong." They laughed out loud.

"Are we cool?" Shaun asked cautiously.

"Yeah, we alright." They did their customary fist bump.

"Bro, I'm really glad for you. You seem really happy. You deserve someone great. I haven't seen you smile this much since... well, let me think... the day you dumped Macy."

They cracked up laughing. "Yeah, bro. I'm happy. She's smart, intelligent, and easy to talk to. Her vocabulary is much larger than, 'Can I have your black card?'"

They did a high-five on that. "I thought maybe you had forgot about your own Christmas party."

"Naw. In deep conversation. She was engaged before."

Shaun lifted his brow. "Oh yeah?"

"Yeah. Her fiancé was killed in a motorcycle accident a few months before their wedding."

"Wow. That was deep. Man, she dropped that on you already?"

"Yeah, but it was my inquisition that got it

started. She wears this necklace and I noticed it had a ring on it. I inquired as to the significance."

"Oh. Okay." Shaun seemed to hesitate. "When was the accident?"

"It was a few years back."

"So, bro, you think she's over that… and ready to be in a relationship?"

Aaron gave his brother a side glance. "She said she was, and until she shows me otherwise, I believe her." Aaron wondered the same thing, too, but time would tell if she was really ready or not.

"Alright, man, let's lighten up this conversation." Shaun sighed. "We still on for our poker night with the fellas?"

Aaron's face beamed. Ecstatically, he said, "Nope. Having dinner with Simone."

Shaun's head jerked. "Wait. You dissing us for dinner? Did I hear you correctly? No poker with the fellas?"

"Yup, you heard correctly. And I'm not dissing y'all for dinner. But I'm dissing y'all for Simone. There's a big difference."

"Dang, man. Already?"

"When was the last time a woman's invited me over for dinner and cooked for me?"

Shaun paused for several seconds. He thought about his response and kept silent. Although Shaun was happy for his brother, he was a tad bit jealous. He thought about the idea of settling down for a moment, and soon dismissed the thought. *Naw. Not yet.*

"Exactly," Aaron interjected. "That long. I'm not passing up an opportunity to spend time with her and enjoy a home-cooked meal."

"Mama would probably take offense to that."

"You know what I mean."

"Yeah, bro. I do."

"Sorry, but the fellas will have to do poker without me."

"Man, is it like that?" Shaun probed more. "You really feeling her like that already?"

Aaron blushed. "Feeling her, sprung, nose open, locked down, whipped. Go ahead and call it whatever you want. When the Lord brings a good woman into your life, you don't let her go."

"Wooooww. Daaaaaang. I can't even argue with you on that."

"Come on, man. Let's do this. I got a date."

The doorbell rang just as Simone was about to put the garlic crab in the oven. She looked at the clock. It was too early for Aaron. She had at least another two hours before he arrived.

"Who could that be?" She walked to the front door and peeked out the peephole. A man with a white hat and blue polo shirt stood at the door.

"Who is it?"

"Oakland Florist. I have a delivery for a Lady Simone Herron."

She had a slight flashback... *Lamont? Naw, couldn't be.*

She unchained the lock, opened the door, and greeted the delivery guy. JOE was printed on the name badge he wore. "Hi, I'm Simone."

"Okay. Let me go to my van. I wanted to be certain someone was home. I'll bring them right out."

She whispered to herself, "Bring them out? What does he mean by that?"

Smiling, Joe returned with a bouquet of red roses, purple alstroemerias, and purple Monte Casino Asters. "Here's the first vase." He handed them to Simone. She took them inside and placed them on the foyer table. By the time she came back to the door, Joe was waiting with another bouquet of roses. This time, the vase was filled with lavender roses, pink spray roses, pink waxflowers, and variegated pittosporum.

His smile widened. She accepted them and placed them alongside the other vase. The last vase Joe brought to the door held a dozen white roses. "There you go. You must be one special lady. Enjoy your day."

With that, Simone shut the door and walked toward the table looking for a card, feeling stunned.

The card read:

Can't wait to see you. Aaron.

Simone felt a big, cheesy grin spread across her face. Not one, not two, but three dozen roses. Her heart fluttered. She strolled into the living room and took a seat on the couch. The room looked so beautiful, it took her a few minutes to compose herself.

Simone was enraptured. Out of all the women he could have selected, he'd chosen her. She was blessed and she knew it. Although they were only beginning to know each other, their connection was strong. Their conversations on the phone were getting longer. They talked about everything from their faith to goals and ambitions.

She picked up the vase with the red roses and moved it to the dining room table. It made a beautiful centerpiece. The vase of white roses went on the kitchen island; the color contrast matched quite well with her décor. Simone left the lavender roses in the foyer so they would be the first thing her guests noticed.

She rearranged the roses and went to call Aaron. Grabbing her phone off the kitchen island, she selected his number and waited for the connection.

She could tell he was smiling when he answered. "Hi," he said in his deep baritone voice.

Simone felt like a giddy high school teenager. "Hi, Aaron. Thank you for the roses. I love them. They're really beautiful."

"You're welcome, Simone. I'm glad you love them."

Simone practically melted at the sound of his husky voice. This man was definitely a keeper.

I should be there shortly. You want me to bring anything?"

"Nope. I have everything. Make sure you come hungry."

"I can do that. Okay, let me finish getting ready. See you soon."

"All right. Sounds good."

She ended the call and placed the garlic crab in the oven. She wanted to call Kendra and tell her all about the roses, but she didn't want to rush the conversation. Tonight's dinner menu consisted of roasted garlic crab with shrimp, garlic noodles, and French bread. For dessert, she settled on homemade pound cake from Sweetie Pie's and chilled sparkling cider to drink. Once everything was prepared, she transferred the food to warmers and placed everything on the kitchen island.

She was all set... at least, her meal was.

After much contemplation, she'd decided on a denim dress with a pair of black leggings. Simple but cute. She touched up her makeup and sprayed on a little of her favorite perfume. Tonight, she wore her hair in finger coils. She loved the diversity of styles she could do with her natural hair. Simone took a final look at herself in the full-length mirror. Once she was satisfied with her appearance, she returned to the living room.

She took three pieces of wood from the log holder, placed them inside the fireplace on the grate, lit the wood, and watched it slowly catch.

Aaron couldn't take his mind off his date with Simone. His workout at the gym felt like it lasted hours longer than normal. His mind kept drifting back to her. No matter how much Shaun talked, Aaron managed to tune him out. Even the noise from the music playing throughout the gym couldn't filter into his thinking. How could this woman have such an effect on him? He wasn't sure, but he was going to enjoy the journey.

He pulled his car into the garage and went inside his house, eager to take a hot shower. Once there, his mind traveled back to the conversation he'd had with Shaun about poker night. Aaron smiled and shook his head. He was proud of himself and thankful to God that his struggle with gambling was under control.

He stepped from the shower, dried himself off, and tucked the towel around his waist. It didn't take him long to slip into his washed blue jeans, white polo shirt and jean jacket. On the way out, he grabbed the necessities: keys, wallet, phone, and since Simone was talking smack, a deck of cards.

Once settled in his seat, Aaron texted Simone to tell her he was on the way. *Leaving Now. BTW I'm gonna school you in spades. LOL*

She replied, *Can't wait. BTW I'm the teacher. LOL.*

Aaron cracked up laughing. He could only envision her smile when she typed those words. He shook his head. *She's something else. I'm really digging her.* He bobbed to the music and grinned all the way to her house.

Shortly thereafter, he pulled into Simone's driveway ready to eat, enjoy her company, and teach her a lesson or two on smack-talking. Aaron rang her doorbell and stood at the door with his hands stuffed deep in his pockets, waiting patiently for her to answer.

He could hear the chains rattling. "Hey," he said as the door swung open.

She stared at him for a second, smiled, then stepped back. "Hey yourself."

He walked in, captivated by her beauty. The outfit she'd decided on was perfect for her body.

Aaron towered over her by a few inches. He grabbed her by the waist and kissed her. "How are you?"

She ran her fingers along his muscular forearm. "I'm doing well. I'm glad you're here. How are you?"

He rested his head against hers. "Better now that I've seen you." Aaron inhaled and exhaled her sweet scent. "You smell good. What kind of perfume are you wearing?"

She smiled. "Today, I have on Peony & Blush Suede by Jo Malone. It's actually one of my favorites."

"I'll have to remember that."

"Do that, counselor. I won't object. Come on in." She grabbed his hand and led him through the foyer to the living room.

"Got the fire going, I see. It feels good."

"Yeah. I thought it would be nice, since the weather has been downright cold."

"You got that right."

She led him to her kitchen and gestured for him to have a seat. He removed his jacket and draped it over the back of one of the chairs. Instead of sitting, Aaron walked over to the island and took the lid off one of the chafing dishes.

Simone studied him as he crossed the room. His broad shoulders swayed gracefully with each step. His eyes widened at the sight of those large crab leg claws. When he spotted the tiger shrimp, he licked his lips. "Ooohh-weee, they're calling my name. This looks delicious." He covered the chafing dish and removed the lid from the second warmer. "Wow. What have we got here? Mmm, I can't wait to taste this."

"Garlic noodles. I hope you like it."

He lifted his head, following her every move throughout the kitchen. For a moment, he envisioned her in his own kitchen, getting the dinner plates and glasses from the cabinet and the silverware from the drawer.

He walked up behind her. Unaware of his proximity, she jumped in surprise when he wrapped his arms around her waist. Aaron whispered in her ear, "Simone, you're so beautiful. I'm glad I broke my rule. You mean everything to me." His warm breath caressed her ear.

Stepping back he said. "Let me help you with this." He grabbed the dishes from her hands and placed them on the island along with the silverware. Simone got the glasses and the chilled cider from the freezer.

Without any hesitation, Aaron grabbed his plate and scooped up a large amount of garlic noodles and stacked a heaping of crab and shrimp on top. His eyes rested on her. "You said bring my appetite, right? And I have."

"I did say that." She smiled and shook her head at his voracious appetite. "Yes, I did."

"I love seafood."

Simone's smile widened. "Really, now? I'll remember that."

After dinner, she took him on a tour of the house. They retired to the living room, where Aaron threw another log on the fire.

He held out his hand to her. "This is a good spot. Let's sit here, enjoy the fire, and talk."

She couldn't resist his request, and happily intertwined her fingers through his.

"I want to make sure you're okay. You've shared some really deep stuff with me." He scooted closer to her and wrapped his arm around her waist. "He took a breath. "It seemed like some parts of your past are still too painful to discuss."

Simone peered at him and pushed a few curls of hair behind one ear. "Aaron, you're the first man I've allowed to get this close to me in years. And you're the only man I've felt comfortable sharing the pain of my past with. Losing Joshua was one of the most difficult things in my life. Everything I ever dreamed about died with him."

He squeezed her waist, giving her the reassurance she needed to continue.

"Believe me, I've had plenty of days where I cried myself to sleep, stayed in the bed all day, and shut myself off from the world, trying to understand why it happened. When I got to the hospital, he was gone. It's taken me years to get to this place of rediscovering myself and wanting to move forward."

He waited for a few minutes before gently asking. "Do you still love him?"

She paused and thought about the question. "I don't know how to answer that truthfully. Everything that I have now, I have because he'd already planned for our life together. Even in his death, he was still loving me. It seems cruel to say I no longer love him, as if what we had wasn't true. I *can* say the love Joshua and I shared is no longer holding me back from loving again. I wouldn't be willing to try this—" Simone moved her hand back and forth between the two of them "—if it was; that wouldn't be fair to you. I'll always have the memories of him. Those can't be erased. Don't worry, though. I'm ready to try this thing called love." She reached for his hand and smiled. "So to answer your question, yes. I'm ready to be in a relationship with you."

Aaron swallowed hard to get the knot out of his throat. He didn't know if it was her soft voice, the words she had spoken, or the heat from the fireplace, but his insides were turning summersaults. The way she looked into his eyes dispelled any doubt he had in his mind about her. He wondered how she would respond to him when he share with her his problem with gambling.

"Good. I'm glad to hear that. That deserves a toast, don't you think?"

She held up her glass. "To us."

"To us," he said, clinking his glass against hers. He leaned over and sealed the toast with a kiss.

"I've been doing most of the talking, Aaron what about you? Do you have anything you want to share?"

He coughed and took a sip of his drink to clear his throat.

"Are you okay?" She asked.

"Yes. I'm fine. You asked if there's anything I

want to share. As a matter of fact, there is. He took a deep breath. "I've been struggling with gambling." He waited for her facial expression to change or her eyes that once glowed to become dim—something that would tell him she was displeased with this new information.

The corner of her lips curved up. "Okay. You want to..... elaborate more?" She paused. "Can you give me more details—like what kind of gambling?

He shook his head in agreement. "Yeah. I better." Aaron gave her the backstory to his struggle, when it started, how it progressed over the years and how he's getting help from his pastor. Simone was the second person that now knew about his secret.

She brushed her lips against his. "Thank you for telling me. I know that was hard to admit. I'd prefer you to tell me now than I find out later. You've owned up to your wrong and I'm proud of you for getting the help you need."

He chuckled. "You needed to know that I'm not perfect and I do have my flaws but I'm working on me. So now you still ready to try this thing called love?"

Simone smiled. "Yes I am."

"Good. I'm glad to hear that. So, do you have any plans for next Saturday?" Aaron inquired.

"Um, next Saturday? No, I don't. Why?"

"Jill Scott is performing at Yoshi's. I thought

that if you didn't have plans, you might like to go. That is, if you like Jill Scott."

Her eyes lit up when he mentioned Jill Scott. She grinned from ear to ear, as if she'd won the lottery. "Oh my, really? Jill Scott?" Simone nodded her head. "I love Jill. I'd love to see her. What time is the show?"

"Show starts at seven, but if it's okay with you, I thought we'd have dinner first."

"Oh, yes. That's perfectly fine with me. I haven't seen Jill in years and I can't remember the last time I've been to Yoshi's." She shifted to a more comfortable position. "Now, you ready for me to kick your butt in spades?" Winking her eye, she gave him a heartwarming smile.

He laughed and nodded his head. "I'm ready to teach you a lesson or two."

Chapter 27

Later that night, when Aaron arrived home, he and Simone talked for another few hours. He sank into bed and pulled up the covers. His mind traveled back to dinner, their conversation, and the wonderful evening he'd had with her.

But were they moving too fast? They were spending a lot of time together, and although their relationship was just developing, he knew he was already becoming attached. Could it possibly be the fact that he hadn't been in a genuine relationship in so long? Whatever it was, it scared him.

Unbeknownst to her, she occupied his thoughts. He'd chosen her over his poker night with the fellas, and had even considered settling down. *Unbelievable. Undeniable.* He hadn't been looking to be in a relationship. He'd been content with his life the way it was. Plus, he had his own

Goliath to conquer. For whatever reason, that hadn't mattered to him before—dating someone and dealing with his problem at the same time—but now, Aaron wanted to deal with the gambling. He needed to be a better man for Simone. *A whole man. I can do bad all by myself.*

He had buried himself in work and everything else that could occupy his time. Then she came along. That first touch at the elevator, the first time he laid eyes on her... he couldn't put the brakes on even if he wanted to. His mind needed to catch up to what his heart had already done.

He pondered everything that could go wrong. If things didn't work out, how would it affect their working relationship? Would she eventually turn out like Macy? Could he stand to see her every day, knowing he couldn't hold her, kiss her, or even talk about their future? Could he handle that?

She hadn't given him any reason to be cautious. In fact, the little things she did only enthralled him more. He loved the way she tucked her hair behind her ear. The way her eyes sparkled when she talked about something she enjoyed. Her sultry voice.

Man, you trippin'.

Shaun was always telling him he had trust issues. Aaron had to be true to himself and admit Shaun was right. He shook his head at the thoughts running through his mind. Why was he second-guessing himself? He didn't need to guard his heart from Simone. He'd already given it to her. There wasn't anything he could do about it.

He turned over, reached for his phone on the nightstand, and flipped through the selfies they had taken at dinner.

His lips curled into a smile. Her beautiful brown eyes reminded him all too well why he wasn't able to get her out of his mind. He would push aside all the fear and doubt and embrace the possibility that Simone was a perfect fit for him. And if things worked out with him and Simone, his mother would be happy. He'd be able to give her the grandkids she wanted and the daughter-in-law she'd been praying for.

Simone entered her bedroom. To ward off the chill, she flipped the switch on the automatic fireplace. She slipped into her silky grey satin pajamas and crawled under her duvet. It was the end of a perfect evening, and hopefully, the beginning of many more days with Aaron. She thought about how her day had begun, the flowers from a man who could easily sweep her off her feet. Caring, considerate, and thoughtful; those were the qualities she most admired about Aaron Blackman.

Simone grabbed her phone from the nightstand, checked the time, and called Kendra. If she called now, she might catch her before she went to sleep.

Simone activated the speaker button. "Hey, sis. What you doing?" Simone said to Kendra.

"Hey there. Well, considering the hour, I'm about to go to sleep. So if I start slurring my words, you know why."

They shared a laugh. "Oops. My bad. We can talk tomorrow."

"Girl, quit trippin'. How you doing?"

Upbeat, Simone replied, "I'm doing so well."

"Sissy, I hear your joy. Do tell. How was your evening with Aaron?"

"Thought you'd never ask. It was amazing... first, he sent me three dozen roses. The sight of them took my breath away. I have to give it to him; he sure knows how to win cool points. We ate, and might I add, we ate good."

"Stoooop it. Did you say three dozen roses?"

"Yesss, girl. Three dozen. And the food was good. I must say, I killed it."

They giggled. "That's awesome. I'm so glad you're happy. You deserve it. Everything seems to have fallen into place. Your job, your house, and now, you have a man."

"I guess I forgot to mention it... that night at the Christmas party I told Aaron about Joshua and the significance of my necklace."

Silence traveled over the phone line. Kendra said, "Really? So soon? How did he respond?"

Simone repositioned herself across the bed. "Well, the door opened when he asked about it. Of course he was surprised about what happened. He questioned if I was really ready for a relationship and if I still loved Joshua."

"Hmmm. Why do you think he asked that?"

"I guess as a precaution. It was a question we both needed to answer. We've both had relationships that haven't turned out the way we planned."

"I do remember the scene in Las Vegas with his ex and what he said about not getting involved with anyone at work. I can only imagine how it was at his job." A few seconds passed before Kendra spoke. "But sissy, your situation is so much different. What you've experienced takes time to heal. You went through a lot."

"Yeah, that's true. We're going to take it slow and see where it goes."

Kendra giggled. "Take it slow. Really? I seriously doubt sending three dozen roses is taking it slow. And y'all been spending every waking moment together. Slow? Please. Tell that to somebody else."

Simone laughed at the comment. "Aww, girl. Don't hate. Celebrate."

"Whatever." Kendra yawned.

"Well, sis, let me let you go. We'll talk tomorrow."

She yawned again. "Okay. Sounds good. I feel myself slowly shutting down."

"Oh wait! I almost forgot. Shaun asked about you."

Kendra came back to life like she'd been injected with a jolt of electricity. "Wait. You wait until I'm near snoring on the phone to tell me that?"

Simone cracked up. "Girlfriend, I thought that would give you another burst of energy."

"You so wrong. But anyways, Shaun asked about me? When? What did he say?"

"Wow." Simone smiled. "When did he ask? Yesterday. 'How is Kendra?'"

"Oooohh, it's like that? If I wasn't so sleepy, I would keep probing, but we'll definitely discuss this again."

"Sounds good. Good night, sis."

They ended the call. Simone thought about what Kendra had said. She agreed about needing time to heal; her pastor's counseling had helped her with that.

But in all honesty, Simone was plain scared to love again. Allowing another man to come and invade the place Joshua used to occupy was difficult for her to accept. She'd built a wall to protect her heart, the one thing she could control. Her pastor told her she had to eventually find a way to face her fears, conquer her challenges, and accept that it was okay to move forward.

That day was finally here. Simone realized it was okay to be happy, to live and love again. She welcomed the possibilities of sharing her future with Aaron Blackman.

She smiled at the thought that the Bay Area's most eligible bachelor was no longer on the market. He was all hers. Life was good.

Chapter 28

Aaron was on cloud nine. He'd had dinner last night with the most beautiful, caring, trustworthy woman in the world, who could throw down in the kitchen to boot. Clients were signing contracts, projects were moving right along, and property was becoming available for purchase.

His counseling sessions with Pastor Williams were going well. Aaron felt stronger each time they met. Pastor Williams was correct. The sessions, scriptures, and prayers had made a major difference in Aaron overcoming his problems with gambling. Because Pastor Williams felt Aaron was doing well from counseling, he'd switched their biweekly sessions to check-in calls.

Since Aaron and Simone had officially become a couple, he was sure Holly would've been the first to gossip, but surprisingly, she hadn't. Aaron was positive Macy knew all her hopes of getting him back were completely shattered. And Lamont... all Aaron could say was, "Bye, Lamont."

He stepped off the elevator, all smiles.

"Good morning, Aaron," Holly said as he approached her desk. "Mr. Kane is waiting for you in the sitting area."

Aaron frowned. He glanced over in the direction of the sitting area. Mr. Kane was reading a magazine.

He turned back to Holly. "Does he have an appointment?"

Holly checked the calendar. "No, sir. I don't see him on your calendar."

Aaron sighed heavily. A client coming in without an appointment was never a good sign. He skimmed through the other messages Holly had given him. "Please check my calendar and see when my next appointment is."

Holly scanned his calendar. "Your next appointment isn't until after lunch."

He rolled his eyes. "Okay."

"What would you like me to tell Mr. Kane?"

Another moment passed before he spoke. "Nothing. Have him sit and wait. Give me ten minutes. Pull the Nevali file and bring it with you when you escort him in."

"Yes, sir. Will do."

"Good morning," Simone said as she walked into the office.

A smile played across Aaron's face.

Simone and Holly's eyes met. "Good morning," Holly replied.

He nodded. "Good morning."

Simone smiled and returned the gesture.

Aaron was about to head to his office, but Mr. Kane saw him standing at the desk. The man tossed the magazine onto the table and rose to his feet. With determined steps, he hurried to meet Aaron. He came to an abrupt stop when Aaron turned around and faced him.

"Hey, Aaron. Perfect timing. Did your receptionist tell you I was here?"

Aaron greeted him with a handshake. "How are you, Mr. Kane? Yes, she did. I was about to have her bring you into my office."

"Can't keep a billionaire waiting, can you, Blackman? I got money to make." Mr. Kane trailed Aaron down the hallway to his office.

"Would you like anything to drink?" Aaron asked.

"No, thank you."

Mr. Kane took a seat in front of Aaron's desk and crossed his legs. Aaron removed his coat and hat and hung them on the coatrack. He placed his briefcase on his desk and sat in his leather chair.

Aaron cleared his throat. "Mr. Kane, what brings you in today?"

"Aaron, we have a problem." He sighed. "I'm putting a lot of money on the table for this project, and the last thing I need," he paused to catch his breath, "is for it not to go according to my specifications."

Aaron's body tensed. *Oh, here we go.* His eyes widened, but he kept his voice steady. He leaned forward. "What kind of problem are we talking about?"

Mr. Kane reached inside his attaché case and pulled out a set of blueprints. "These right here. These aren't the designs I agreed upon. I don't think they even belong to me." He handed Aaron the blueprints and showed him the difference between the drafted plans and the ones he'd received.

Aaron gawked at him. The pompous man was dressed like Mr. Brown from a Tyler Perry play, talking to him like he pulled the strings and called the shots. Aaron glanced at the blueprints. In his most professional voice, he said, "Mr. Kane, let me have my design team take a look. I'm sure it's a minor mistake. It will be corrected immediately. Let me assure you that your investment is secure. We are doing our utmost to keep this project free of any unnecessary mistakes, delays, or errors—within our control, of course."

Mr. Kane twisted in his seat. "I sure hope so. I hope this doesn't happen again. I don't want to think I hired the wrong firm to do this project."

A knot formed in Aaron's stomach. "Is there anything else you wanted to discuss?"

"No. That was my concern. By the way, I have my accountant looking over the financials."

"No problem. When I get the corrected blueprints, I'll send them over to you, Federal Express."

"Sounds good." Mr. Kane hoisted himself from the chair, shook Aaron's hand, and hurried out of the office.

Aaron slammed his palms against his desk. He hated feeling like he was being dangled around because of money, especially when there was nothing he could do about it.

After Mr. Kane left, Aaron instructed Holly to call a meeting with the entire department. He didn't know which was hotter, the temperature in the conference room or the heat coming from his body. He knew he had to compose himself before everyone assembled. Tense, he sat at the head of the conference table, hands folded, waiting patiently for everyone to enter. Once they all arrived and were seated, the meeting began.

"Okay, everyone, I know this is an impromptu meeting and we all have plenty of work to do, so it won't be long. We know how important the Nevali project is to the firm, and how, we as a firm, strive to do our best, making sure our clients are happy." Confused expressions all around confirmed no one had any idea what Aaron was talking about, or where he was going.

"I had a visit from Mr. Kane." He cleared his throat. "Our client for the Nevali project. He chewed me out. The man questioned our ability to get the smallest things accurate. For instance, someone sent him another client's drawings. Sending out the wrong designs to such a high-profile client—to any client—is not good."

There was a heavy sigh in the air.

"To us, that might be small and trivial. To Mr. Kane, it shows our lack of attentiveness. We can't afford to be careless with our jobs. The last thing I need is for Mr. Kane to come back in this office and question if he picked the right law firm or not."

He sighed. "I want to be fair-handed, but I will not accept mediocrity from any of you. Careless mistakes could cost us money and I can't have that. I'd hate to lose anyone over something so trivial. Remember my no-excuses policy?"

Everybody nodded in agreement. Well, everyone except Simone. Her eyes widened. She hadn't heard about her boss's no-excuses policy before.

Aaron studied Simone's facial expression. She was thorough, detail-oriented, focused, ambitious, and could handle any task assigned—a jewel. She was what the firm needed. She was what *he* needed.

When Aaron had pretty much given up on any genuine relationship, she'd popped right in. Perfect timing. She had done something to him no other woman had—stolen his heart and had him considering marriage. She was the kind of woman his mother would love to call 'daughter.' The kind of woman he'd love to have his children. His lips curled into a smile just thinking about it.

Shaun took over. "If there aren't any questions, I believe we're done. We'll keep you posted on our progress." As people left the room, he eyeballed Aaron. "It must have been a really good dream. Were you on some secluded island or something?"

"What you talking about, bro? My mind was on the project."

"Um. Really? You were daydreaming. Your mind left the project ten minutes ago. Let me guess—was it about the woman with the black suit and the white blouse, who was sitting right in front of you in the meeting? The one who makes your eyes sparkle every time you look at her? I guess I would be like that, too, if I was in love."

Aaron jerked his head and raised his eyebrows. "In love? Ain't nobody said nothing about being in love." *It's too soon to be in love. Nah. It ain't so.*

"You don't have to say a word. The billboard you're wearing says... 'I'm in love with Simone.'" Shaun laughed so hard he cried.

"You got jokes, huh? I don't have time for your jokes. Besides, we have work to do." Aaron shook his head. "This meeting is adjourned."

Shaun retorted, "And I rest my case."

They looked at each other and broke out into laughter. Aaron sat at his desk and pondered what Shaun had said. He couldn't be in love with a woman he barely knew. Nope, it was too soon.

Daydreaming was just that; an insubstantial fantasy, an idle contemplation.

His cell phone beeped. Simone had sent a text. *Hi. Thinking about you.*

Aaron smiled. He leaned back in his chair and texted back. *Thinking about you, too.* "This is why I can't get no work done."

Chapter 29

Simone couldn't contain her excitement. She'd been waiting all week for their date. Aaron stood at the door, dressed in a dark blue suit and an open-collared light blue shirt. Hair freshly cut low, he looked like he'd just finished a photo shoot with GQ magazine.

Her breath caught. *Oh my, what a gorgeous creature.* "Hi. Come on in. You look good."

He smiled. "Hey, love." Aaron bent to kiss her on the cheek. "You look stunning. How are you?"

"I'm fine."

"Yes, you are, baby. Yes, you are," he continued with a wink. "Ready for a night at Yoshi's?"

"I am. Let me grab my coat and purse, and we can go. I'm starving."

Aaron helped Simone into her seat, shut the door, and got behind the wheel. They listened to

Anthony Hamilton's latest CD, their heads bobbing in sync with the music as they sang along. When they didn't know the words, they made them up. Twisting in their seats, they faced each other and laughed.

'What I'm Feeling' came on. Instead of singing the words, they listened. From Simone's peripheral view, she could see Aaron glance in her direction, not saying a word.

The song mentioned love. She wasn't sure if he was feeling it, but she sure was. *No, Simone, way too soon for that.* She forced the thought away, but it didn't take long for other thoughts to fill her head. *Remember... Aaron might leave you, too.*

She turned toward him. "Aaron, I didn't know you could sing."

He looked at her for a brief second. "I can't sing. I'm frontin'." They shared a laugh.

As they walked into Yoshi's, they scanned the restaurant. By the looks of the crowd, Aaron was glad he'd made reservations. In the heart of downtown Oakland, Yoshi's was a place for the young and old. Close to the beautiful waters of the Pacific, it was the ideal spot for those who loved all things jazz. Several of Aaron's friends and business associates approached them. He greeted them all and introduced Simone.

The hostess greeted them and led them to their table. Women's heads turned in their direction. Some shot envious glances at Simone; others admired the delightful piece of chocolate who had his fingers tightly intertwined in hers.

Before they claimed their seats, Aaron found great pleasure in watching the heads of women turn away when he brushed his lips against Simone's. "That's for all the haters."

The hostess handed them the menus and told them what the specials were. The waitress, a young red-haired woman, brought some water with lemon wedges and placed them on the table. She returned shortly and took their orders. They ordered sushi rolls for appetizers. Aaron chose the tiger shrimp tempura for an entrée, and Simone ordered grilled salmon.

She leaned forward. "Thank you."

A slow smile worked its way across his face into his eyes. He reached over the table and clasped her hand in his. "Thank me for what?"

The heat from his hands made her stomach flutter. "For bringing me here. I've been excited all week."

"This is only the beginning, my beautiful Simone. You deserve this and so much more."

A wave of strong emotions jolted through her body. While their meals were being prepared, they asked each other question after question. She chuckled. "We sound like a remake of *Think Like a Man*. Have you ever seen that movie?"

Aaron laughed. "Oh, my gosh. Steve Harvey did that for real."

Simone looked down. When she looked up, her expression was somber. "Aaron, why me? You have a catalogue full of women you could pick from."

He coughed to clear his throat. "Whoa. Well, my first thought is—why *not* you? But I can tell this is important to you, and since you've asked a two-part question, I'll answer it in two parts. Why you? Well, Simone. I won't lie. The first thing that caught my attention was your beauty." He took a breath. "You are beautiful; however, the more we get to know one another, there are other qualities that draw me to you. You're intelligent, and you have this confidence about yourself that's quite appealing. You're fun to be with, and I enjoy spending time with you."

He leaned in. "Now, to answer your next question. Contrary to what you think, I don't have a catalogue full of women. I try to be very selective with the women I date." He paused. "With the exception of what's her name...."

Simone filled in the gap. "Macy."

"Yeah, her. I totally missed it on that one. But in all honesty, I picked you because... I wanted to. Plain and simple. You're who I want to date. Now, does that answer your question?"

Simone took in a deep breath and smiled. "Yes, it does. Thank you."

"Now, on a lighter note, have you ever been sailing?"

"Sailing. No, I haven't. I don't even know anyone who has a boat."

"Well, now you do. I have a small boat on the pier. When the weather gets better, I'd love to take you out on the water." He sipped his water. "You not afraid of the water, are you?"

Her eyes widened. "Oh, no. As long as I'm on the boat and not in the water, I'm cool."

They laughed. "Not a swimmer, huh?"

"Nope. Never learned."

He grinned. "Umm. Well, maybe I can teach you one day."

From the look in his eyes, she knew he was serious. Once again, he was drawing her in.

She lifted up her glass and took a sip of water before answering. "Oh, and how you plan on doing that?"

He kept his smile wide. "I have a swimming pool at my house, and if you want to shoot some pool, I have a game room, too. So we have plenty of things to do to occupy our time together." His eyes twinkled.

She smiled. "I have a swimming pool, also."

"Wait. You bought a house with a pool, and you don't know how to swim?"

"Yeah. That about sums it up."

He grinned. "Well, there are two options. I can come over to your house and teach you, or you can come over to mine."

"We shall see." She blushed, lowering her eyes.

A few minutes later, the waitress arrived with the appetizer. They bowed their heads, and Aaron blessed the food. All during dinner, he studied her. He only had eyes and ears for her. Every time they stared at one another, his face broke out into a smile. He tried hard to tame his feelings, but it seemed like they had a mind and will of their own. He yearned to be part of this woman, to be everything to her and for her. He had no doubt he could make her happy.

The more time he spent with her, the more he realized how much they had in common. They were both health enthusiasts, loved traveling, loved sports, and had a spiritual connection. For the first time in a long time, he was feeling alive and happy.

Aaron checked his watch. They only had about fifteen minutes before the show. He signaled for the waitress and paid the check. Aaron stood and walked over to Simone's side, assisting her with her chair. He moved in close behind her as she stood to her feet. Aaron wrapped his arms around her waist, closed the distance, and nipped at her neck.

She gasped.

He whispered in her ear, "I couldn't help myself. It was too tempting to pass up." His smoky voice sent shivers down her spine.

Aaron placed his hand at the small of her back and led her into the show. The greeter escorted them to their front row seats. Aaron pulled out her chair, then sat next to her. Under the table, they held hands tightly.

When the room darkened, the voice of the emcee resonated through the mic. "Good evening and welcome, everyone. You're in for a treat. This is a perfect night for the sweet sounds of jazz coming from none other than the sultry, talented Jill Scott. So, sit back. Relax. You are in for a dynamic evening. Without further ado, I present to you... Jill Scott!"

The audience went wild. Jill came on the stage. "Hello, Oakland." She paused. "How's my Oakland family?"

A fan hollered back. "We doing good, since you here!"

Someone else hollered out, "We love you, Jill!"

She smiled. "I love you, too."

They stood, danced, sang, and clapped as she performed. Before Simone knew it, the two-hour show was over. It went by faster than she had expected, but Simone couldn't have asked for a more perfect evening.

Aaron didn't want the evening to end. "Would you like to take a walk at the pier? If it gets too chilly, we can leave. Can your feet handle it?"

"You're a joker, too, I see." She punched him playfully on the arm. "Thanks for reminding me about that foot massage you still owe me." She inhaled a cleansing breath. "I'd love to take a walk with you, Aaron."

He linked his fingers through hers as they walked across the street to take a stroll on the pier. The night air was perfect; her small jacket sufficed in keeping her warm.

They stopped walking once they found an empty spot. It was a clear night, no clouds in the sky. Captured by the beautiful, majestic stars that twinkled and filled the space above them, they were silent as they stared into the sky.

"Amazing. It's beautiful, isn't it?" He pulled her close, wrapped his arms around her waist and kissed her softly on the cheek. "I've been enjoying your company. Spending time with you tonight has been such a great pleasure."

His beautiful brown eyes held warmth and knowledge. They sparked her curiosity and a longing to know him better. What other mysteries did this man hold? "I feel the same. This has been a perfect evening."

Aaron moved in front of her and pushed her hair behind her ears. He cradled her soft face in his hands. Her pulse quickened as he drew her into his arms. "I wish it didn't have to end."

She whispered, "We have forever."

He quickly lowered his head. His lips touched hers. He intended it to be a short kiss, but it didn't work out that way. She stole his breath when she wrapped her arms around his waist and refused to let go.

Once they eased out of the embrace, he kissed her on the forehead. "You make me lose all sense of reason when I'm with you."

Shaun was right. In a short amount of time, she had made an impact on his life. If someone had told him six months ago he'd be in this position now, he'd have laughed in their face. He knew at times she still struggled with the memories of her past, but he was willing to do whatever it took to make the relationship work. She'd said they had forever, and all he had was time on his side. She was worth every minute. He was truly living a blessed life.

Simone was exactly what Aaron needed.

Chapter 30

Aaron stepped out of the shower and dressed. He grabbed his things and backed out of the garage to work. He listened to one of his pastor's messages on Romans 8:28.

He drove down the highway, listening to the message and saying his amens. Pastor Williams's messages were always on point and on time. He remembered how messed up his life had been with the gambling and the drama with Macy. That scripture had changed his life dramatically. His business was prospering, he was growing spiritually, and God had blessed him with a great woman who genuinely cared about him; not for what she could get out of him, but for the person he really was.

She gets me. They could talk for hours. He had already shared his own personal struggles of gambling with her. Aaron had grown to trust her and care for her. Maybe he was even growing to love her.

He hadn't been this cheerful in quite some time.

His cell phone rang and interrupted his muse. He clicked the phone icon on the steering wheel.

"Hello."

"Aaron, good morning. This is Holly."

"Good morning. What's up?" He couldn't imagine why Holly was calling, knowing he was on his way into work. He didn't have anything pressing on his calendar or any clients coming into the office until later that afternoon.

She muttered, "Aaron, Mr. Kane is here to see you. He keeps coming to my desk, asking when you will be arriving. If he keeps pacing back and forth on that carpet in the sitting area like he's doing right now, we might have to bill him for new carpet."

Aaron rolled his eyes. *What is it now?* "Okay. Tell Mr. Kane I'll be there within the next fifteen minutes." He paused. "Holly, pull the file."

With a heavy sigh, he ended the call. He drove the rest of the way to work praying, *Lord, my morning cannot start like this.* He had an unnerving feeling about the meeting, but he didn't know why.

Fifteen minutes later, he pulled into the parking lot. He grabbed his briefcase from the passenger's seat and took the elevator up to his office. When the elevator doors opened, instead of seeing

Simone's beautiful face or being greeted by Holly, he was met by Mr. Kane, who had fire in his eyes.

Aaron forced a smile. "Good morning, Mr. Kane."

"Aaron," Mr. Kane grunted.

Aaron instructed Holly to hold all his calls. From the look in Mr. Kane's eyes, Aaron could tell he hadn't come to pat him on the back. The back of Aaron's hair stood up as Mr. Kane trailed him into his office. *Why does it feel like I'm about to get a beat-down?*

"Come on in and have a seat." Aaron sat in his chair and observed Mr. Kane pacing back and forth.

"No, thank you. I'll stand." The man blew out a terse breath. "Blackman, I trusted you with this project. And this is how you repay me?" His voice was shrill, harsh.

Aaron was about to respond, but Mr. Kane held up a hand, silencing him. Aaron's eyes widened, but he remained calm.

"Were you trying to rip me off, or what?" He peered at Aaron and cleared his throat for the tenth time.

Aaron's jaw tightened. He was getting furious. There was a long moment of silence between them. Aaron quickly rose to his feet. He stood at least two inches over the man. With one punch, he could send the man into his next dream. Aaron gave him an exasperated look instead. "Mr. Kane, what do you mean, 'trying to rip you off'? Blackman and Blackman is a reputable organization, and I take offense. I would strongly recommend you explain your statement."

Mr. Kane tossed the financial reports on Aaron's desk. "Gladly. Those are the financials we received in my office. My accountant looked them over and informed me that the bottom line is over the original budget by four million dollars."

Aaron frowned. "That can't be correct. I looked over the reports myself and verified the amounts before they were sent to you. There must be some logical explanation." Aaron shook his head. He felt like a scratched record. The last time Mr. Kane was in the office, Aaron had given him the same response. His heart rate increased as he glanced over the report. "I need time to look this over and see where the mistake is."

"Don't bother, Blackman. Time is money, and mistakes like this are costing me." He paused to take a breath. "I've decided to take my project to LW Associates instead. I hear Lamont is one of the best in the Bay Area, also."

Aaron's face tightened. "Mr. Kane, give me until later today to see what happened. I'm sure the mistake will be corrected."

"Blackman, you sound like a broken record."

Aaron's anger rose several notches. His level of tolerance diminished. "Mr. Kane, do I need to remind you that we have a signed contract?"

"No, you don't need to remind me at all. Sue me then, Blackman." He turned and walked out of the office, slamming the door behind him.

Aaron collapsed in his chair. *What happened?* He was in disbelief. *Did he say he was giving the project to Lamont Willis?* He leaned back in his chair and loosened his tie. *One of the biggest projects of my career slipped out of my hands... because of a mistake.*

All the time and long hours wasted, not to mention the money the firm was planning on making. He sighed heavily as he stared, bewildered. He sat in confusion, replaying the last few minutes in his head. The more he thought about it, the more annoyed he got. *Why does Lamont Willis's name keep popping up?*

Lamont was his archenemy—professionally and personally. Out of all the real estate developers in the Bay Area, Mr. Kane had selected him. *Why?* Aaron pounded his fist on the table. The man was a scumbag and a cheat. *How did he manage to steal this project away from me?*

Aaron thought about the last time he'd seen Lamont. *How could I forget? He came to pick up Simone for lunch.* He remembered the smirk on Lamont's face. A twinge of irritation crawled over Aaron's skin.

Aaron and Simone had looked over the financials together. They were all in order. Everything was correct. So, what happened between Simone leaving his office and Mr. Kane receiving the package? Something wasn't right. It didn't add up. Could she have bungled the reports? But why? *No. Aaron. She's too meticulous. She would have never made that kind of mistake.*

His mind traveled to the times all three of their paths had crossed. Lunch at Le Cheval. *Maybe that would explain her nervousness that day.* The conference in Las Vegas. He'd seen them talking. Lamont came to the office to pick her up for lunch. The roses—she'd never divulged their sender. *I'd bet good money they were from Lamont.*

It was obvious Lamont was attracted to her, but she'd led Aaron to believe she wasn't interested in Lamont.

Knowing Lamont, he'd use anybody to vex Aaron, including Simone. *Aaron, you've lost your mind.*

Hmm, have I? Could they be working together? If they were, she was really good at fooling him. He felt a tightening in the pit of his stomach. His skin crawled.

His eyes flew to their picture on his phone. The selfies they had taken at Yoshi's. His feelings were all over the place. One moment, he dismissed the thoughts of her and Lamont conspiring together. The next, he pondered the possibility.

Nah. Not Simone.

He was emotional, but he had to know the truth.

Aaron marched into Simone's office and threw

open the door. She jumped in her seat as he slammed it shut. She spun in his direction, and he stared her down with dark, piercing eyes. "We need to talk."

Simone's head jerked at the sound of his voice. Something was noticeably wrong with him. Shocked by his behavior, her brows lifted. "Excuse me. Are you alright? What's wrong with you?"

Aaron walked toward her desk, he stood and stared at her. "No, I'm not alright. I had a visit from Mr. Kane."

Her eyes narrowed. "Okay, but why are you coming in my office, slamming the door, and raising your voice at me? What did Mr. Kane do that has you all ready to explode on me?"

"He showed me the financials that you sent to him. The figures were manipulated. Can you explain that?"

Her mouth dropped open. She couldn't believe what she'd heard. Simone came from behind her desk and stood directly in front of him. "Let me get this straight. Are you accusing me of manipulating the figures?" She folded her arms across her chest waiting on his response.

"Well, you were the last person to have the file."

"Aaron, there has to be a mistake. Let me take a look at it again. I can show you."

His nostrils flared. "No. It's too late. Why did you go behind my back and alter the figures?"

She frowned. "Aaron, I have no idea what

you're talking about. Think about it. Why would I do that?"

He eyed her skeptically. "That's the problem. I have thought about it."

"Aaron, what's gotten into you?" She held her hand up to silence him. "Never mind. I think you should stop right there before you say something you'll regret."

He moved closer to her. "Come clean, Simone. Are you working for Lamont? Did he recruit you to sabotage the project? To ruin my life?" His once beautiful dark eyes had turned hard and cold. "I thought you were different."

The way he was studying her cut her to the core. Inside, she was shaken. "What is that supposed to mean?" Simone stared at him. "Aaron, this is ridiculous. And what you're saying is so foul. I don't appreciate your tone." She paused. "And, no. I'm not working with Lamont. How could you even think I would do such a thing? What have I ever done to make you think that low of me? I'm Simone... not Macy."

How could he believe the worst about her? She cared for him, had opened her heart to him. Was ready to love again—and now his words had shattered her heart into pieces. She was crushed.

She'd had enough of his accusations, his stubbornness. She knew him well enough to be sure that once he made up his mind about something, nothing she could say would change it.

She made an attempt to leave, but he blocked her path.

"Your assignment is finished. You're done here. You can leave now. You've accomplished what you were sent to do." His pulse revved up like a race car at the Indy 500. "You're fired."

Simone could no longer hold back her tears. The man who'd once wiped her tears away, was now the man responsible for causing them to flow like a river. The anger behind his words sliced her in half.

He'd made himself quite clear when he managed to end their relationship and fire her all on the same day. All in one sentence. She looked at him through a cloud of tears.

His cold eyes stayed glued to her as she began to pack her things. He stopped her before she could finish. "You can leave. I'll have Holly send them to you. Go. Please."

She shut her eyes for a brief second. She hoped it would all be a dream when she opened them. This could not be happening to her, not after everything she'd gone through to get to this point. She opened her eyes, stunned.

His smile was gone. His eyes had darkened; no hint of infatuation remained. This time, when she attempted to leave, he moved and let her by.

Despite the anger and hurt, she remained calm. Simone grabbed her purse. She headed toward the door to the lobby and turned back to him. "Aaron, you were right about one thing. I am different from Macy. You won't find me trying to get you back." She paused. "And after you realize your mistake, don't even *think* about calling me."

Her candid words fell on a stony heart. She turned and walked away. She could feel him staring at her, but he was the one who called the shots.

Out of his eyesight, she leaned against the wall, reached inside her purse, pulled out some tissue, and blotted away the tears. Inside, she was a nervous wreck. The once short walk down the corridor felt like a track field. Her knees wobbled as she hurried toward the elevator. She hit the down button, ignoring Holly's voice calling out her name. Once the elevator doors swung open, she entered and turned around, catching Aaron's eye for the last time.

Chapter 31

Aaron racked up the pool balls for the third time. He lined the pool tip with the cue ball and smashed it forward. Aaron tried unsuccessfully to force every thought of Simone away. His thoughts always led back to her. The tears in her eyes eroded the tablet of his heart.

"I don't even have to ask what's wrong with you," Shaun said.

"There's nothing wrong with me. I'm letting out a little tension."

Shaun took his turn. "I wonder why."

Aaron gave his brother an icy stare. "Go ahead and say what you want to say, even though I told you to stay out of my business."

Shaun dismissed his brother's request. "Okay. I'll say what I want to say. Man, you wrong about

Simone. She has to be innocent. Didn't you once say everything is fixable?"

Aaron gave Shaun a stern look. "Yeah, but there is always something that can't be fixed, and this is it." He took a deep breath. "We lost a big contract because of her."

Shaun took a swig of his drink. "Brother, you lost more than that. You lost a great woman that cared about you, adored you. I'm sure she was falling in love with you. I know you feel the same about her."

Aaron rolled his eyes. "A woman who played me."

"I reject that statement. That's where you're wrong, counselor. You made assumptions about a situation that you have absolutely no facts to support."

Aaron took a sip of his drink. He studied his next play on the pool table and took his turn. "Don't need any facts. The handwriting was on the wall."

"The only handwriting I see on the wall are the words 'Aaron messed up... big time. Aaron pushed a good woman out of his life. Aaron's a complete fool. Aaron's—'"

"Watch it, brother," he cautioned.

"You said yourself you didn't give her a chance to explain. Maybe she does have—"

"A good explanation?" Aaron completed Shaun's sentence.

Shaun nodded. "Yeah. You should have heard her out. This is one case you have definitely lost, and I will not defend you."

Aaron's nostrils flared. "Are you done?"

"No. I'm not done. So, you do admit you were falling in love with her?"

Aaron positioned himself across the pool table, aimed at one of the balls and took another turn. He took a moment before answering the question. "Nah. I wasn't."

Shaun laughed hysterically and shot him a look. "Yes, you were. Let me correct myself. You're in love with her. That's why this is bothering you so much. If you didn't love her, you wouldn't be acting like this. Maybe it's your guilt kicking in."

"I told you I'm letting out a little tension. Will you take your turn, please?"

"Hmmm. Call it tension if you want. You acting like a junkie needing a fix. Let me drop this on you and then I'll be finished. You gave Lamont full access to her again."

Aaron cringed. "When did you become an expert love therapist? Let's enjoy the game and not talk about my complicated love life. And, please. Don't mention Lamont's name."

Shaun lifted up his hands in defense. "The last time I checked, you don't have one and I rest my case."

Aaron scowled. "Good. Now, can we finish our game of pool?"

But Shaun was right. So what? Yeah, he loved her. More than he cared to admit. Trying to get Simone out of his mind was like trying to get the white out of milk. It was simply impossible. He wished even more that he could dismiss what Shaun had said, but he couldn't do that either. *You were wrong*, his conscience accused him. Maybe his guilt was kicking in. He had hurt her and scolded her in a matter of a few seconds.

Aaron mulled over the last words she'd said to him before she walked out of her office. "And after you realize your mistake, don't even *think* about calling me. You won't find me trying to get you back." *No problem. Fine, Lady Simone. I know I'm right.* How did she do it? Why pretend to care about him? How could something that felt so perfect turn out this way? He'd let his guard down. Once again, Aaron vowed not to allow another woman to soften his heart.

How could he be wrong? *Nah. I'm not.*

... But, what if I am?

She would never forgive him, especially for how he'd treated her. It was too late for him to be second-guessing himself now. So why was his stomach in knots and his head throbbing?

Exasperated, Aaron slammed his pool stick down on the table.

"You okay?"

He took a deep breath. "Nah, Shaun. I'm not okay." He walked out of the game room and headed to the nearest medicine cabinet to take two aspirins.

Simone had spent the last few days curled up in bed next to a box of Kleenex. It was so unlike her to lay around in her loungewear all day, but considering what had happened, she deserved it. She watched marathons of *Power*, *24* and anything else that would entertain her. Anything except shows that had to do with love.

She crawled out of bed, went to the bathtub, and turned on the water. The jets were what she needed. She pulled some lavender and chamomile bath gel from the cabinet and generously poured some into the hot running water. The blend of essential oils and natural ingredients would enhance her mood. It didn't take long for the fragrance to infuse the water. She slid right in and let the jets massage her body.

One hour later, she reluctantly removed herself from the comfort of the jets. In a better mood, she grabbed a novel and sat in her sitting area, reading to avoid her own thoughts.

Her mind replayed her last conversation with Aaron. She kept hearing herself say, "You won't find me trying to get you back." The look of shock on his face confirmed she had pierced his heart.

Good. Satisfied that she'd hurt him a little, it was enough for her to keep stepping.

"You're fired." *Really, Aaron Blackman? Whatever.* She tried to dismiss every memory of him. *Shoot. Go away, please.* Why could she not get him out of her system? Deleting him out of her phone contacts was easy. Tossing every picture of them in the trash—easy. Deleting every email and text—easy. But forgetting how he made her feel when he touched her, remembering his soft kisses, his powerful arms holding her, and his smile... she was boiling mad thinking about him.

She refused to shed any more tears, especially for a man who considered her the enemy. He had hurt her tremendously, crushed her heart, and sent her away in tears without even giving her the opportunity to fix things.

The pain of his words made her question her own decision to allow her heart to be open again. *Never again.*

When Simone shared with Kendra what happened between her and Aaron, she suggested Simone return to New York. Simone was eager to escape. She didn't want to chance running into Aaron around Oakland, or Lamont, either. The last thing she needed was for Lamont to get wind of her and

Aaron's breakup. She was done with them both. Simone scowled. "Men," she grunted.

A trip back to New York away from Aaron Blackman suited her fine. She wasn't tied down to anyone or any job now. She could come and go as she pleased, and that was exactly what she was going to do.

Her chest tightened as she fumed about the accusations Aaron had thrown at her. He was a liar. Obviously, he didn't care about her as much as he said he did. But when he discovered his error and tried to come back around—because he would—he could kick rocks, for all she cared.

Simone had been seething since she'd walked out of her office. She slammed the book down on her sofa. "So much for relaxing," she grumbled.

Disgusted, she sat back on the couch and stared at the ceiling. Anger swelled inside her all over again. "Your assignment is up," he'd said. How could she have given her heart to someone who so easily trampled on it? *No-excuse policy. What a joke.*

Her cell phone rang, breaking her from her reverie. "Hey, sis. How you doing?" Devon asked.

"I'm okay... finished up my last bit of packing earlier."

"Great. Anything you need me to do while you're gone? Hurt Aaron, perhaps?"

They laughed. "Do you mind going by my office—" she sighed "—correction... to the Blackman and Blackman law firm... to pick up my personal items?"

"I gather you rushed out before you could pick up your stuff?"

Simone scoffed. "Well, not quite. Aaron hurried me out while I was packing and told me he would have Holly ship me my stuff. The nerve of him."

"Are you sure you want me to go? I'm liable to break his jaw for hurting you. Please give me permission to give kick his butt, sis."

"Devon...."

"I knew you wouldn't, but I had to give it a try. My heart breaks for you, sis. You've been through so much. Now, don't get me wrong. You're a survivor, so, I'm fully confident that when you return from New York, all will be well. For now, I'd like to use Aaron Blackman's face as a punching bag."

"No. I don't want to have to bail you out of jail." She laughed. "Besides, you need your hands for your dental practice. I'll email you the list of items to pick up. You'll need to call Aaron beforehand and tell him you're coming to gather my stuff."

"Okay. No problem. I can't wait to see his face."

She gave Devon the address and phone number to the office. "I wish I could be a fly on the wall. I'll give you my house keys when I see you tonight at Mom's. You can drop the box off while I'm gone."

"Sounds good. And don't worry. I'll take care of the house and everything else."

"Thank you."

Chapter 32

Aaron sat at his desk and stared out the window. He tried hard to concentrate on his work, but his thoughts kept drifting back to Simone. How was she doing? Was she throwing darts at his pictures? Had she already tossed them in the garbage? *Probably*. He wondered where she was.

He rubbed the back of his neck. His head was still throbbing. Maybe, it was because Devon was coming in shortly. He'd called and announced that he was dropping by to pick up Simone's personal things. Her brother was a few inches taller than Aaron and about fifteen pounds heavier, and he appeared to be all muscle. Aaron could only imagine how angry he must be at him for hurting his sister. He thought about calling security, but that would probably irritate Devon even more.

He prayed her brother would get her belongings and quietly leave, but he really didn't believe that was going to happen. He had so much nervous energy.

Many times, he'd picked up his cell phone and looked at her number. He'd been tempted to call to hear her soft voice, but he could never go through with it. He wondered if she even thought about him. Probably not, after what he'd done. As much as he hated to admit when Shaun was right, he couldn't deny the fact that his actions had opened the door for Lamont to step back into her life. Jealousy surged inside him as he pictured Lamont touching her. Aaron nearly gagged.

He hoisted himself up from his desk and decided to go into her office. He hadn't been in there since she left. There was no reason to. She was gone because of him. Holly had offered to pack up Simone's stuff and send it to her, but he told her no. It wasn't like he thought she was going to return. For some reason, he wasn't ready to remove her personal items.

As he crossed the threshold of her office, he realized that her sweet fragrance still lingered. His breath caught. It was the perfume he'd bought her—one of her favorites had soon become one of his. The air was clean and fresh, a mixture of jasmine, rose, and gillyflower. Her face popped in his head. She was the woman who had changed his life, who had gotten him to do what no other had.

He leaned his shoulder against the doorjamb

and took it all in. He canvassed the room. Nothing had been disturbed. Seeing her office released a floodgate of memories he'd have preferred to forget—memories that would stay bottled up in his heart.

Sensing the presence of someone behind him, Aaron spun around and met Devon's cold, unwavering stare. They continued to gaze at one another until Aaron broke the silence.

"Hey, Devon. How are you?" Aaron was going to offer a handshake, but reconsidered when he saw the anger in Devon's eyes. A knot formed in Aaron's stomach. He wished he had called security for backup... just in case.

"I'm good. I came to get Simone's stuff. I'm going to need a box."

"Yeah, sure. I'll bring you one." Aaron stepped aside and allowed Devon to enter her office. He went to the copy room to retrieve a box. When he returned, Devon was standing near Simone's desk.

"Here you go." Aaron handed him the box. He wanted so desperately to ask about Simone. He had to continue resisting the urge. "Let me know if you need anything. I'll go back to my office."

Devon peered at him. "Okay, but I'm sure I won't. Thanks anyway." He turned his back on Aaron, took out his list, and proceeded to check off everything as he put it in the box.

Hesitantly, Aaron sauntered back into his office to try to get his mind off the fact that

Simone's brother, who now hated him, had the answers to his most probing question. He glanced at the time and cringed. Devon would only be in the office a few more minutes.

"Enough of this," he said out loud.

The anticipation of not knowing how she was doing was killing Aaron. He didn't care if Devon tackled him, punched him, or put him in a choke-hold, he was going to ask. He hurried back into her office and stood in the doorway, watching Devon pack away her belongings. "How is she? How is Simone?"

A long silence filled the air. Aaron walked in and shut the door.

Devon turned around slowly and looked at him with a penetrating gaze. "Why do you want to know? If memory serves me correctly, you're the person that hurt her. Right?"

Aaron swallowed hard to get the lump out of his throat. The look Devon gave Aaron made him regret drawing his attention. Devon was correct. He *was* the reason for her pain. He was the reason Devon was standing in her office packing her personal belongings. But that didn't mean he'd stop caring about her.

"Yeah, I hurt her and—"

Devon raised his hand to stop him from continuing. "Ummm. I'm not the person you need to be confessing to. But, to answer your question..." He gave a dramatic pause. "Call her yourself and find out. I didn't come here to be probed about my sister. I will tell you this, though. I asked her if I could break your jaw, but she said no. Maybe that will give you some indication of how she's feeling."

Aaron's eyes widened. He felt like he'd been punched in the gut. He crossed his arms, realizing his error. "You're right, Devon, my bad. I'll call her myself."

"Yeah, right. Now, let me ask you a few questions. You down for that?"

Refusing to be intimidated by Devon's tone and size, Aaron nodded. "Yeah. Go ahead."

"Tell me how you could hurt her like that? I watched the two of you at the Christmas party. I saw how you two looked at one another. She hadn't smiled like that in years and you come along and crush her like that." Devon shook his head. "Men like you don't know when a good woman's right under your nose. You accused her of some crazy stuff. You know what, my sister don't need you or this job. You're a complete fool."

Why were Shaun's same words coming back to haunt him? Sweat dripped from his brow. "She loves you... well, I don't know about now. But she did."

She loved me? Aaron hadn't felt this low in years.

"Now, let me finish what I came here to do... before I..." He collected himself. "I only have a few more items to check off her list, and I'll be done."

"Sure." Aaron was mortified. At least she

didn't send Devon to the office to break his jaw or give him a black eye. *My sweet Simone would never do that. My Simone.*

If she's so sweet, how could you accuse her of treachery without giving her a chance to explain?

He heard her voice in his head. "When you discover your mistake, and you will, don't even bother calling me," she'd said. Nope, she was no longer his.

"All right, I'm all done," Devon said. He slipped the list back into his pocket and sealed up the box with tape.

Aaron walked over to the desk, looked around, and noticed a flash drive. He grabbed it off her desk. "Wait. Did you forget this? It belongs to Simone, right?"

Devon pulled out the piece of paper. "Nope, not on my list. I got everything on the list she asked for."

"Oh. Okay."

Devon picked up the box and started toward the door. He pulled the door open. "If you ever get back in the good graces of my sister… you'll have to get through me." With those words, he gave Aaron one last look and walked out. Thirty minutes later, relieved that he was still alive, Aaron sat at his desk, signing contracts, reading emails, and thanking God Devon had walked out of the office with only a box and not one of his teeth.

Curious, he grabbed the flash drive he'd taken from Simone's desk and inserted it into one of the

USB ports on his computer. A dialog box appeared. He clicked on the option folder to view the files. Every project she worked on had its own folder, including the Nevali project. He clicked on the folder and searched for the financial reports. He pulled up the report from the company's database and compared the two.

For the next few hours, Aaron busied himself comparing the figures line-by-line. He noticed that some figures had, in fact, been altered. Not only that, the dates of the reports were different. The date of the report from Simone's flash drive was the same as the date of his letter to Mr. Kane, but the date on the company's report which was queued from Holly's printer was the following day.

Maybe someone else within the organization had altered the figures and sent that report to Mr. Kane, in hopes that the project would be sabotaged and Simone would be blamed. But who? *Who could be that ratchet? That conniving?* Something twisted in his gut at the thought.

He moaned, "Oh no." Considering how small their office was and the number of staff members who had access to the files, it couldn't be anyone but... "Holly." Aaron slapped his palm against his forehead. "Of course. She and Macy are friends."

He let out a heavy sigh. Aaron rested his elbows on his desk and cupped his face in his hands. He stared at the evidence before him. He had accused Simone of working with Lamont and intentionally sabotaging his life and business. Aaron muttered, "What have I done? She'll never talk to me again."

Now he felt like the scumbag he'd accused Lamont of being. He had no idea how to fix this. For the second time today, her words haunted him. *Don't call me when you discover your mistake.*

He called Shaun into his office and showed him the information, including his idea about the possible person who may have been the mastermind behind the entire plan. They contacted IT, who provided them with a detailed report of the print jobs queued from Holly's computer on the day in question. It was confirmed that she did print out the report

They met with Holly, showed her the evidence and waited for her to respond.

Her voice broke, and a tear slid down her face. "I'm so sorry. I had no idea it would cost the firm the contract with Mr. Kane. When I realized it was wrong, I tried to retrieve the package, but it was too late; the mail had already gone out. I'm soooooo sorry."

Shaun handed her some Kleenex and asked, "But why would you do that? That's what we want to know."

Holly paused before speaking. "I let Macy talk me into it. I didn't know you were going to fire Simone. We just thought it would put a little tension in your relationship, and then Macy would have a better chance of getting you back"

Aaron rolled his eyes. "Well, Holly, looks like y'all's plan did a whole lot more than anticipated." He sighed. "You're fired."

"Don't you have something to do? Somebody to make up to?" Shaun said.

"Yes. I do."

Aaron grabbed his keys, hurried out of the building, and headed to Simone's.

Twenty minutes later, he stood on her porch ringing the doorbell. To his dismay, the person who answered the door was the man who'd wanted to break his jaw. *Lord, you have a sense of humor.*

Devon chuckled and gave him a half-smile. "Yes. Can I help you?"

Stuttering, Aaron said, "Hey, Devon. I'm looking for Simone."

"She's not here." His tone was as sharp as it had been at the office. His dark stare appeared more sinister.

"Okay. Look, man, I know I'm not your favorite person right now. But, I need to speak to Simone. She's not answering any of my calls."

"Well, well, well. I did say you would have to get through me, didn't I? I didn't think it was going to be so soon."

"Torture me all you want, Devon. I don't care. Kick my butt. I deserve it. But, I'm a man on a mission. I hurt your sister. I've got to talk to her. I need to see her. I need to make things right between us. If it's the last thing I do on earth. I have to find her and win her back...." Exasperated, he ran his hands over his hair. "Will you tell me where she is? Or... at least let her know I'm trying to reach her."

Devon crossed his arms. "Now why would I do that?"

Aaron inhaled deeply. "Because I love your sister and I know she loves me, too. Yes, my actions caused her pain, but I'm going to do whatever it takes to make it up to her."

Devon stared intensely at Aaron.

Aaron held his gaze.

After what felt like an eternity, Devon stepped away from the door and invited him in.

Devon interrogated Aaron about his intentions regarding Simone like a practiced attorney.

Finally, able to convince him that he really wanted to make amends and would cause his sister no further pain, Devon relented and told him Simone was in New York.

"She's in New York? I should have guessed," Aaron responded.

"Yep. New York."

Aaron paused. "Man, how am I going to find her in New York?"

Devon's eyes widened. "I have no idea. I'm not

giving you her info. I don't think she's going to be too happy when she finds out you looking for her."

Aaron nodded in agreement. "You might be correct, but that's not going to stop me from pursuing her. C'mon, man, I need your help. Please. Can you call her for me? I'm not leaving here until I speak with Simone."

After considering his options, he agreed to call Simone on Aaron's behalf.

"What do you want, Aaron?" Her tone was dry.

"Simone, how are you? It's so good to hear your voice."

Dead silence traveled over the phone.

"Simone, are you there?"

"Yeah, I'm here. I'm waiting on you to say something worth my time."

She was cold, but he wasn't going to let her tone discourage him. Somehow, he was going to break through. "Simone, I'm so sorry. I was wrong. Please allow me to fly to New York to see you. I need to talk to you. I don't want to have this conversation over the phone."

"I'm not sure that's a good idea."

"Simone... please. I'm begging. I know I'm asking you to do something I didn't give you the opportunity to do. But I need to make things right."

"Fine, Aaron. You can come."

Aaron let out a heavy sigh. "Thank you, Simone. I'll catch the first flight out to New York."

She gave him her address and the directions he needed to get to her place. He hurried and left her home, placed a call to his travel agent, and booked the next flight to New York.

Chapter 33

After finally getting through the horrendous New York traffic, Aaron pulled his rented car into the garage and parked in one of the available spots for visitors. He completely understood why everybody took the subway. The traffic was worse than the Bay Area.

He sat for a moment, inhaled deeply, then got out. He walked into the lobby and entered the elevator. His heart raced as he watched the number of each floor increase. When the elevator stopped on the seventh floor, the doors opened. He quickened his steps down the hall to her apartment. Aaron stood at the door, waited a few seconds, and finally rang the doorbell. His heart thumped twice as fast at the sound of the chain rattling and the door opening.

"Hi." Aaron stood with his hands stuffed deep

in his coat pockets, praying for himself, praying for them.

Taking a deep breath, Simone responded, “Hi.”

“May I come in?”

She paused for a second. To Aaron, it felt like time stood still. She stepped back. They looked at one another without saying word.

Aaron licked his lips. His eyes traveled down the length of her body. He admired her perfectly manicured, red-painted toenails. Her jeans hugged toned thighs and accentuated her curvaceous hips.

Seeing her again only reinforced how much he needed her, wanted her, and missed her. He loved this woman. For some reason, the pull was even stronger than before. It took sheer willpower to fight back the urge to grab her by the waist and kiss her. He looked into her eyes. Nothing but hurt there, no hint of desire at all. With an icy stare, she held his gaze. He wondered if he should cut his losses, turn around, and take the next flight back to California.

Aaron didn’t know what was colder, the look she gave him or the fifty-degree weather in New York. This was not going to be easy. Why did he think it would be? Not after what he had done. She’d finally opened her heart and his actions, without question, had caused her heart to become hardened.

The door swung wider. She turned and walked inside. He followed. Aaron closed the door, removed his coat and hat and laid them on the chaise. Simone led him through the living room into the kitchen. She gestured for him to have a seat. He shook his head slightly. He preferred to stand. He watched her every move. She stood with her arms crossed, leaning against the kitchen island. She offered him some tea which he gladly accepted. He took a sip and placed the mug on the table.

A smile teased the corner of his mouth, but soon disappeared when she didn't reciprocate. Simone wore a pained expression. Aaron's heart dropped. He was the reason she'd lost her smile.

"How have you been?"

"I'm okay." He heard her say, but her eyes held great pain. "And you?"

He took a step toward her. "Not good. Not good at all without you. I've missed you like crazy."

She cocked her head to the side and glared at him.

Without giving much thought to her expression, her coldness or the anxiety in the air, Aaron reached for her and drew her into an embrace. She put her hand on his chest, intent upon pushing him away, but the warmth of his muscular arms around her waist made it difficult to fight.

She resisted for a second, then finally relented when he kissed her. The kiss was different than before. It was an 'I messed up and I know it' kiss. He held her tighter and deepened the kiss when he felt her surrender. He eased out of the kiss and rested his head against hers. "I'm sorry. We found your flash drive. It was Holly that made the changes."

"What? Holly? Somehow that doesn't surprise me." She blinked back the tears that threatened to fall, but it was too late. They escaped. "So, that makes everything okay? You blamed me, Aaron. You looked me in the face and accused me of sabotaging your company and your *life*."

He felt the water flow down her cheeks. His lips traced each tear. "Simone. Please. I'm sorry I hurt you. I was wrong about everything. Forgive me for hurting you."

Her eyes popped open. "Stop. Let me go, Aaron." She attempted to pull out of his hold, but he would not yield.

"You think it's that easy? You can come in here and apologize and boom, we back to the way things were?"

He took a deep breath. "Relax, Simone. I hear you. You said you were going to give me time to make things right."

She glared at him.

Aaron chuckled. "I did fly out here to apologize, but I also wanted to see you. I wanted to hold you and kiss you. To tell you I've missed you. To tell you I'm sorry. To tell you I love you."

"Love me. Really?" She laughed, sarcastically.

He wasn't going to let her anger drive him away.

He was determined he wouldn't leave without her. His jaw tightened. "I'm not naïve, Simone. I know things can't go back to the way they were. Too much has happened. I want things better. I was wrong for not listening to you. For not giving you the opportunity to talk. I make no excuses. I own up to it. My actions hurt you."

"Duh. Really? That's an understatement."

Somehow he had to make things right before he hopped on the plane in the morning. *Dear, Lord, help!*

She sighed. "Aaron, I don't know."

Contrary to what she said, her words didn't match what he saw in her eyes—fear. He knew he was fighting an uphill battle. His words didn't appear to soften her heart at all.

"Simone, sweetie. I know I hurt you, and I would give anything to take those words back, but I can't. I can only hope you will accept my apology, truly forgive me and give us—give *me*—another chance. I don't want what we have to end. You are the best part of me. I know you might not believe me, but it's true."

"Aaron, you're absolutely correct. I don't believe you. You don't treat the people you care about the way you treated me. You threw my character in my face. My integrity. My feelings for you. You love me, you say? Yet, when things went south, you didn't even trust me or give me a chance to defend myself." She shook her head at the memory of her last day in the office.

Man, this woman doesn't pull any punches. She was giving him all she had and then some. As painful as it was to listen, she was right. A knot formed in his stomach.

"Aaron, I need time to think things through. A lot has happened. I'm not sure anymore."

His heart sank. He wasn't expecting that response. He'd made a mistake. He'd apologized for it. They loved each other. Why couldn't they move on? He was confused. He couldn't understand why she was making this much harder than it had to be.

Aaron's voice softened. "Simone, you're right. I'm guilty as charged." Her honest words cut his heart. He had no defense. He stared at her. "Okay," he relented. "I'm going to give you time to think things through, but while you're thinking, think about this. I can't promise you I won't make any more mistakes, I'm human. I can't promise you, you won't get mad at me... again. I can't promise you I won't get on your nerves with some of my ways. But I can promise you this—I will cherish you with all my heart. I can promise you that I would never deliberately hurt you. I can promise you I will grow in love with you and love you with all heart. I can promise you I will be a better man because of you. I promise to give you the kind of love you deserve. And if I don't know how, teach me how to love you."

Tears rolled relentlessly down her cheeks. Aaron reached over and wiped them away with his thumb.

"My plane leaves in the morning. I'm staying at the Times Square Hilton, room 601. He looked deeply into her eyes. "I would love leaving here knowing we're back together. I know things can work out between us."

He kissed her on the forehead and turned to leave. Simone trailed him as he walked toward the chaise. "Aaron, are you telling me you want me to give you an answer by morning? You're not giving me much time to think."

He looked back over his shoulder. "It doesn't take long to decide if you want me or not. You either love me or you don't." He slipped on his coat and hat, then shut the door behind him.

"You said what? Run that by me again?" Kendra waited on her friend to explain the rationale behind her statement. Simone gave her the run-down of everything that happened with Aaron, every little detail.

"I told Aaron I needed time to think things through." Simone lay across the living room floor, in front of the fireplace, with a cup of tea and a box of Kleenex beside her.

"Ummm. Okay. Let me see if I got this right.

Aaron flew all the way from California, hunted you down to apologize and ask for another chance, and you told him you'd *think* about it?"

"Kendra, you don't have to make it sound like that."

"Girl, you know I like to keep things one hundred. And, you know you my girl, right?" Simone knew Kendra was about to read her the riot act. "I need you to listen to what I'm about to say. Can I get you to do that?"

"Okay, sissy. I know I'm your girl, and even if I didn't want to listen, you'd find a way to get your message across anyways. So, go ahead."

"Why, thank you. I appreciate that. Sis, you have a man that obviously cares a great deal for you. He adores you and has confessed to loving you. If all he wanted to do was to apologize, he could have done that over the phone. He didn't have to fly all the way to New York for that. Simone, the man wants you. Do you know how many women are waiting for you to get out of the way so they can come snatch his fine butt up? Flaws and all. You can blow it if you want. Sis, true love doesn't always come knocking a second time. Sissy, I could hear the excitement in your voice when you talked about him. It's been years since I heard you talk about a man as much as you talked about Aaron. Don't do something you'll regret."

Simone sipped her tea and considered what Kendra was saying. "You have one of the Bay

Area's most sought after attorneys trying to get with you. Okay, sis, he screwed up. And, I'm not making any excuses for him. But, come on now, he deserves a second chance." Kendra took a breath. "From what I can see, it appears you want to run at the first sight of trouble or stay out before he leaves you later. Sissy, are you running again? Is this déjà vu?"

Simone rolled her eyes. "Excuse me. Did you forget what he did? I am not running. How can you even say that? Bestie, you don't even know what you're talking about." Silence filled the air.

"Nope, I didn't forget. Not at all. I remember what he did. But you told me he apologized." Kendra kept her tone gentle. "Simone, this is ya girl. And yes. I do know what I'm talking about. We've known each other for years. Remember, I was with you the entire time you dated Joshua and then I saw you deal with his death. I witnessed the effect it left on you emotionally. Sissy, have you told Aaron everything? Does he know?"

Her question hung in the air. Then Kendra said, "Didn't Pastor tell you to face your challenges? Well, here you go. The perfect opportunity. You are going to have to deal with this issue if you are ever going to have a genuine relationship with that gorgeous male specimen."

The water dam broke. Simone dabbed her face with some Kleenex and gave herself a moment to soak in the truth. *The truth sets you free.* She had to admit Kendra was right, once again. She hadn't really faced her issues head on and she hadn't told Aaron everything.

Kendra's voice invaded her silent thoughts. "Girl, there are no perfect couples, perfect relationships, or perfect people. Did you stop to think that he is willing to put up with all your weaknesses and shortcomings? And he doesn't even know what they are."

Sobbing, Simone managed, "You're right, Kendra. I need to deal with it. I have to deal with it." In her heart, she knew Aaron was a good man who really did care about her. She had been unfair to him by not sharing her fears.

Kendra blew out a breath. "Where is he now?"

"Times Square. He's at his hotel. His flight leaves in the morning."

"Okay, so are you calling for Uber, or am I? Because I think you need to go see him and tell him everything. If he's still interested in your crazy butt after you talk to him... keep him for life."

"I am, sissy. Let me ping Uber right now. I'm going to see him."

"That's what I'm talking about."

Simone ended the call, hurried to the bathroom, washed her face, brushed her teeth, and got dressed in record time. She opened her Uber app and requested a car. Noting the arrival time of the driver, she grabbed her coat and hurried out to meet the car.

While riding to his hotel, she prayed God would give her the exact words to say. She believed He would. She'd come too far to go back now.

Aaron stepped out of the shower and dried himself off with a plush, white towel. He put on a pair of black drawstring pajama pants that hung low on his narrow hips and threw on a black hoodie. Tired and exhausted, he lay on the bed and replayed the entire afternoon in his head. He was surprised that after all he had said and done, Simone still needed time to think. *What in the world was there to think about?* He was going to take that as a no and be done with it.

He'd get on the plane, go back to California and try to forget everything that happened. *Try to forget her.* But how could he? She was incredible. She was everything he'd ever wanted and more.

Yet, she gave him no sign that she was willing to reconcile. For days, he'd been miserable without her. His once merry heart was now crushed. Granted, it was all his own doing. But still, he couldn't wait to see her, talk with her, and make plans with her. Now all he wanted to do was get on the plane and never look back.

His phone rang. "Hey, bro. How'd it go?"

"Women." Aaron shook his head.

"Oh. I take it that it didn't go too well."

"Yep, that's exactly correct. She said she needed time to think."

"What is there to think about?"

"If she wants to be in a relationship with me or not."

"Hmm, I see. Wow. Man, I'm sorry to hear that."

Aaron wanted to change the direction of the conversation. "I'm all packed and ready to go. My flight lands at noon."

"Yeah, I got you covered. So are you going to talk to her again?"

"Nope. I'm taking that as a no. I told her I was leaving in the morning. She hasn't called or come by."

"Naw, Aaron. That ain't you, bro. You're not a quitter. You adore her." Shaun paused. "Shoot, you gave up a night with the fellas for her. I know you mad and hurt, but let's talk this through."

"Whatever."

"Alright, think about this. Maybe, maybe, she scared. You dealing with a woman whose fiancé died. I'm no counselor, but that might have something to do with her decision, or should I say lack of decision. You should think about it before you give up on her and the relationship. This is not like you giving away clothes. It might be hard getting her back."

Aaron stood and walked over to the window. "Scared. Scared of what?" He waited a few seconds before he spoke, "Man, remember? We were in a relationship."

"I know, but what happened between you two at work must have triggered something in her. That's my two cents' worth."

"Alright, man, I'll take that into consideration. But what exactly would she be afraid of?"

Shaun snickered. "You don't sound too convincing, but I'mma leave it alone... for now. Alright, bro, I'll see you tomorrow. Oh, by the way, the project is moving right along. Mr. Kane is once again a happy man."

"Well, finally... some good news." The call ended.

Shaun was correct about one thing. Aaron wasn't too convinced about his theory, but what if he was right? What would she have to be afraid of? And if Shaun was correct, why wouldn't Simone talk to him about it? She could tell him her fears. She could confide in him. Trust him. Obviously, she wasn't ready.

Aaron shook his head. It was too much information to deal with right now. But, the more he tried to dispel Shaun's theory, the more intrigued he became with it. He walked over to the desk and sat down. He powered up his laptop and went on his own hunt to satisfy his curiosity. Maybe Simone didn't tell him everything. Maybe he didn't have the entire story. But, why not?

He didn't know where to begin so he typed in

different words: scared, loss of a loved one, grief. When he typed in 'what causes fear', he got his answer. And there it was. Abandonment. Other words popped up: desertion, leaving, rejection.

His mouth opened wide when he read more about the pattern of behavior. *They look for flaws. When they find someone who might be a good partner, they start looking for their faults. They look for what's wrong instead of what's right. They are always the one to leave.*

He read it again. Finally, it registered. *She thinks I'm going to leave her... again. Like Joshua. She thinks I will desert her. She should know I would never do that.*

But you did.

Shaun was right. She was scared. He picked up the phone. He wanted to call her to find out if this was true or not. He hit the *cancel* button. As anxious as he was to dial her number and reassure her that he'd never leave her, he couldn't. If what he found in his reading was correct, she was going to have to be honest with him. She had until morning to contact him. Meanwhile, he packed his bag and readied himself for his flight first thing in the morning.

Without warning, there was a knock on his hotel door, and he opened it, figuring it was some kind of room service mistake. But there she was, beautiful as ever: Simone, absolutely stunning. Her scent could make him forget that she'd broken his heart.

Their eyes held. It had only been a few hours since she'd seen him, but her heart pulsed like it'd been years. She studied him, wondering if he was going to let her in. She broke the silence.

"Hi. Can I come in?" Her voice cracked.

"Hey. Yeah." He opened the door wider and stepped aside. She walked in. He gestured for her to have a seat.

She declined, took two deep breaths, and cleared her throat. "Can I have some water, please?"

Aaron lifted his brow. He could tell she was nervous. He wanted to sweep her off her feet, swing her around, and be her knight in shining armor. Instead, he held his composure and did as she asked. He grabbed a water bottle from the refrigerator, twisted off the cap, and handed it to her. She took a big sip.

"You got something you need to say?"

"Yes, I do. Plenty." She paused. "I'm a runner. I run at the first sign of trouble. At the first opportunity to say goodbye, I'll take it."

He tilted his head to the side. "Runner? You want to explain that?"

"The day Joshua died, we had a disagreement. We were planning to have dinner to talk about it, but that never happened. I didn't get the chance to talk to him and make things right or even say my last goodbye." She swallowed hard and continued, "So from that point on, for any potential relationship with any man that approached me, I looked for a way to say goodbye first."

Silence filled the air. "With other guys, don't get me wrong, it hasn't been but a few since Joshua, I was looking for a flaw in them. Any flaw, so I could leave. And believe me, I found them."

His eyes widened in surprise. His mind shifted to the article he had read earlier. *They look for flaws. When they find someone who might be a good partner, they start looking for their faults.* Her voice intercepted his thoughts. "But you're different." She took a step closer to him.

Aaron interjected, "Different." He raised his eyebrow. "What do you mean different?"

"I wasn't looking for your flaws, but you provided an escape clause for me to use. You revealed your flaws to me without me even looking. When we had that big blow-up at the office and you fired me, remember? Accused me of working with Lamont. That was my opportunity to run and keep running."

She took a breath. "You gave me the perfect reason to say goodbye... on a silver platter. You made it real easy for me to walk away, to go back to the way I was. To look for flaws in every man, find them and leave before... they leave me. But instead, you showed up here. You asked for a second chance. You told me you loved me, and I said I had to think about it."

He nodded in agreement. "Yeah, you did, and I took that as a no."

"I'm sure you did. I would have, too." With her eyes locked on him, she took another step closer. Her heart pounded faster as she pressed closer and then stopped. "But I don't want to run anymore."

"Is that right? How do I know you won't run at the first sign of trouble?" He crossed his arms and leaned against the desk. He had no intentions of making this easy for her. The script had been flipped.

She guessed he was giving her a dose of her own medicine. "I'm here, aren't I? I could have let you leave in the morning without saying a word. Things could end right here. But, no. I'm standing in your hotel room, in the wee hours of the night, trying to convince you that I don't want our relationship to end." She paused. "Not only that, I could have said goodbye to you the day you told me about your struggle with gambling."

"Okay. Go ahead."

Go ahead? Simone squinted her eyes. She couldn't believe this man. Was he really going to continue punishing her? *Stand your ground. You know he cares about you. He loves you.* "I won't run anymore. My running days are over. I don't want to say goodbye to you. I *can't* say goodbye to you. I love you, Aaron Blackman."

When she spoke his name, he lost it. He quickened his steps toward her, closed the distance between them, yanked her to him, and covered her mouth with his in a hungry kiss. Aaron broke the contact. "You have no idea what you're doing to me right now."

Her breath caught. "You're distracting me from finishing."

He chortled. "My bad. Go ahead."

She continued. "I can't promise I won't make you mad. And I can't promise you I won't make any more mistakes. I'm human."

He chuckled at her confession.

"I can't promise you I won't get on your nerves. I can't promise you I won't say something wrong. But I will promise you this: I will never give up on you or our relationship. I promise I won't run from any problems we might have. I accept you, flaws and all, and you're accepting mine."

He kissed her tenderly on both cheeks "Okay. What else?"

She giggled lightly. "I promise to grow in love with you and love you with all my heart. I promise to give you the kind of love you deserve. And if I don't know how, teach me how to love you."

He kissed her on both earlobes. "Okay, Simone. You finished?"

She whispered, "I have more, but it can wait, since you're making it hard for me to concentrate."

"Good," he crooned. "There will be plenty of time to talk later."

As the longing became unbearable, Aaron's

soft lips met Simone's. She wrapped her arms around his neck and held it in place. He covered her face with tender kisses before he claimed her smooth lips once again, the lips that now belonged to him.

He held her tight and whispered in her ear how much he'd missed her and how glad he was that she came to see him. He eased out of the embrace, lifted her chin, and looked deep into her eyes. "I want to know everything about you: your likes and dislikes, where you like to travel, what makes you smile, what makes you sad. Promise me that you'll talk to me about everything."

She nodded. "I will."

"Your time here in New York has ended. Fly back with me in the morning. Let me call my agent and let her do her magic and get you a ticket. Is that okay with you? Your life is with me now."

She would gladly do what he asked without hesitation. "Yes, Aaron. I'd love that."

"I love you, Simone Herron."

"And I love you, Aaron Blackman."

Tomorrow would be the first day of another new beginning.

About the Author

Paulette Harper's story is different from other authors. She didn't grow up with the aspiration to become a writer. When she decided to pursue a writing career, she knew of no other author who could guide her through the process. Those she shared her aspirations with looked at her with disbelief. Although they may not have openly questioned her goals or aspirations, she knew that in the back of their minds they questioned her success. It was the kind of skepticism that whispered, "Oh yeah, we've heard that before!" But she never allowed their disbelief to influence the direction she believed God was taking her.

Paulette wrote that statement in 2011 when her second book Completely Whole, a Readers' Favorite Award winner, was released. She followed her award winning book with others: *Living Separate Lives*; her children's book, *Princess Nevaeh*; and her *Write Now Author's Manual, Tools and Resources for Success.* Her story *The Courage to Stand* is included in Vanessa Miller's collaboration *Love. Hope. Faith. Stories that uplift, inspire and enlighten.*

In addition to being an author, Paulette is an inspirational speaker, as well as a writing workshop instructor. She has a passion to coach aspiring authors and speak into the lives of women from every walk of life. Her literary works have been spotlighted in a growing number of publications, including CBN, Real Life Real Faith Magazine, and Black Pearls Magazine. She has also appeared on numerous local and online radio shows.

Paulette resides in Northern California. To book a speaking engagement or learn more about Paulette, go to her website www.pauletteharper.com or connect on social media at or info@pauletteharper.com.

Author's Note

Book Reviews

Did you enjoy *Secret Places Revealed*? Please consider writing a book review on Amazon, Barnes & Noble and Goodreads.

Book reviews are important to authors and it only takes a few minutes to write one.

A review doesn't have to be long. A few short sentences or a few words to describe the book works just fine.

Book Recommendations

Since you enjoyed reading *Secret Places Revealed* will you help me promote it? Here's how you can help.

- Kindly recommend it to books clubs and other readers.
- Ask your library to carry a copy.
- Order another copy to give away instead of passing *Secret Places Revealed* around.
- Share it on social media as a book recommendation.
- Invite me to discuss the book either by Skype, Facebook Chat or a visit to your city.

Subscribe

Please join my mailing list for updates on events and future book releases.

www.pauletteharper.com

Thank you so much!!